Chris Niles

Grace Falco

GW00691125

PAN BOOKS

First published 2006 by Pan Books
an imprint of Pan Macmillan Ltd
Pan Macmillan, 20 New Wharf Road, London N1 9RR
Basingstoke and Oxford
Associated companies throughout the world
www.panmacmillan.com

ISBN 0 330 43524 8

A CIP catalogue record for this book is available from
the British Library.

Typeset by Intype Libra, London
Printed and bound in Great Britain by
Mackays of Chatham plc, Chatham, Kent

Acknowledgements

The idea for this book came from the dinner table of John O'Brien and Jamie Lehrer and I wish to take this opportunity to thank them – yet again – for their steadfast friendship and for owning a house with an interestingly seedy history.

I'm very fortunate to work with Abner Stein, Rosemarie Buckman, Jessica Buckman, Vicky Bijur and Sarah Turner, who provide the best back-up that any writer could wish for.

Sarah Tombaugh provided valuable insights into the world of architecture and David Corbett patiently answered incredibly stupid questions about white-collar crime.

Roderick Huntress gets ten out of ten for being an excellent husband and human being and for never once asking, 'So, how's the writing going?'

Lastly, I would like to express my sincere thanks to the real Grace Falco, who unhesitatingly allowed me to take her name and have my evil way with it. Because of her generosity I wish to emphasize that the characters in this book are a product of my own imagination and are not based on any actual person.

Grace Falco

One

The big old house was white, two-storeyed with grey shutters. A porch wrapped around front and back. It exuded stolid New England dignity; it had earned its right to be there.

It was surrounded by an acre of lawn, trimmed close. Mature oak and maple trees dotted the yard. A swing hung from the largest, quite motionless. Grass had grown beneath it.

The house stood on a rise next to an intersection but no traffic moved along the four roads that rippled over hills and into the distance.

There was one light on in the house, on the back porch. There were no lights within. Nobody moved, inside or out.

The evening was exactly what one expected of night-time in the country. There were sounds, but they were sweet, calming sounds of rusticity, not the teeth-grinding sounds of the city. No car alarms, no police sirens. In the distance, if you concentrated, you might hear a dog warning off an imaginary prowler, a night-bird calling, a truck clutching down to first gear.

There were houses nearby, but apart from the odd lighted window they showed no sign of life. It was late after all, way past midnight. Farmers were early risers, and so too, when they could be prised away from their twenty-four-hour doormen and Citarella delivery service, were the Manhattanites who liked to play at being farmers at the weekends.

The Milky Way arced above the bucolic tableau. Light from further than the human mind could comprehend, falling almost like a blessing. The stars were thickly clustered and so bright that it was difficult to pick out constellations; far easier, and more wonderful, to comprehend the whole, a big, starry carpet unfurling in space.

The barn had recently been painted a rusty blood red.

It was not really a barn, anyway. Not in the real sense of the word, because the large farm it had once served had been chipped away by the inevitable economic forces of modern life. The process had begun when the potato crops moved out west to Idaho and it had been finished off by the development of highways that brought the wealthy Bostonians and New Yorkers to the Berkshires for weekend peace of mind and made it more economically sensible for farmers to sell up than plant.

There were just a few acres attached to the big house now, most of them either forested or fallow, so the barn was no longer needed to store feed or to shelter animals. Now one half of it served as a garage and the other half as a place to keep bikes, canoes and pool equipment.

There was a car in the garage. A Jeep Cherokee.

It was maybe five years old but it had been well taken care of. It was clean inside and out, and the paint-work, a classy silver grey, had no nicks or scrapes.

A man sat in the front seat, hands loosely clasped in his lap, his head cocked to one side as if he was straining to hear somebody speaking softly.

But there was no other person in the barn. He was alone, the only noise the low hum of a well-tuned motor. To the rear, one pipe had been connected to another with the help of duct tape. The second pipe curved stiffly out of the exhaust – it was new, bought specially for this purpose – into the rear left window.

The crack left by the partially opened window had also been sealed with tape. It probably wasn't one hundred per cent effective – it had been a rushed job – but then it didn't need to be. The garage doors were tightly shut, and the building had been constructed by craftsmen and well maintained by the farm's three or four owners.

Carbon monoxide, the by-product of incomplete combustion of fossil fuels, kills as effectively as any noxious gas. One may become dizzy or have chest pains or a headache before passing into unconscious-ness, but in this case the person behind the wheel felt no discomfort because a generous helping of sleeping pills had already placed him beyond any meaningful sensation.

And even though he could no longer speak for himself, the circumstances indicated, accurately, that his rapidly ebbing life had indeed washed up in a desperate place. Perhaps if he had been more sentient he might have spared a few moments' reflection to pinpoint exactly where his life had gone so badly wrong.

But then again, probably not.

He had never been one for reflection or the weighing up of consequences. He had never seen the point in looking back and posing that soul-jabbing question, 'What if?' And in that respect his death was a perfect reflection of his life. Because his death had been avoidable, just like all the other mistakes he had made.

Two

Earlier that evening

The parking attendant brought the Jeep round to the apartment building. He slid out and tossed Mitch the keys.

'Thanks.' Mitch pressed a twenty into his hands.

'You're welcome.' The guy checked the denomination unobtrusively before the note vanished into his front pocket. 'Thanks,' he said again, surprised. Mitchell Browning was not known among the staff of the building as a big tipper.

Mitch shrugged, turned to the doorman. 'Any sign of her?'

'I sent the elevator up, sir. She's on her way.'

Mitch checked his Tag. They were late; it was five thirty. They were going to hit godawful traffic. Damn her. If there was one thing he hated it was lateness, it drove him batshit. And Grace would be late for her own funeral.

He felt the familiar tightening of his jaw, reached up to pinch the bones apart and then stopped.

Relax, he told himself. Enjoy the drive. Enjoy the night. Who cares if it takes five hours? It's not like you have any other pressing appointments.

'What's so funny?' Grace said as she struggled out

of the elevator with her heavy suitcase. He could never persuade her to do what he did and leave a spare set of clothes up at the house. That would imply a level of acceptance by her of their weekend arrangements and she wasn't prepared to do that.

'What's that look?'

'Nothing.'

'You're angry with me.'

'I'm not.'

'I know that look, Mitch.'

Mitch sighed. He hated this. Hated the way she always tried to second-guess him. 'Just worried about the traffic, that's all.' He took the bag from the doorman and hefted it into the trunk. 'And I've had a hard week. I'm tired. It's nothing to do with you.'

Grace's expression softened, she put a hand on his arm. 'Sorry,' she said. 'I know things have been tough for you.'

You don't know how tough, sweetheart.

He felt a pang of remorse; he promptly shunted it aside. Remorse was just one of the many luxuries he could no longer afford. Nope, it was all much, much too late for any nuanced emotion.

Funny how quickly life could strip down to its essentials.

My own needs first; anybody else can go hang. What he had to do now was set himself in drive and go heedlessly forward. Do what he had to do.

'That job is killing you.' Grace settled into the front seat, fastened her seat belt and put her bag on the floor in front of her. Louis Vuitton, brand new.

Hundreds of dollars worth of tacky stamped leather and gilt.

He felt a flash of annoyance at Grace and her free-spending ways. *She got you into this mess*, a little voice said. *No she didn't*, the other side of his conscience responded. *You did that all yourself.*

But she didn't help, the voice snapped back.

'Oh, be quiet.'

'Pardon?' Grace's eyes darkened in panic. She hated it when he got mad.

Mitch was unaware that he'd spoken out loud. That was one of his problems lately; he was finding it hard to distinguish between his inner and outer life. Between his real memories and things that he'd dreamed up. This must be the definition of madness, he thought. He knew that, on some level, reality was a mental construct, but you were really in trouble when you couldn't convince yourself what that reality should be.

'Nothing, darling. Just talking to myself.' He squeezed her hand. Not too much longer to play the loving husband.

When he dropped her hand she reached for the radio, flipping it off NPR and on to Lite FM.

He hated Lite FM. He hated lite anything.

But he didn't say anything. He put the key in the ignition and reached to fasten his own seat belt.

'That job is going to kill you,' Grace said again as the opening notes of a particularly egregious Kenny G song assaulted him.

He thought of ten sharp retorts and said none of

them. He concentrated instead on the traffic, a sluggish, barely moving stream. He caught the eye of a guy driving a car with TLC plates, a liveried cab – notoriously the worst drivers in a city that prided itself on bad driving. Amazingly, the guy let Mitch in.

'Yeah,' he said. 'Well, we all gotta go some time.'

Three

Hong Kong, one year earlier

Poppy Adams put down her chopsticks and rested her hand in her lap, flicking her thumbnail with her index finger, a sign since childhood that she was under stress.

'You're going home.' She stiffly repeated the words that Philip Ross had just said to her, trying to inject them with a little life, but failing. They fell flat on the table in front of her. She felt as if she should pick them up out of the fried shrimp.

'It's the offer of a lifetime.' Philip's handsome face displayed no turmoil, not one hint of regret. He had elegant hands, long fingers, square-filed nails. They were poised, holding chopsticks over the shrimp like a designer bird of prey.

'It sounds like it.' Poppy forced herself to smile, hoped it didn't seem too staged. 'Just what you've always wanted.'

'Right. I'm thrilled.' Philip said the words in a measured tone, like he wasn't thrilled at all but somebody had put a script in front of him and told him to go right ahead and read the words. 'Although of course I'm going to miss Hong Kong.'

But not me. The unguarded thought filled Poppy with sadness.

'And all my friends here.' Philip smiled and reached across the table for Poppy's hand. For a moment she considered withholding it, like a spoiled child. But she didn't. She held out her hand for his and they remained linked this way, above the food and the teapot and the beer bottles, for what seemed like a very long time.

Why do I love this man? Each time she asked herself that question, she couldn't think of a thing to hang her answer on.

One of the things that had first piqued her interest was Philip's manners. He could always be relied upon to behave correctly. He stood up when she came into the room and helped her off and on with her coat. He wrote beautiful thank-you notes. She had kept the first one he had sent her after a dinner party where she had cooked pasta in her tiny apartment and her guests had eaten sitting cross-legged on the floor. By no stretch of the imagination could it have been described as a formal event and yet Philip had expressed his thanks using a fountain pen and blue-black ink, something that she dimly remembered her mother telling her was extremely good form.

The note had intrigued her. Good party manners for most of the hard-drinking reprobates she hung out with meant calling the following day to apologize for their behaviour. But not Philip; for one thing, he never had anything to apologize *for*. In the months that she'd known him, she'd never seen him angry or drunk or even hilariously happy. It was as if all his emotional responses were set to 'mute'.

Despite this, her interest had grown to fascination

and one quiet day, without her really noticing, it had slipped across the border and become love. And when that happened, it had become a problem.

Poppy believed that life was tough enough without using men as an instrument of punishment. She wasn't into emotional game-playing or sitting around waiting for the phone to ring. Normally she thought of relationships as a tug of war; both sides had to be pulling approximately equal amounts to maintain the tension necessary to keep it interesting. But Philip didn't play by those rules so she had been forced, for the first time in her life, to be less than honest.

She spent a great deal of time and effort concealing her love from him because something told her that he would be able to spot it. That was the trouble with quiet people: you never knew what they picked up when everybody else was yakking away. So Poppy put herself on a Philip diet. She didn't see him more than twice a week and most of those times other people were around. The times they slept together, she never stayed the night. She didn't leave so much as a stray hair at his apartment. She didn't push him into telling her what he thought of her, she didn't ask any more of him than he was willing to give.

It was hard, hard work, but until this moment she had believed it would eventually pay off.

So much for that.

The restaurant on Lama Island was one of Hong Kong's most popular. Crowds of Chinese and Westerners were packed into big round tables. It was loud and hot. The food, in a city where excellent was the norm, was outstanding.

Poppy had a view of the dock. She watched a boat dock and the gangplank flop down, delivering another gaggle of chattering, eager diners.

'All your friends here. Of course.' She had to physically fight the impulse to yell out, *What about me? You could at least pretend to be sad, you supercilious shit.*

No, that wasn't fair. Philip had never given her any indication that they were anything other than buddies, buddies who slept together occasionally. He'd never made false promises. He'd never said anything just to get laid.

And just because she loved him didn't mean he had to love her back.

It was a problem all right.

Poppy had no reason not to believe she had a fighting chance. She had coppery red hair, dark blue eyes and a curvy five-foot-five frame that called to mind the feminine glamour of old Hollywood movie stars. She had what she thought was the sexiest job in the world – foreign correspondent. She'd been to all sorts of exotic places and had amusing stories to tell about them. She was a blast at parties, at dinner, at softball games, anywhere really. She was thirty-two, the well-rounded product of a loving home, carried no emotional baggage. There were lots of guys she could have had. Lots.

The waiter slapped down a huge plate of fried water spinach, made soggier by garlic sauce. Poppy's favourite dish. She looked at it and felt sick.

What about us? She wanted to say the words. Felt like she had to grab them, strangle them before they spewed out of her mouth.

She swallowed and didn't say it. Couldn't say it now, after all this time of pretending he was nobody special. How ironic.

Besides, it was early days. He wasn't leaving for another fortnight. Perhaps he'd change his mind. She pictured him racing off the plane at the last minute and into her arms – a real Meg Ryan movie moment.

But then what? He wouldn't give up his job offer to stay in Hong Kong and she couldn't very well just pack up and go to New York. She had a great gig right here. They were both ambitious, that was one thing they had in common.

Sighing, Poppy picked up her chopsticks.

'Everything OK?' Philip asked. 'You look a little peaky.'

'Hangover,' Poppy lied, with a blitheness that surprised her. She couldn't look at him. Instead she loaded water spinach on to her plate, a great big slag pile.

Just because her heart was breaking did not mean that good food should go to waste.

Four

New York City, two weeks later

Philip felt an unexpected sense of confusion as he stepped off the plane at John F. Kennedy Airport, the feeling he sometimes got when he woke up in a strange place and couldn't for a moment make sense of his surroundings.

It was just the terminal, he reminded himself, and its shabby, impermanent sense of corporate sameness that one saw all over the world.

His father and Mitch were waiting for him at the baggage carousel, just as they had threatened. Mitch held a cardboard sign that read, 'The Prodigal Son'.

There were manly handshakes and then, after a brief pause, hugs.

'Good to have you back,' his father said simply. The old guy was deeply tanned and looked a little thinner, Philip thought. A little more aged.

Mitch was not thinner. He was about the same height as Philip and even though he wasn't fat, the general physical impression was one of roundness. Philip noticed that he had gained a little gut recently – a reward for all those hours logged behind a desk – but it sat unobtrusively on his broad, stocky frame.

'Hey, buddy.' Mitch hugged him hard, almost lift-ing his feet off the ground. 'Just as ugly as ever.'

He was strong, Philip thought, he could take me, and then immediately wondered why he'd thought that. Mitch would never want to take him. They had been friends since college.

The carousel wheezed into motion and, like a gift from the benevolent god of baggage-handling, Philip's bags were first to come tumbling down the belt.

The traffic was hell. Philip sat up front with Mitch and his father stretched out in the back, unfolding a copy of the *Times*. They were motionless somewhere in Queens, marooned in a landscape of unimaginative buildings. It was a hot day and drivers had their windows down. Competing hip-hop and salsa rhythms were beating from the cars around them.

The traffic began edging forward. Up in the dis-tance in the oncoming lane, Philip could see police lights, an ambulance and two cars with their fronts bent out of shape. Both drivers, a man and a woman, were shouting into their cellphones, gesticulating the semaphore of the angry and frustrated.

'Ridiculous,' Philip's father said from the back seat. 'There's no need for our lane to be going slow at all but people will rubberneck.'

'Other people's misfortunes are the very best kind, William,' Mitch said cheerfully. 'You know that.'

They crossed the Williamsburg Bridge and headed west on Delancey. Philip had never liked this part of town, it didn't feel right to him. The streets were too broad and the buildings too short, especially after chaotic, cramped Hong Kong. He felt exposed, disappointed, as if he'd been tricked into coming back to the wrong city.

Discomfort spiralled into panic. I shouldn't have come back, he thought, I've made the wrong decision. I should have stayed in Hong Kong.

He put a hand on the door handle, imagining himself jumping out on to the street and running away – to another place, Chicago perhaps, or London – where he could lose himself again.

But that wasn't right. He hadn't gone to Hong Kong to lose himself. That was absurd. He had nothing to run away from.

He breathed in and out slowly, telling his mind to relax.

'Everything OK?' Mitch glanced over at him.

'Sure.' Philip moved his hand back into his lap. Forced it to unclench. Set his shoulders back and relaxed the muscles of his face. He was home now, in the city that he had known all of his life. He was surrounded by people who loved him, there was no need to be . . . what was the word? He searched and found that he could not put a name to his feeling. It was something more than unease, more like a premonition. But it couldn't be a premonition. He was not prescient in the slightest; the only gut feeling he'd ever had was indigestion. No, it was just stupid panic attacks that were going to stop now that he was home and surrounded by familiar things. Hong Kong had been different; nobody could blame you for having panic attacks in Hong Kong. Too many people and too little space did that to you. New York was a sylvan paradise compared to Hong Kong.

Mitch turned right, heading up Broadway and into familiar territory, and Philip's fear died away. He name-checked his list of blessings: a great job, his friends, his father, his own apartment. There was nothing to worry about. The life that he had always imagined was right here. Just waiting.

Mitch negotiated the swirling mess of traffic calmly. He'd always been an unflappable, confident driver. Suicidal bike messengers, taxi-drivers, clueless out-of-towners swerved and braked in front of him but seemed to have little effect on his concentration or mood. A pedestrian stepped out into the street, not looking, chattering on his cellphone. Mitch stood on the brakes, stopping with a few inches to spare. The pedestrian gave him the finger and Mitch responded with a friendly salute.

A few minutes later he pulled up outside Philip's apartment in the flower district.

'What are you guys doing next Friday night?' he asked, casually, as he turned off the engine.

Philip shrugged, looked at his father, who shook his head.

'Nothing, I guess.'

'I don't have any plans,' his father said. 'Oh no, wait a minute, I think I've got a hot date with the Discovery Channel.'

'Cancel it,' Mitch said. 'I want you to come over to my house. There's a woman I want you to meet.'

'Why?' Philip's father leaned forward from the

back seat. He was an incorrigible gossip. 'Why do you want us to meet her?'

'Because she's the most amazing person and we're getting married.'

Five

William Ross mixed a Ketel One martini and placed it in his son's hand.

'Got some supplies in,' he said. 'Just the essentials.' He smiled and flopped into the chair opposite Philip, although flop probably wasn't the most accurate description. None of his son's furniture encouraged any posture other than one suggestive of paying strict attention.

Architects had weird ideas about furniture.

'Place is looking good, eh? Your pal James was the dream tenant. I didn't even have to threaten life and limb to get him to move out. Mind you, I don't think he was here half the time.' William Ross took a sip from his drink and pretended to look at the glass, although he was really taking inventory on his son. He tried not to worry about him. Some days it was difficult.

'Thanks, Dad.'

'It's good to have you home.' William Ross tried the direct approach. Sometimes it worked. He knew his son loved him, but demonstrative wasn't right at the top of his list of qualities.

'It's good to be home,' Philip said, stretching his legs out, relaxing a little.

'When do you start work?'

'I've got a meeting with Herb on Friday.'

'Philip Ross Architecture. I'll drink to that.'

'Yeah.' Philip's face creased into a smile. He looked like his mother when he smiled, William thought with a twinge; he was still surprised to find that he missed her after all these years. He wondered if Philip would have turned out differently if she had lived. Perhaps if she'd been around, Philip would not have felt it necessary to react so vigorously to his father's loose manners and don't-care attitude. But what the hell, he'd done his best, no point in torturing himself. He took a generous belt of martini. As a young man he'd lost too many of his friends in a pointless foreign war and he had learned early that regret was a wasteful, indulgent emotion. He had done his best with Philip, considering the circumstances, with no mother. He hadn't even dated another woman, despite many offers, until five years after his wife had died. He had devoted himself entirely to his son and his welfare. Not that he suspected Philip would have suffered from a little Saturday night neglect. Even as a very young child he had been happy locked away in his room with his books and only the most educational of toys.

'So what about Mitch?' Philip said. 'Marriage. Out of the blue. Just like that?'

'I hope he's holding the stag party somewhere decent.'

'I don't think he's having a stag party.'

'We have to go to a strip club. It's only proper.

Most of the decent ones have moved out of Manhattan but I know of one that's not too deep in Queens.'

Philip lifted an eyebrow.

'He used to like them, I seem to recall.'

Philip contemplated biting and decided against it. He was feeling relaxed now – jetlag and vodka will do that. His silly anxiety attack had been processed and safely filed away. 'Perhaps we should leave the stag night arrangements to the groom,' he said.

'I can handle it,' William said.

'I'm sure your contribution to his marital happiness will not go unrecognized.'

'It's the least I can do.' William beamed at his son over the rim of his glass. 'What did he say her name was again?'

'Grace Falco.'

'Who is she?'

'I don't know. I haven't spoken to Mitch in a few weeks. I was running around like a lunatic getting everything wrapped up in Hong Kong. He did send me an email saying he had some news but he wanted to tell me in person. I'd forgotten about it, to be honest.' Philip sipped his drink and felt the stress of the journey slip away. 'I wonder what she's like?'

Parties.

Philip wasn't socially adept at the best of times, and walking into a room full of people determined to have a good time held a special anxiety for him. He had felt that way all his life, and the accomplishments

and experiences of adulthood had not left him any better inclined – or equipped – to cope. Most cocktail-party chatter bored him. He hated to have to listen to people droning on about their careers, their diets, their workouts, and he often wondered why on earth they thought that the minutiae of their lives was interesting to others. He had never seen the point of talking for the sake of hearing oneself speak.

But this was different. Tonight he was meeting the life partner of his cherished friend, and with that thought in mind he paused on the threshold of Mitch's apartment and told himself that he would be as charming and social as he could manage.

He couldn't see Mitch – or indeed anybody that he recognized – in the sea of Upper East Side Prada patrons, so he made his way to the drinks table, stopping to drop his present off with a pile of others on a table in the living-room.

A waiter was pouring honey-coloured wine and Philip accepted a glass. Still no sign of Mitch or his father, although William was probably still sulking because Mitch had canned the stag night idea.

'You must be Philip.'

She held out a hand. 'I'm Grace Falco. Mitch is trapped but he sent me over to say hi. He says you hate parties.'

Philip took her hand and shook it. 'Congratulations. I hear you have stolen my old friend's heart.' The words had a more gallant tone than Philip would normally have taken and he could see by the way Grace's eyes narrowed that she was searching their meaning for implied criticism.

'We fell in love,' she said, the defensiveness not quite masked by a bright artificial smile.

Not such a good start. Philip looked around the room, searching for his father. He was always the perfect social lubricant in these situations.

'You've known Mitch since, like, forever?' Her accent was a strange amalgam of New York and Planet Posh; she was trying too hard, Philip thought.

'Since we were undergraduates.' He searched his memory without success for a witty anecdote about his and Mitch's good old college days. 'How did you meet?'

'I met him in a bar. Just around the corner, actually. Lulu's – you know it?'

'By reputation only.' He didn't mean the words to sound as condescending as they did; it just popped out. Lulu's was a ghastly, sleazy singles bar, the favourite refreshment place of frat boys and women who worked in public relations.

'It was my lucky night. I was a bit drunk or else I'd never have got up the courage to talk to him.' Grace laid a familiar hand on Philip's arm. 'Thank God for alcohol, eh?'

Philip was saved the trouble of replying by Mitch's arrival. He came up behind Grace, flung an arm around her shoulders and popped a kiss on her cheek. 'There you two are! I thought I'd better not leave you alone too long or you'd steal her away from me. Isn't she a stunner!'

'She certainly is,' Philip said. In fact he had barely registered Grace's appearance because she looked exactly like every other woman in the room. The

Upper East Side uniform consisted of the designer style of the minute draped on too-thin bodies and accessorized with identical handbags and shoes. This season was the hobo bag but it could just as easily have been the Birkin or the Kate Spade. Grace's dark brown hair was ironed flat. She had light blue eyes under finely plucked eyebrows. She was wearing a lot of jewellery. Her cheeks were shiny and her lipstick was too red.

Mitch whispered something in Grace's ear and was rewarded with a laugh. It was a loud, gasping sound that sounded like a hyperventilating donkey.

Common, Philip thought, and immediately chided himself for being uncharitable. He was keenly aware that he was much too critical – an occupational hazard for an architect – and that he should not be judging a woman he had just met.

Another guest claimed Mitch and Grace's attention and Philip was left standing alone, wondering whether this was the reason for the dull sense of unease that had enshrouded him since he had returned to the city. Not even the long runs he had taken along the West Side river path every morning could budge it.

He shook his head.

Or maybe it was just nerves about the job. The job was big. And important. He was designing a boutique hotel – one that its owner wanted to be a magnet for supermodels and hip-hop impresarios. The first architect had already been sacked and Philip had been brought in to do everything that he had failed to do. The developer, Herb Slotkin, was a friend.

On the one hand he was very excited about the job – if he pulled it off it was going to get him to the place he wanted to be: not slaving for ninety hours a week and no health benefits at one of the big name firms, but running a thriving company, making his own name. If it went well, he'd be living the life he had dreamed of since he was a teenager. If it didn't . . . he shook his head. He hadn't even started the work; it was much too early to be thinking about failure.

He looked across the room. Grace Falco had her arm around Mitch. She was saying something to a woman with spider-thin limbs and laughing. That laugh.

'Hey.' His father put a light hand on his neck. 'Everything OK? You look like somebody just punched you in the gut.'

'Everything's fine, Dad,' Philip said, feeling a rush of envy for his father. How he wished he could be as joyful about life as William was.

'What do you make of her?'

Philip shrugged. 'What do you make of her?'

'I asked first,' his father shot back.

'I shouldn't . . .' Philip looked around to see if anybody was listening. Nobody was.

Philip looked at Grace and Mitch again. She was hanging off his arm and had one hand on his head, ruffling his hair. Mitch had a stupid grin on his face and he was flushed, whether from booze or excitement Philip couldn't be sure.

'She's not like any of the others,' William Ross said. Mitch came from a distinguished family who had lived in New England for hundreds of years and his tastes tended towards the preppy.

'Dreadful,' Philip said finally, and it was a relief to get the word out. 'Absolutely dreadful.'

Six

Philip was making coffee and toast when his father came stumbling into the kitchen, eyes half closed. He groped the fridge door open, reaching inside for the orange juice.

'It's here, Dad.' Philip held out a glass and a couple of ibuprofen.

'Ah, you're a good son.' His father slapped the pills to his mouth and downed the glass of juice in one. 'Did you get the number of that girl last night? Stacy?'

'It's written on your arm in felt-tip pen,' Philip pointed out.

William slowly opened his eyes. 'And so it is.'

'Isn't she a little bit young for you?'

'She didn't seem to think so.' William sounded smug, despite the thickness in his voice.

Philip snorted, but was distracted from what he was going to say by the beep of the coffee machine. He began pouring. His father practically snatched the first cup out of his hand.

'It should be you that's doing this, not me.' His father slopped milk and sugar into his cup and stirred it vigorously.

'Picking up drunk girls in bars?' Philip poured

himself a cup and sipped it black. 'Really, Dad, sometimes I think your standards are unattainably high.'

'You know what I mean.' His father sat down at
the kitchen table. 'Have fun, loosen up.'

It had been William's idea to go bar-hopping after
Mitch's party. Normally Philip would have made an
excuse and begged off, but last night he had wanted
to hang out with his father.

The toaster popped up and Philip put the toast on
to plates. The two men busied themselves with peanut
butter.

'Do you think Mitch is doing the right thing?'
Philip said after he'd cut his toast into four neatly
equal squares. 'He has only just met her.'

William stopped ripping chunks out of his toast
and looked up at his son. 'I fell in love with your
mother the moment I met her. I loved her till the day
she died. Beyond.'

'How did you know that it wasn't infatuation?'

'That's like asking how you know whether it's right
to breathe or not. You just know what's the right thing
to do.' His father put his toast down and licked his
fingers, which were greasy with peanut oil. Philip
flinched at the sight. 'So he's marrying a woman he's
only known a few weeks. It happens all the time.'

'It wouldn't happen to me.'

'That's because you live life like a chess game.
You're always calibrating and triangulating, figuring
out what the next move will be, and the one after that
and the one five moves after that. Most people don't
live like that. Most people just see something they like
and they say to themselves, "Hey, that looks like fun,

why not give it a whirl," and sometimes it works out and sometimes it doesn't.'

'I don't think it's going to work out.'

'You're not the one marrying her,' his father said, holding his empty coffee cup out for a refill. 'Now take pity on a dying man.'

A week later Philip was accosted by a strange woman on the street. She said his name.

He stopped walking and focused on the person standing in front of him.

'Grace Falco,' she said, not able to keep the amusement out of her voice. 'Mitch's fiancée. You came to our apartment.'

'Oh, ah, Grace. What are you doing downtown?' Philip had just come from a site meeting with his client and his mind was not on Prince Street, where his feet were.

'I come down here fairly often. The border controls aren't too stringent and they accept uptown currency.' She held up a bouquet of shopping bags. 'Wedding shopping.'

'Lovely.' He forced a casual, friendly smile. She was dressed in tight low-cut jeans, which showed a foot or two of gym-smoothed navel, and a spaghetti strap top. Her hair was pulled back in a ponytail. Philip tried to think of something to say.

'Looking forward to the big day?'

'Of course.' Grace's eyes narrowed in puzzled amusement. 'Who doesn't look forward to their wedding?'

'Lovely,' Philip said. 'Well, er, Grace, so nice to see you again.'

Grace said nothing and she didn't move. She stood there, regarding him with curiosity. Her cool manner unnerved Philip and he did something he didn't often do – he rushed to fill the silence.

'Look, er. Why don't we grab a cup of coffee?'

Why the hell had he done that? He didn't want to have coffee with Grace Falco. What on earth would he say to her?

Grace's body weight shifted from her left to her right foot and he thought at first that she would say no. It occurred to him that perhaps their antipathy was mutual.

'Coffee sounds good,' she said at last. 'Mitch says you're family, so we should take the chance to get to know one another.'

The coffee shop was nominally Italian but Philip took one sip of the grey, watery offering and pushed it aside.

'I was in Hong Kong for a couple of years. I got out of the habit of drinking so much coffee. Now unless it's Peet's I can't stomach the stuff.'

Grace gently bobbed an Earl Grey sachet in her mug. 'You're a connoisseur,' she said, her tone neutral. Mitch had told her that Philip was 'very proper'. She should probably behave herself.

'No, just a fussy prick.'

She paused, waiting for the apology.

'Excuse my French.'

'It's all right. I don't speak French.' Grace set the teabag carefully aside. 'What would you like to know about me?'

The direct approach took him aback, as she had intended it to.

'Shall we run over my schools? My work?' she continued before taking a ladylike sip of tea. She really shouldn't be doing this because she had a very busy day ahead and because Mitch had assured her that Philip was a terrific guy. But she couldn't resist it. There was something about him that irritated her. She hoped Mitch wouldn't want to see too much of him after they were married.

'What makes you think I want to know those things?'

'Just a feeling.'

Philip swallowed and drew the rejected coffee cup closer to him because he needed something to do with his hands. She was right. That was exactly what he wanted to know.

'Can I ask you a question?' Grace leaned forward and he could see more of her breasts than he wanted to.

'Ah, sure.'

'Do you still have the sweatshirt?'

'The what?'

'The college sweatshirt, you know, the tribal affiliation, the one that says you're cleverer and brighter and richer than the rest of us?' She said it with a smile.

'Now you're making fun of me.' Philip took a sip of the dreadful coffee. He did have the sweatshirt. But what was so wrong with that?

Grace shrugged.

'I'm sorry,' he said. 'We seem to have got off on the wrong foot.'

Disappointing, Grace thought. He caved immediately. Very disappointing. A little verbal ping-pong would certainly have redeemed the shining hour.

'What's there to be sorry about?'

'You're marrying my best friend. We're going to be seeing each other.'

Don't bet on it. The words were on the tip of her tongue. She so very nearly said them. But he was Mitch's friend after all. That counted for something.

'Mitch tells me you're very career-focused,' she said, because few people could resist the choice between telling their life story and sitting through somebody else's.

'Architecture is more of a calling.'

It gets better, Grace thought. *He's pompous and self-important.*

'By which I mean you don't usually make lots of money so you have to really love what you're doing.'

In the silence that followed, Grace could see that he was trying to think of an unobtrusive way to steer the conversation back around to her. He wanted to firmly slot her into his social hierarchy. He wanted her labelled and filed under white trash.

Not today, buddy, she thought. *More forceful men than you have tried to extract my secrets and you've caught me on a day when I'm simply not in the mood.*

But Philip opted instead for more recent history.

'So tell me about you? How'd you meet Mitch?'

'I already told you that. We were drunk in a bar. I picked him up.' Grace put her teacup down and wiped her lips with a napkin, leaving a red, greasy lipstick smear. 'Took him home, fucked his brains out.'

Philip paled and said nothing.

How disappointing. Mitch had told her he had a sharp wit. Fish in a barrel, she thought, opening her handbag for her lipstick and a mirror. A pompous supercilious fish, what's more.

She reapplied her lipstick right there at the table and got more pleasure from watching him wince. Bad Grace, she thought, snapping her Chanel mirror shut and dropping it back in her bag. Perhaps she had overdone it; after all, Mitch wanted them to get on. But what the hell, she had to get her kicks where she could.

'You know, this has been fun,' she said, gathering up her bags, 'but I must fly. I have a dress fitting in half an hour.' She scooped up the check, threw a couple of dollars tip on the table and patted his arm. 'Don't worry, honey, the drink is on me.'

Seven

'Philip, darling. How perfectly delightful to see you.'
Francesca Browning kissed Philip on both cheeks and
enveloped him in a discreetly expensive fragrance.
'How are you?' Francesca was Mitch's sister and a
beautiful, brittle bundle of bisexual neuroses.

'Franny, you look gorgeous as ever.'

'Thank you, darling, I love the way you lie.' Francesca was dressed, as always, in black. Her hat was
the size of an umbrella. She was smoker thin and her
raven hair was longer than Philip remembered. It fell
to her shoulders, from where it flipped up jauntily.
She was a beautiful woman, although Philip had never
known her to take a compliment.

'How is the glittering world of fashion?'

'Fashionable. What do you think of the bride?'

Philip swallowed. 'Not sure yet. What do you
think?'

Francesca clicked her tongue.

'You don't like her?'

'I didn't say that.'

'But you have your doubts.'

'They haven't known each other that long.'

'Well, sometimes you don't need to.'

'Oh come on, Philip, you're a realist. Half of all marriages just lead to divorce lawyers getting nicer swimming pools.'

Across the room Philip could see Grace talking to another guest. Mitch was facing a different direction, talking to another person, but they were holding hands.

'The blushing bride,' Francesca said, affecting a southern accent. 'Oh, my lord, do you think Little Bo Peep was aiming for demure?'

Grace's dress was blinding white, with off-the-shoulder puff sleeves, a fitted bodice and a wide ballerina skirt. Her hair had been curled and was piled up in ringlets and fixed with a band of tiny white roses.

'It's not too bad,' Philip said mechanically, because arguing with Francesca was a habit.

'Yes, it probably looked very nice in *Neurotic Bride Monthly*.' Francesca waved his argument away with the flick of her gloved hand. 'What's new with you?'

'Except for my whole new life? Nothing much.'

'I didn't mean work. Why didn't you bring a lovely girlfriend back from the Far East?'

'So you could steal her? Do I look that stupid?'

Francesca laughed. 'You don't look stupid, darling. You look gorgeous and debonair as always.'

Philip bowed slightly, acknowledging the compliment.

'It is funny to think that my family is getting bigger for once,' Francesca said.

Her parents had been killed in a road accident when she and Mitch were eighteen. It had happened just before Philip had met them both, in his first year at Brown. Francesca seldom referred to it and Philip was oddly flattered that she had. Francesca wasn't an easy person to know or love – too many sharp edges and barbed comments. He squeezed her elbow.

'Your turn next.'

'Good lord, Philip, can you see me married with children? What could I possibly teach a child except how to make a proper martini?'

'Martini-making is a useful skill.' He caught sight of his father across the room chatting up a young woman in a too-tight dress. The old goat never missed a trick.

'What about you?' Francesca asked. 'Marriage and kids on the horizon?'

'My heart belongs to nobody but you, Franny.'

Francesca fanned herself coolly with one hand. 'Gallantry. How thrilling in this cynical day and age.'

He enjoyed the day. The wedding was extravagant but he knew that Mitch liked to throw money around and that it pleased him to have his family and friends enjoy his largesse.

He spoke to Grace only once. He took both her hands in his and said congratulations and she said thank you as she kissed him on the cheek. Very demure, very best friend of the groom. Perhaps she wasn't so bad after all.

Both she and Mitch seemed terribly happy and Philip realized that he was happy for them. That day, as he ate and drank and chatted with people he hadn't

seen in some years, the feeling of unease that had
roiled his gut since he arrived back had finally moved
on. He had started on the hotel project and was
relishing the challenges it presented. He looked forward to getting up and going to work each day. In
addition to that, he was settling back into life in
Manhattan, starting to feel like it was his town again.
Maybe he'd follow Mitch's example and find somebody he could begin to think seriously about a future
with.

Eight

Three months later

The hotel started to take shape. There were the usual problems of a large construction job – dealing with the demands of city code, construction crews, neighbours' complaints and the foibles of the designers on the job, but Philip enjoyed it all. As the weeks slipped by, more often than not he found himself collapsing into bed at the end of an equal parts exhausting and exhilarating day and realizing that he had thought of nothing else except work from his first waking moment.

One day he got an email from Mitch. *Come up to the house this weekend.*

Just like that.

Love to but I'm snowed under, he wrote back. A reflex. He'd been so busy for so long that he'd been feeding that response to all his friends without even thinking about it.

A few minutes later, the phone rang.

'Just come up for the day then,' Mitch said. 'The ponds are frozen, we'll go skating. Franny's coming. It'll be just like the old days.'

Philip had fond memories of Mitch and Francesca's big old house in the Berkshires. He'd been going up there ever since college. He stared at the sketches glaring at him from his computer monitor. They were for a new commission he'd just received. He was excited about the job but couldn't get his ideas and his client's to shape up into a coherent whole. Perhaps he did need to get out of town and recharge.

He picked up his car from the garage very early Saturday. The West Side Highway was empty. He punched Puccini into the CD player, stepped on the gas and made good time to the Taconic Highway.

It was a gorgeous crisp day in the Hudson Valley. The trees had lost their fall colour, but after several years in Asia Philip had a new appreciation of winter's stark simplicity. It was good to be home, he thought.

North of Poughkeepsie he took 44 East and trundled through the prosperous farmland of Dutchess County, stopping at Millbrook for breakfast – eggs, toast and criminally weak tea. Out of force of habit he checked his watch when he left the diner, mentally deducting from the journey time the twenty minutes it had taken to eat. He knew exactly how long it took to get to Mitch's house from Manhattan, but it didn't stop him from perpetually trying to shave some time off.

At Armenia he took 22 North. It was ten o'clock and the traffic was heavier, moms heading to the supermarket, families for the bijou ski slopes that dotted the area. He wound down the window, breathed deep and let the freezing air buffet his face.

*

North of Canaan he turned east once more and the car responded to the final stretch of the climb. The trees were tall around here and the frozen ponds added to the stillness of the atmosphere. He turned off the CD player.

The place where Mitch had grown up stood at a crossroads on a hill. The epitome of prosperous recreational New England, it was a big white farmhouse with charcoal shutters and porches on two sides. Two barns, one closed and one open, stood respectfully to one side like uncertain suitors. Behind a five-foot hedge there was a pool and a tennis court. There was also an orchard and a small pine forest.

Philip eased the car into its customary position outside the big barn. Switched off the engine. The front screen door clattered shut and Mitch shouted out, 'He's here!'

Nine

The frozen ground crackled as Philip stepped out of the car to greet Mitch, who was striding across the lawn. He heard the screen door bang shut again and saw Grace standing on the porch, one hand still on the door, an enigmatic smile on her face. 'Great to see you.' Mitch hugged him hard.

'You too,' Philip said. He held him at arm's length and noticed that he'd put on weight. 'Marriage agrees with you.'

'Best thing I ever did,' Mitch said, slinging his left arm around Philip's shoulder.

'Hello, Philip,' Grace said. She was overdressed for the country, he noticed, in too-tight jeans and high-heeled boots. 'Nice to see a fresh face.'

'Grace is still getting used to the idea that this isn't the Hamptons,' Mitch said, ushering Philip inside.

'I didn't say that.' Grace pushed the door shut. 'I never said that.'

'You thought it,' Mitch said over his shoulder, and Philip couldn't tell whether he was joking or not. 'All your friends are in the Hamptons.'

'Just because it's winter doesn't mean you can't go to the beach. Or a few parties.'

Stepping into the house was like coming home. Philip breathed in the sweet familiar smell of woodsmoke, looked at Mitch and grinned with relief.

'Nothing's changed,' Mitch said, understanding.

'Nothing much,' his sister corrected. She was sitting on the sofa in front of the fire, leafing through *Vogue*. 'Hello, darling.' Francesca had spent two years in England at Cambridge University and it showed in her voice when she wanted to be arch.

'Francesca.' Philip crossed to her and planted a kiss on her cheek. She took hold of his hand and examined it briefly.

'How are you?'

'Oh,' she waved a languid hand, 'same old.'

Just as she had been at the wedding, Francesca was dressed head to toe in city black. She had been coming to the Berkshires all her life but she'd made not one single concession to country living in all that time. It wasn't uncommon to see her striding briskly along the road in stiletto heels, a fedora and a fur coat.

Mitch went to the kitchen to get coffee and Philip sat on the sofa next to Francesca. Grace took the chair on the other side of the hearth and smiled brightly at them both. Philip smiled back.

'How was your trip, dear boy?' Francesca asked.

Philip looked at his watch and realized that he hadn't clocked his time when he had turned in the gate as he normally did. 'Pretty good,' he said. 'Not much traffic.'

'We've been all aquiver waiting for you,' Francesca drawled. 'Up since dawn, pacing the metaphorical

42

widow's walk. Grace and Mitch baked cookies. It does get a little slow here on the weekends sometimes.'

'Nothing wrong with that,' Mitch's voice boomed from the kitchen.

'Nevertheless, I'm flattered.' It always took Philip a little time to slip into Francesca's conversational rhythm – it was like playing a clever, skilful game where the ball must not be allowed to fall to the ground.

'Don't be, darling. Fresh blood,' Francesca murmured. 'We thrive on it.' Grace's smile seemed to take on a static quality, which made Philip wonder if they were getting along. Nobody, not even Francesca, denied that she could be difficult. Add in that Mitch was the only family she had left, and Philip could imagine Grace's early married life must not be without its strains.

Mitch arrived with coffee and cookies.

Francesca portioned out a tiny smile and Mitch laughed.

'Well, Francesca will never say it, so I'll say it for her. It's great to have you up here again.' Mitch beamed. 'So tell us what's been happening?'

Philip launched into what he hoped was a witty description of his travails with the hotel. Architecture was the one subject on which he found it easy to be eloquent.

'What about women?' Mitch asked, when he had finished. 'Are you seeing anyone?' he reached over and squeezed Grace's hand as he spoke.

Philip looked down at the rug. There was a perfect round burn mark at his left foot. He had made it when he was twenty – his first and only attempt at smoking.

'Mitch is quite the proselytizer these days,' Francesca said. 'It's enough to warm the hardest heart.'

'And speaking of hardest hearts, how about you?' Philip asked. 'Any romance?'

'It's still open season, darling,' Francesca sighed theatrically. 'And that's the way I like it. Goodness, I can't even choose a china pattern. Imagine how much more difficult it is to settle . . .' she paused as if in search of a delicate enough phrase '. . . matters of the heart.'

The skating pond was about half an hour's drive away. Mitch drove and Philip sat up front.

'How's the job?'

'It's OK,' Mitch said. 'Not really stretching me these days. Been passed over for promotion a couple of times. It hurts.'

'I'm sorry.'

'And I could do with the extra money. Living isn't cheap these days. By the way, you'll have to come and visit our new place when we get settled.'

'You moved?' Philip was shocked. He wasn't that out of the loop, surely?

'Not yet. Next week. Same building, just a bigger place.'

'And a better view,' Grace said from the back seat.

'She's crazy about views.' Mitch changed the car into four-wheel drive as they approached a hill. 'Stares out the window for hours. It's a lot more money but we'll manage it.'

Philip searched his mind to think of something that was wrong with the old apartment. It was about the same size as his, with a fairly big bedroom, a living-room and a decent-sized kitchen and bathroom. By Manhattan standards it was generous.

'Grace wants to make some changes at the farm-house too.' Mitch shifted down a gear as they reached the top of the hill. 'A new kitchen, things like that. We might be calling on you to draw up some plans.'

'Oh,' Philip said, surprised. He couldn't imagine the house ever changing. He didn't want it to change, but he was an architect, so he had to ask the question. 'What sort of things are you thinking of?'

Mitch lowered his voice, although Francesca and Grace were talking in the back seat and not paying any attention to him. 'Just whatever she wants. She doesn't like the place, you see. I've got to make it so she likes it.'

'What are you guys talking about?' Francesca leaned between the seats.

'Talking about how we're all changing. Getting older, re-evaluating our priorities,' Philip said.

'Speak for yourself,' Francesca chipped in from the back seat. 'My priorities haven't changed one bit. All I have ever sought is a hot body, a cool martini and a front-row seat at the Paris shows.'

Grace's hee-haw laugh filled the car as they crested the hill and came in view of the pond.

It was the New England idyll. Kids played hockey. Parents pulled toddlers on sleds. An enterprising person had set up a propane stove and was selling hot chocolate with marshmallows.

Mitch hefted a wicker hamper out of the trunk, followed by a sled on which he had stacked plastic furniture. They were going to picnic in the middle of the pond.

Grace couldn't skate at all, so she clung to Mitch's arm, laughing as he tried to explain the importance of keeping her ankles straight. Francesca shot ahead, a slender streak of practised skill. Philip took the job of pulling the sled. He hadn't been on skates for years and was surprised to find that it was still in his muscle memory.

Most of the skaters were clustered around the edge of the pond. The further out, the quieter it became, just birds and trees and the sun glinting dully off frozen water. Philip realized how much he missed his weekends in the country.

'Are you sure it's thick enough out here?' he shouted to Francesca, who had doubled back and was doing a wide graceful loop with a couple of figures thrown in. Out on the ice, where she didn't have to worry about being sophisticated, she could relax and be joyful. She casually waved a black-gloved hand to dismiss Philip's fears.

'You're making great progress, honey.' Mitch's cheerful voice boomed across the ice. Grace had fallen and was lying on her back. Philip dropped the sled handle and skated over. Mitch was bent over Grace, his hands on his knees.

'You let me go, you bastard,' Grace said, half laughing. 'I trusted you and you dropped me.' She reached out her hands to be helped up and Mitch pulled her to her feet. 'Oh-oh!' She fell backwards again, arms windmilling. Mitch reached out to grab her again and Philip skated away backwards, breathing the still mountain air.

'Charming picture of domesticity, n'est-ce pas?' Francesca skidded to a stop beside him and nodded at Mitch and Grace.

'It's nice to see him so happy.'

'Leave that picnic. Come with me.' Francesca took his hand and led him further out onto the lake.

'I have a little problem,' she said when she'd judged they were out of earshot. 'It's a money problem.'

'Do you need a loan?'

'Don't be silly, darling.' Francesca laid a light hand on his arm. 'Aren't you sweet? No, the problem is a little more delicate than that. Skate with me, indulge my Hans Brinker fantasy, it'll help me think.' They crossed arms as they had used to in the old days and for a few moments the only sound was the crunch of ice under blade. 'I don't know if you know this, but the house is owned jointly by Mitch and me, free and clear. No mortgage, nothing. Not even a low-interest home improvement loan. I'm sure, as a professional in the construction business, that I don't need to tell you it's worth a significant pile of cash.'

'No, you don't,' Philip said, automatically totting up what the place must be worth. High six figures, easily. Maybe seven.

'There's nothing wrong with this house. Absolutely nothing. Every day I'm there I wake up and thank God my grandparents had the foresight to buy it when they did, because there's no way on earth that we could afford it now. Plus there's all our tragic goddamned family history. That house is all that's left of our parents, at least that's the way I see it. I love that place, Philip. As far as I'm concerned, it *is* my family.'

'I know,' he said quietly, wondering where this was leading.

'So last week Mitch told me he's thinking of selling.'

'What! He can't do that.'

'You're damn right he can't, because my name's on the deed. And I told him over my fashionably dressed dead body. And I wonder why he would bother to insult my intelligence in this manner. He knows I would never sell. And I can't afford to buy him out. This week I find out. It turns out that that was just the opening salvo. This morning, after I've been stewing for a week, I find out the real agenda. He wants to raise a mortgage on the place. I think he wants to buy a place in the Hamptons.'

'Mitch hates the Hamptons.'

'Grace wants to be somewhere fashionable.' Francesca spat the words out. 'She wants to hang out in nightclubs with lots of other little Versace tramps who find some rich idiot to buy them three-hundred-dollar bottles of champagne.'

'He'll need your permission.'

'He's not getting it. I told him so.'

'I've had a bad feeling about her,' Philip said slowly. 'On the one hand she seems perfectly nice. On the other . . .'

'Oh, stop being so proper, Philip,' Francesca snapped. 'She's a perfectly nice, perfectly vulgar little gold-digger, and at the rate she's going she'll be the ruin of us.'

Ten

Five months later

Poppy waited for the phone to ring three times before she answered it and when she picked it up she pretended to herself that she wasn't expecting it to be Philip.

'Mate, how's it hanging?' It wasn't Philip. It was her boss, Mick Davis.

'You bastard, why are you bothering me? I just filed.' She channelled some of her frustration about Philip into the pretend rough game she often played with Mick. Mick had a crush on her and he thought he disguised it by treating her as one of the boys.

'I'm bothering you because I've got an offer you can't refuse,' Mick said.

That invariably meant another boring 'economic miracle' story in Taiwan, Poppy thought glumly. Taiwan was her least favourite part of Asia and she hated to do stories about how big fat corporations grew bigger and fatter.

'I can hardly wait.'

'You're gonna thank me for this, mate. Are you sitting down?'

'Yes,' Poppy lied as she poured her third cup of coffee.

'Pete's job is open,' Mick said.

Poppy searched her mental database . . . Pete?

'Pete Kennedy,' Mick said impatiently. 'God, it's not that early in the day, is it?'

Peter Kennedy. Poppy did sit down then. Pete Kennedy was in New York, had been for years. Loved it. No plans for going anywhere. At least that's what he said.

'Why?'

'His wife's got cancer.'

'That's terrible.' Poppy had met Angie Kennedy a couple of times, and liked her. 'What's the prognosis?'

'Looks like she'll be OK, they think they got it in time, but it hit her pretty hard and she wants to go home so they're moving back to Sydney. The good news is the job's yours if you can drag yourself away from Hong Kong.'

Poppy took a deep breath. 'Sounds interesting,' she said, with a coolness that she could almost believe had no connection to the thumping in her chest. 'What about benefits?' Even though her parents were American she had never lived in the States, but she did know that company-paid health insurance was mandatory for peace of mind.

'You'll get insurance and we'll pay fifty per cent of the rent on your apartment and throw in a free trip back home every year. So what do you think?'

'I like the sound of it,' Poppy said, daring to imagine, for a few brief seconds, her and Philip together in New York.

'Good. I've gotta go now, but call me in an hour or so when you've had time to think, consult your runes or whatever you do. Thing is, we need an answer pretty quickly on this.'

There were very few places in the world that actually lived up to their billing. New York was one of them, Poppy decided as the Cathay Pacific plane banked steeply over John F. Kennedy airport, giving her a first-class view of the skyscraper spikes of Manhattan. She was so excited she could hardly breathe. To calm herself down she tightened her seatbelt and re-arranged *Anna Karenina* so that it sat squarely in the seat pocket. It was her favourite novel but she hadn't read a word on the journey. She had not been able to focus on anything except New York and seeing Philip again.

He was picking her up at the airport, at least that's what he had said. She had spent the last several hours preparing herself for his no-show. He was very busy, after all. A dozen times she had mentally rehearsed stepping through the entry gates and scanning the crowds of limo drivers and not seeing him. He would send somebody else, of course. A man like Philip didn't leave you hanging; that would be the height of bad manners. So there would be somebody holding a floppy cardboard slap in the face – with her name misspelled. But she wouldn't cry. She was determined she would not cry.

To her surprise customs formalities were minimal. The customs officers briefly scrutinized her visa and waved her on through with good wishes for the rest of the day.

Poppy picked up her other bag at the carousel. She had two, not including her computer. She always travelled light, even when she moved continents. Most of her belongings were being shipped. She nodded at the older woman who'd sat next to her on the flight, then, taking a deep breath and repeating to herself, 'It doesn't matter,' she stepped through the doors.

He was dressed, Cary Grant style, in a light grey suit. His pose was relaxed and elegant, right hand on the left elbow, left hand cupping his face in a contemplative manner, as if he was posing for a portrait. He was oblivious to the chaos surging around him and seemed to be in deep thought. He didn't notice Poppy until she was standing right in front of him.

'Fancy meeting you here.' She hadn't intended to sound flippant but it was a well-used defence mechanism and she found herself falling back on it without thinking.

At that moment, as Philip embraced her and seemed, she thought, genuinely pleased to see her, she thought she was the happiest person in the entire city.

'Somehow I never pictured you as an Alfa Romeo driver.' Poppy stretched out in her seat with a bag of bagels in her lap. She'd only been in the city a few weeks but she knew she was experiencing a perfect Manhattan moment – heading out of town on a flawless summer morning with the top down.

'How do you mean?'

Philip looked relaxed today, she thought, in an open-necked shirt, a pair of jeans and suede loafers.

Poppy shrugged. 'Well, in psychological terms, cars are aspirational, and Alfas are sexy and fast but unreliable.'

'And I'm none of those things?' The traffic stopped at 76th Street and Philip glanced sideways at Poppy with one eyebrow raised.

'It's a compliment.'

'I'm not sexy? That's a compliment?'

'You know what I mean. Reliable.'

The traffic started again and Philip's eyes returned to the road. Poppy was glad because it meant he couldn't see her blush. She was embarrassed by the fact that she blushed easily – it didn't go with her image of herself as a hardened reporter.

'I see you as more of a Volvo man,' she said, not being able to resist.

'Why?'

'You're careful and precise.' Poppy ripped her bagel into quarters and passed one piece to him. He shook his head. 'And of course you like good design,' she added hastily.

Philip paused a moment before replying. 'This car was my first ever impulse purchase. I saw it in a car yard when I was eighteen. It was love at first sight. I didn't have the money for it so I persuaded the garage owner to let me work for him till I paid it off.'

Poppy stroked the burgundy leather seats. 'Love at first sight? Are you telling me there's a reckless heart beneath that stony, intellectual exterior? Good Lord, stop the car! I've got a story to file.'

'I am a man of unfathomable contradictions,'

Philip said. He was in a very light mood today, Poppy thought with relief. The pressures of working on the hotel had been enormous lately, and often when she saw him he was exhausted.

'What did you do with the car while you were in Hong Kong?'

'I left it with my dad on the strict condition that he only use it to drive little old ladies to church on Sundays. A condition which he was happy to fulfil.'

He sounds like fun – the words nearly escaped but she bit them back. Philip often mentioned his dad, but she hadn't yet been invited to meet him and she didn't want to fish.

Instead she asked, 'What about your mom?'

'She died when I was six.'

'I'm sorry,' Poppy said. She couldn't imagine life without her mother; they spoke on the phone at least four times a week. 'That's a terrible shame.'

'It was. My dad and she had the rarest of things – a happy marriage.'

'You think it's rare to be happily married?' Poppy said, curious and eager to take advantage of this rare confessional moment.

'Well, look at the statistics. Fifty per cent divorce.'

'That still means fifty per cent don't divorce.'

'But are they necessarily happy? People stay together for all sorts of reasons.'

Sometimes his cynicism was just wearying, Poppy thought. And she'd had plenty of practice dealing with cynical people

'That doesn't make them less valid. And what is happiness anyway? A few days out of a lifetime in my experience. Most of the time we're not happy, we're just getting on with stuff. The times we are happy is because happiness has found us, not the other way around.'

'Are you saying I don't have a right to pursue happiness? As an American I'd have to disagree. It's in the constitution.'

'I'm saying you can pursue it all you like,' Poppy said. 'Doesn't mean you're going to hang on to it once you find it.'

The house was dressed up for a party. Chinese lanterns hung from the trees and the verandas. Extravagant bunches of flowers were scattered around the grounds in large terracotta pots and a marquee was set up in the middle of the lawn, complete with a dance floor. White-jacketed staff scurried to and fro bearing trays of food and arranging furniture. There was no sign of the hosts.

'Pretty flash,' Poppy said. 'You do this every year?'

'Yes, but not normally as flash as this,' Philip said dryly. 'Before he met Grace, Mitch's birthday parties were no fancier than a keg and a few bottles of cheap wine. The barbecuing was generally done by whoever thought they were sober enough to handle fire.'

'Sounds like my kind of do,' Poppy murmured.

'Let's go inside,' he said. 'I'll drop the present off.'

The house interior was cool and dark and also lavishly decorated with flowers. The floorboards had been polished and there was a fresh coat of paint in the living-room, a very pale pistachio green. There was new furniture, and paintings on the wall that he didn't recognize. Mitch hadn't followed up on his plan to redo the kitchen yet, but he had definitely made some changes.

He took Mitch's present and put it on the table in the library.

'What'd you get in the end?' Poppy asked, because Philip had been agonizing over the correct gift.

'Some more glasses to match the wedding ones,' Philip said. 'Steuben,' he added absently. 'They can take them back if they don't like them.'

'They'll love them,' Poppy said, taking his hand. 'Since our hosts aren't ready for us yet, why don't you show me the grounds? I need to stretch my legs after the drive.'

Philip was about to reply when they heard a crash in the room above them.

'You've got to stop spending.' It was Mitch's voice. 'You don't know when to stop.'

A second person, it sounded like Grace, said something in response, but her voice was muffled. It sounded as if she was crying.

Mitch said something else, it sounded like ' . . . blood out of a stone', and then there was another crash and the tinkle of broken glass. Philip started up the stairs.

Poppy moved faster. Her arm clamped on to his, so firmly that it hurt and surprised him.

'Don't interfere, Philip. You'll only embarrass them if you go up. C'mon, let's skedaddle before they find out we're here.'

'But . . .'

Poppy shook her head. 'No,' she said. 'Now come on. Let's go outside, take a walk around the grounds and then pretend we've just arrived.'

'A bit different from the old days.' Francesca sat down next to Philip with a nod that took in the marquee and the caterers and the flowers. Dinner had finished, the staff had cleared away and people were dancing.

'Things change,' Philip said.

'My, how they do.'

Something in her tone of voice was different. The ironic distance was gone. Philip looked at Francesca closely. She was drunk. 'You OK, old girl?' he asked gently. 'Want me to take you upstairs?'

She shook her head impatiently, ignoring the opportunity for a lewd comment. 'I've been meaning to talk to you, Philip. I want you to do something for me.'

'Sure.' Philip drained his coffee. The DJ was playing a disco number and Poppy was doing the twist with an old guy in a seersucker suit. You could never accuse her of not mingling. 'Is it about the mortgage?'

Francesca waved a hand. 'I put a stop to that. Told him flat out he couldn't do it. There was a terrible scene but the house is safe, that's the main thing. No, I need you to talk to Mitch. Find out what's bugging him. He won't talk to me.'

'Why not?'

'He thinks I don't like Grace.'

'Is that true?'

'Yes, but not for the reason he thinks. He thinks I'm jealous of her taking him away from me, but I'm more worried about what's happening to him. Mitch isn't himself these days, Philip. He's withdrawn and moody. He was never moody before. And he shouted at me the other day.'

'And you think Grace is responsible?' Philip was thinking about the fight that he and Poppy had overheard.

'I don't know,' Francesca said. 'All I know is that he's closed himself off to me and he's never done that before. He's my little brother, for God's sake.'

'What do you think it's about?'

'Well, I have a theory that . . .' Francesca stopped speaking as Grace came up.

'Not interrupting anything important, am I?'

'Not at all, Grace,' Francesca said wearily. She slumped as if exhausted by the energy of her own thoughts and fears. 'I was just going upstairs to work on my hangover.'

'We haven't cut the cake yet,' Grace said. 'The caterer's about to bring it out any moment. And I can't find Mitch.'

Francesca pushed her chair back and stood up. She seemed surprised to discover that she was quite steady. 'I'm not up for it. Call me next week, Philip,' she said as she walked across the lawn.

'Some thanks I get for all this work.' Grace's voice was tense. She stared at Philip accusingly.

'I'll go and find Mitch,' Philip offered.

*

Mitch was sitting in a deckchair by the pool watching an inflatable mattress bump against the filter. A glass of whisky dangled from his fingertips.

Philip sat down beside him. 'This is the part of the evening where you get to blow out the candles and make a wish.'

Mitch didn't move. He looked up and even in the darkness Philip could tell that his eyes were filled with pain. 'God, I've made a massive hash of things.'

'What do you mean?'

Mitch drew a deep breath and his breath shuddered. 'I'm living a lie, Philip, and it's killing me.'

Philip put a hand on his friend's shoulder. He'd never seen Mitch in this state before. 'I'm sure it can be sorted out,' he said. 'Why don't you tell me what the problem is?'

'It can't be sorted out, that's precisely the problem. I can't get out of it.'

The two men sat in silence. *He realizes he's made a mistake about Grace*, Philip thought.

'Anything can be sorted out,' Philip said. 'Why don't you tell me how I can help?'

Mitch drew another shuddering breath and seemed about to reply when the pool gate creaked open and stiletto heels clicked annoyance along the cut slate. 'Mitch? Is that you? C'mon, sweetie, the cake's ready and everybody's waiting. Some people are driving back to the city tonight so we've got to let them go.'

Mitch looked at his wife and then at Philip, his expression opaque.

'I'm sure they won't mind waiting a few minutes,' Philip said. 'If you want to talk.'

'I'm sure they really will.' Grace's voice snapped with frustration.

'OK.' Mitch hauled himself to his feet with the tired gestures of a much older man. 'Let's blow out some goddamn candles. God knows I could use that wish.'

The party petered out. Guests left in clumps, getting in their cars to drive back to the city. Philip and Poppy were among the last to leave.

The caterers had cleared up effectively, so there was little to do. Grace said the briefest of goodbyes and didn't walk to the car with them. Philip knew she was annoyed with him. *Tough*, he thought. *I'm Mitch's friend, not hers.*

'Call me if you want to talk. Any time.' Philip hugged Mitch before he got in the car.

'I will,' Mitch said as he waved them goodbye.

But he didn't, and that was the last time Philip saw him.

Eleven

One month later

It was six in the morning and a watery dull grey dawn pushed steadily against the darkness. Francesca's car was parked in the driveway of the house. She stood beside it, knuckles tapping softly on the bonnet, lips pursed, eyes on a point far in the distance.

Despite the long drive from the city and the lack of sleep she wasn't tired. Tiredness was inconceivable after what she had seen in the barn. Tiredness was for normal people with normal lives and normal concerns – pension plans, mortgage payments, weight gain. Tiredness wasn't an option for people whose heart had just been ripped out and thrown away.

After tonight – *if* she could get through this – Francesca knew that nothing about normal life would ever bother her ever again. Not her upstairs neighbour who liked to do aerobics at five thirty every morning. Not even her snotty, backstabbing assistant who undermined her authority every chance she got. Not even reality television. After this – assuming there was an after – nothing would touch her. She would be free.

Why me again? The words forced themselves out of her in a whimper. But she knew they were a waste of emotion. From now on she had to channel all her energy into getting through. Later she would be angry at her brother for checking out and leaving her with a godawful mess to clean up. But for now it was step by step. Call the cops, then start arranging the funeral. It wasn't as if she hadn't done it before.

The old house was still, silent and looked peaceful.

Peaceful, Francesca thought. *What a joke.*

She went into the kitchen, making sure not to bang the screen door and wake Grace. She had no idea how she would break the news to her.

The note her brother had written lay on the kitchen table, propped up against the fruit bowl. She opened it.

Grace, I'm so sorry, Mitch.

'Bastard,' Francesca muttered as she picked up the telephone and called the cops.

After she'd made the call she put on a pot of coffee because she needed something to do with her hands.

'Francesca, what are you doing here?' Grace was standing in the doorway wearing a satin nightgown and dressing-gown. 'I thought you weren't coming up until tonight?'

'I drove up. I couldn't sleep.'

'Do you know where Mitch is? He didn't come to bed at all.'

'Grace, sit down. I have some very bad news.'

Grace stared hard at Francesca. 'What are you doing here so early?' she asked again.

'I told you, I couldn't sleep. Grace, please sit down. I need you to . . .'

Grace advanced warily towards the table, where Francesca was sitting. Then she saw the note.

'What's this?'

'It's a suicide note, Grace. Mitch is dead.'

Grace picked up the note gingerly, as if she was expecting it to be hot. She read the words.

'It's to me,' she said dully. 'But this can't be right. He was fine last night. A little preoccupied, under stress, but he . . .' She looked at Francesca and her face tightened into a scowl. 'It can't be. You're playing a horrible trick. I always knew you hated me. Do you think I didn't notice? With your snide little comments and your . . .' Shaking her head, Grace seemed to run out of steam. She reached blindly out for a chair.

'I would never joke about something like this,' Francesca said in a voice so low that Grace could hardly hear her. 'I would never.'

'Where is he?'

'Grace.' Francesca moved towards her, arms out. 'You don't need to see him, honestly.'

'Where is he?' Grace stood up, knocked the chair over. It clattered against the cabinets. 'Jesus Christ, he's my husband!'

'Grace, please, let me take care of this, OK?'

Grace shrank from her. 'You smell of exhaust fumes. Oh my God!'

She was out the door, her dressing-gown flying. Francesca dropped her coffee cup and ran after her.

Whatever else she did, she had to stop Grace from

witnessing the terrible picture that she had seen in the barn.

'I met Mitch at college.' Philip adjusted his glasses and looked up briefly at the crowd that had taken every seat that the funeral home could provide. 'We shared a couple of classes and his room was across the landing from mine. The night we met was a Saturday and, like many of my classmates, I had only one thing on my mind. *Unlike* many of my classmates, that thing was study.' He paused briefly for the polite laugh that rippled around the mourners. 'I had seen Mitch around, of course, and I was in awe of him. He was the guy that everybody seemed to know. He was the one who had by some spooky, osmotic process picked up the inside running of college almost immediately. I think he'd broken up with two sophomores by the time most of us had found out where the cafeteria was.'

Another polite ripple of laughter.

'So when he turned up at my door at seven thirty on a Saturday night with a six-pack and two girls called, I think, Jennifer and Sandy, and offered to take me to a party, I was extremely flattered. I couldn't imagine what he saw in me, the shy kid from New York whose idea of fun was a difficult Russian novel.

'Needless to say, Mitch's idea of fun had nothing to do with Russian novels and lots to do with dancing, loud music and girls. I remember every detail of that night, even all these years later. Mitch had this great gift of cutting through to the things that mattered. In his mind it was irrelevant that we had just met – he said we were going to be friends and so we were.' Philip glanced down at Grace, who was gazing up at him, her face a pale blur of pain. Funny that he had not realized they did have one thing in common – they had both bonded with Mitch instantly.

'Later, when I found out that Mitch's parents had died less than a year previously, I was even more amazed at his approach to life. It was almost as if he had decided to live not just for himself but also on behalf of his parents, whose lives were taken at a young age. The result was that you felt invigorated just being around him. And you hoped that a tiny bit of his vigour and his ... love ... would rub off on you.'

Philip paused and looked up. The room was quiet. He could see Grace and Francesca looking tiny and shrunken in the front row. His father was just behind them, head to one side, biting his lower lip, formally unfamiliar in an expensive-looking dark grey suit.

He looked down at the rest of what he had written. It was garbage, he realized with dismay – a collection of words that sounded right but yet were meaningless. They didn't convey Mitch's spirit any more than did the urn full of ashes.

He cleared his throat and looked up at the crowd once more. 'I would like to say that I have been able to extract some meaning out of Mitch's death, but I can't. And I know that these occasions are supposed to provide some measure of closure for the living. The truth is, I don't feel any closure. I don't know what happened to that cheerful loving young man I knew,

I don't know at what point we lost him or he lost himself. When I compare the picture I hold in my mind of Mitch at college and put it alongside the adult, I don't even know if they're the same person.

'The truth is, I'm angry at Mitch for depriving me of his company and his love and his amazing big-hearted laugh, and angry at myself for not seeing and not knowing and not somehow being able to step into the terrible breach that he saw as so enormous that there was no option except to jump in.'

Philip resumed his seat between Francesca and Grace. Francesca, who had abandoned her customary black and wore vermilion, put a gloved hand on his arm.

'I'm sorry,' he said in a low voice. 'I just couldn't put any spin on it.'

'Say whatever you like,' Francesca whispered. 'There's only me left now and you know I don't care.'

Philip glanced at Grace, who looked as if she had aged twenty years in the last few days. She was looking down at Francesca's hand on his arm and her pinched, sorrowed face seemed to contract even further.

A fraction of hesitation and then Philip reached out and put his arm around her. Her head fell on to his chest as she let out a quiet sob.

Twelve

Two months later

'Have another canapé.' William Ross pushed the plate towards Poppy. She accepted one, tucked her feet under her and leaned back so that the swing moved ever so gently. It was a perfect Indian summer day. They were sitting on the front porch of William's eccentric Victorian house in Nyack, sipping wine and watching the Hudson River roll by.

Philip pulled a face behind his father's back which Poppy refused to acknowledge. She had been warned that William was an enthusiastic but quite terrible cook.

'Thanks, Dad, I'm full. They're absolutely delicious, though,' Philip said when his father offered him the plate. Poppy had noticed that Mitzi, William's Maltese terrier, had been the grateful beneficiary of a couple that had 'fallen' to the ground.

'I'll have another one, William.' Poppy scooped a second snack up and swallowed it with a smile. 'They're simply wonderful.'

'I like you,' William said. 'No food issues.' He used his right index finger to carve quotation marks in the air. 'There's nothing that bores me more than food issues.'

Poppy smiled. 'I went on a diet once when I was a teenager. It made me crabby and one thing I hate worse than feeling fat is feeling crabby.'

'Good on you.' William resumed his seat and beamed at Poppy. He was handsome. This was where Philip had inherited his good looks from. William's hair was gunmetal grey and cropped close to his head. He had a hooked nose that made him look like a Roman senator. He wore army shorts and a T-shirt that revealed tanned skin and a body that was in great shape. He was a real old flirt, Poppy noted happily. And she was making a good impression.

She took a contented sip of wine. The last couple of months had been rough, but they were inching through. Philip's suffering had revealed his vulnerability and their relationship had deepened. He hadn't actually said that he loved her but she felt that he did. A new Philip had emerged, she thought. He was more open, and not so quick to judge. He had invited her to meet his father and they were getting on like a house on fire.

Things couldn't be better.

William poured himself another glass of wine and sat on the wicker sofa next to his son.

'A colleague gave me some tickets to *The Lion King* Friday night but I've already made arrangements. You can have them if you want. I know it's not exactly up your alley but it might be fun.'

'Sounds great,' said Poppy, who loved noisy Broadway musicals.

Philip shook his head. 'I can't do Friday night,' he said. 'I have plans.'

Poppy frowned. She hadn't heard about any plans.

'I'm helping Grace out,' Philip said. 'She's moving into a new apartment and she wants me to help her put up some shelves.'

'On Friday night?' Poppy was glad William asked the question because she didn't think she could have kicked it out there with the right amount of insouciance.

Philip shrugged with just a shade too much casualness. Poppy felt a chill at the base of her spine. She set her wineglass down carefully on the coffee table and folded her hands, waiting for his answer.

'That's the only time she can makc it.'

William glanced at Poppy. He was sharp, she thought. He knows exactly what I'm thinking.

'I thought you didn't like her, Philip.'

'It's nothing to do with like, Dad. She's my best friend's widow. She's alone and she needs help. What am I supposed to do?'

Poppy looked down at the floor. Part of her hated herself for being so mean-spirited. Of course Grace needed help, and Poppy wasn't a jealous person, not at all. But all the same, this news hit her like a punch in the stomach.

'I'm sure she won't mind if you put up her shelves another time,' William went on. 'Explain the situation. Tell her you'll stop by Saturday.'

'I promised her,' Philip said, getting up. 'And I'm not going back on it, OK? So just leave it alone.' He held out his hand to Poppy. 'We should get back,' he said. 'The traffic on the bridge'll be hell.'

Poppy couldn't resist a look at William, who gave a tiny shrug.

'I should know by now,' he said lightly, 'never to try and talk my son out of something once he's made up his mind.'

'I have all these great plans but too late I realize I have not one handy bone in my body.'

Philip kissed Grace on the cheek, a gesture that was becoming easier the more time he spent with her, and he wondered why it was that he had not noticed before how beautiful she was.

She had lost weight in the months since Mitch's death, but whereas before he'd thought her fashionably skinny, now he saw in her gauntness a measure of noble suffering. There was less make-up now, or at least it was more subtle. She no longer lined her eyes heavily and shaded them in blue and gold and she had let her hair grow. It now fell below her shoulders. And she looked good in simple clothes, better than all the high-fashion gear that he loathed. Tonight she was wearing a white T-shirt, Juicy track pants and purple Converse sneakers.

She waved a drill in one hand and a sheet of instructions in the other. 'I hope this won't take too long. You've probably got plans for the evening. I don't want to keep you.'

'Don't be silly,' Philip said. 'I have no plans.'

Not strictly true. Poppy had eventually passed on the Broadway tickets when she'd discovered that two old friends from Hong Kong were making a flying visit. She was taking them out for dinner at Schiller's Liquor Bar and then they planned a sedate trawl through the bars of the Lower East Side.

'Call me, when you're done,' she'd said. 'We won't be going anywhere fast.'

Philip had promised that he would. And when he'd said that he had fully intended to.

'There's no hurry,' he said again.

'Good. I got some wine. No need to suffer just because we're doing chores. Can I invite you to step into the kitchen?' Grace made an exaggerated movement towards the kitchen, which couldn't really be called a kitchen at all. It was a nook, in a studio apartment that wasn't much bigger.

Grace's living standard had fallen drastically since Mitch had died. She had been forced to moved out of the apartment on 76th Street and into a fifth-floor walk-up in Yorkville, a sublet. The neighbourhood was one that Philip didn't much care for – it was full of badly designed high-rises tenanted mostly by recent college graduates with a taste for beer, sports and cheap chainstore clothes. The bars and restaurants of the neighbourhood reflected their lack of discrimination. But Grace had found this apartment though a friend of a friend. As far as anything could be described as such in Manhattan, it was pretty cheap.

Grace poured two glasses of wine, chattering all the while about the changes she was planning to make. Philip listened, checking every now and then that the smile was still on his face. The place sure needed help, but he wasn't sure that a coat of paint would be able to effect the necessary alterations. A wrecking ball, perhaps.

Grace's new apartment was cramped, scruffy and dark. The windows were so encrusted with grime that barely any light got in, although this was in one way a blessing because the view, usually the compensating factor of a walk-up, was squandered by a huge apartment complex of minimal architectural merit. The walls were so ineffectual in blocking sound that Grace said she could hear her next-door neighbour's toaster pop up.

But Grace seemed to like it. Or at least she refused to allow Philip to feel pity for her.

'Cheers,' she said, stuffing the cork back in the bottle and lifting her glass to lightly touch his. 'Here's to . . .' And then she faltered for a moment. Her eyes looked wildly around, as if she was frantically trying to think of something to be happy for.

'Friends,' Philip said as Grace's eyes filled with tears. 'Old friends.'

'Of course,' she said, dashing the tear quickly away. 'Typical me, can never see the terrific things that are right in front of me.'

Philip's heart stirred. It was as if an ancient buried longing for something that he couldn't name was pushing its way up into his consciousness. In the time since Mitch had died there'd been days when he'd feared that his heart was about to crack open and everything inside it come pouring out. This left him feeling as if he could no longer trust himself to stay in control.

Tears came to his eyes.

'Look at us,' Grace said. 'Aren't we a pair?'

To take her in his arms seemed like the most natural thing in the world.

They held each other for what seemed like a long time. Then he pushed her away, angry at himself for feeling guilty. He hadn't done anything wrong. He was comforting the wife of an old friend; that was all.

'Come on,' he said. 'Those shelves aren't going to put themselves up.'

The wall was a mess, so the process took longer than he had expected. Grace offered to help but he turned her down. He didn't want her any closer than absolutely necessary. The feeling that he had somehow betrayed Poppy nagged at him, although he knew it was ridiculous.

Grace seemed to pick up on his discomfort. She sat cross-legged on the floor, fingering her wineglass but not drinking from it.

'I never told you what happened the night Mitch died,' she said suddenly

Philip said nothing as he screwed in the first bracket.

'He had decided to spend the weekend in the country,' she said. 'I didn't really want to go but Mitch said he'd go crazy if he didn't get out of town. I just didn't feel like driving all the way up there and we had a big fight before we left. Usually if I didn't feel like going we didn't go. But this time he'd already decided, I guess. He had it all planned out.

'The traffic was a beast. It was pouring rain and

the roads were jammed; it seemed like every single person in New York City was trying to get out of town, that was partly why I didn't want to go. By the time we got to Brewster we were both pretty cranky so we stopped for a burger and a Coke. He just bolted his down and jumped back in the car and started driving, fast this time. I had to tell him to slow down, I was pretty scared, the roads are narrow and it was dark and raining. He slowed down for a bit then he sped up again. I asked him if everything was OK and he said he was fine but I could tell he wasn't.

'So we get to the house and it's stopped raining but it's dark and cold and I go inside, I'm still mad at him for driving so fast and making me scared. So I go inside and tell him I'm going straight up to bed. He says fine. He's got some things to take care of. And I hear him opening the big barn door and putting the car inside and that was it.'

'Do you have any idea why he decided to do it?' It was the first time Philip had put that question to her. Before, he had always been afraid that she would consider it a reproach.

'There was definitely something up at work,' Grace said, shaking her head as if she had been over this a million times and still couldn't make sense of it. 'There was a lot he didn't tell me.'

'What kind of something?'

'He was very angry about it,' Grace said. 'But he'd never say exactly why. I think he thought they didn't treat him fairly. He'd been passed over for promotion a couple of times. The thing that tortures me is what if our argument that night pushed him over the edge?

What if he hadn't made up his mind until we had our fight?'

'Grace, you can't make somebody commit suicide.'

'My therapist thinks I should just admit I'm angry.'

'Well, aren't you?' Philip said, as he attached the second bracket and rested the bookshelf on top of it. Perfect. He had a very good eye for level and he was proud of it.

'I guess. I don't know. Aren't you?'

'Yes.' Philip put down the drill and squatted so he was at Grace's level. 'I wish the bastard was here right now so I could punch him on the nose.'

He got a little laugh out of her. Encouraged, he took her hands, in a neighbourly, brotherly kind of way, and he looked deep into her eyes. She did have amazing eyes, with long dark lashes. 'It's tough right now but it's going to be all right, I promise you.'

'I wish I shared your optimism,' Grace said, her voice small and flat. 'I really wish I did.'

Thirteen

'Hey, sailor. That was pretty amazing.' Poppy un-wound herself from the sheet and got up. 'Miss me, did you?'

'You could say that.' Philip propped himself up on one elbow and watched her move about the bedroom. She was easy to watch; she had the hard muscles of an athlete, good legs, and her skin was creamy pale. She ran her fingers through her sex-rumpled auburn hair and frowned at her reflection in the mirror.

'How was Mexico City?'

'Now he asks me. It was a disaster. If the phone goes, don't answer it. It'll be my editor, yelling.'

'I wouldn't dream of answering your phone.'

'Or maybe you should answer it and tell him I died or something.' Poppy pulled on a pair of sweat-pants and a T-shirt. 'A mysterious yet fatal disease. That'll put him off his stride for at least thirty seconds. How have things been here?'

'Work, work and more work.'

Not quite true. He'd seen Grace several times in the ten days Poppy had been away. And he'd taken her out to dinner one night, to a terrible Tex-Mex place in her neighbourhood. She was doing better, he told himself, and it was because of his help. He was making a difference for her.

'Seen much of Grace?' Poppy enquired lightly as she opened the refrigerator door. She had promised herself she wouldn't ask. So much for that.

'A couple of times.'

'How's she getting on?'

'Not great actually. She's not having much luck finding work.'

'What does she do?'

'Fashion retail management.'

'Why did she quit when she got married?'

'She got laid off.'

Poppy reached into the fridge, grabbed two bottles of water and took them back to the bed, where Philip had propped himself against the headboard and was watching her with a distant expression in his eyes.

I'm losing him, she thought as she handed him the bottle, and then checked herself. Philip was just doing what any friend would do. He had told her that, repeatedly.

Still, she could no longer deny that she was jealous of Grace Falco and that made her feel small and mean.

What's wrong with me? she thought as she changed her mind about getting back into bed with Philip and sat instead on the side of the bed, holding the cold water in both hands.

'She's really struggling with money. I've had to lend her some so she could buy some clothes to interview in.'

'Oh really?' The cold hand clutching Poppy's heart squeezed even harder. 'Interview clothes,' she repeated slowly. 'If she's that short of cash why didn't she just borrow something from a friend?'

'I don't think she has too many friends. I get the impression she's all alone in the world.'

I'll bet you do, Poppy thought. *I'll just bet you do.*

Fourteen

Frederick Thadeus Marvel sat behind his desk with his feet up. It was a good day, sun shining, birds singing. He had a skim-milk latte within reach and a poppy-seed bagel with light cream cheese and lox balanced on a paper plate on his stomach. His flat stomach now, thanks to Weight Watchers, a daily run and a twice-weekly Bikram yoga class.

He was forty-five years old, recently divorced. He had a kid in college, her name was Sally, she was on the way to becoming a civil engineer and he was pleased with her. He was pleased with his relationship with his ex-wife, Madelaine. They were better friends than they'd ever been the whole time they were married. He was pleased with his new Saucony running shoes, which had not even murmured a protest as he had taken them out on their maiden trot that morning. He was pleased with his new bachelor set-up – a duplex apartment in Fort Greene with a rooftop garden and views of the city and a cute downstairs neighbour with two black pugs and shoulder-length red curls.

Marvel had a weakness for redheads.

He hadn't thought quite so highly of his life a year

ago when he was thirty pounds overweight and his wife had announced she was leaving him. She'd sat him down one evening, handed him a bottle of his favourite boutique beer, told him to get comfortable and explained to him that she didn't need to find herself and there was no other man. She didn't need more space or time to think about the direction her life was taking. She had just decided there was no need for them to be married, especially now that Sally was grown up and gone.

It had been a shock. But after thinking it over, Marvel had been forced to agree with his wife. He had pushed aside his old notions that marriage had to last, no matter what, and had decided to ignore the voice in his head that told him he had failed, and he and Maddie had parted friends. They had sold the big house in Boerum Hill for a satisfying profit, after a semi-serious debate about whether they should divide it into two separate apartments and continue to live there. In the end they decided not to because, in Maddie's words, it was 'too sitcom-y'.

Marvel didn't miss the big house. Truth be told, he didn't miss his old life. He liked being thin and looking younger and not having to worry about neglecting somebody because of all the time he spent at work. He liked his work.

He took a bite of his bagel and chewed slowly, relishing the contrast between the saltiness of the fish and the smoothness of the cream cheese. Low-fat wasn't too bad, not when you considered all the things that were unsatisfactory in this world.

He put the bagel down between bites and flipped

open the folder on the late Mitchell Browning, frowning as he did so. Although Frederick T. Marvel was a long-lapsed and recently divorced Catholic, he still could hear the voice in his head that whispered that taking one's life was a sin against God.

He sipped his coffee and tried to imagine what it must be like to commit suicide. How did you plan it? How did you choose whether to jump or bite the barrel of a gun? How the hell did you word your suicide note?

The coffee was a little cool, so Marvel put it into the tiny microwave oven that he kept in his TriBeCa office. Thirty seconds was all it needed.

Much better. Nothing worse than cold milk. He returned to the file. On the top was a photo of Mitchell Browning. It was a studio shot, head and shoulders. He looks like fun, Marvel thought; the kind of guy who'd strike up a conversation if you met him in a bar. Marvel imagined that Mitch was the kind of guy whose friends would have been shocked at the manner of his death. Not him, Marvel could imagine them saying. Anyone but Mitch. He was never depressed, never down. He loved life.

But Frederick T. Marvel had been in business long enough to know that it was almost always unwise to judge people by their appearance. Look at the photos of murderers. Or serial killers. Can you tell from their faces that they're criminals? With the possible exception of Charles Manson, no.

Frederick T. Marvel had a theory about crime that he would have told anybody if they'd bothered to ask him. Nobody ever had, but he lived in hope that some

day somebody would, so he refined it in contemplative moments like when he was showering or stretching his hamstrings after a stiff run. You never knew,
perhaps one day he'd be interviewed in a magazine.
Weirder things had happened.

His theory was this: leaving aside the sociopaths
and other wackos who did it for the sport or because
their brains were all twisted or because their mothers
had beaten them and locked them in the trunk of the
car when they were six, most people turned to crime
because they couldn't deal with reality.

Middle-class crime, in Marvel's book, was about
the choices people make when it hits them that
they're not going to be millionaires or superstars or
have better sex – whatever it is they think will make
them happy – unless they do something. Something
illegal like ripping off a bank or knocking off the wife.

Normal people, the ones who don't end up doing
twenty to life at your friendly neighbourhood peniten-
tiary, adjust their expectations when life gives them
that little hint. They choose a new path and accept
that they're not going to have a spread in Malibu, a
Swiss bank account and regular three-way action with
Catherine Zeta-Jones and Halle Berry. They make do
with what they have.

Sadly, Mitchell Browning hadn't accepted his lot
in life. He had taken what wasn't his.

Marvel flicked through the file again. He was one
of the few who were acquainted with the fact that
Mitchell Browning was a thief. Browning's good name
was still intact because he had worked for First-
Venture, a publicly listed company whose share price

in recent months had given the board cause for more than a little concern. In these delicate times the board was disinclined to alert the shareholders to the discomforting fact that somebody in their employ had relieved them of ten million dollars. Coupled to that was the larger business climate. Tyco, Enron, Kenneth Lay and Worldcom. White-collar crooks were thick on the ground. FirstVenture was understandably reluctant to be tarred with that brush, which would inevitably happen once the SEC and the FBI started poking around. From there it was a short step to company executives being doorstopped by CNBC.

It was a tricky situation, no argument there. Because even in these days of vastly inflated executive salaries and perks that seemed more commensurate with banana republic dictators than American business leaders, the loss of ten million dollars still stung.

It was a big job. A team of forensic accountants were combing through the company's financial transactions. It could take months. Browning had been clever, not too greedy, taking a little here, a little there. The money guys might never find it all. Marvel was no accountant, but he knew that the lavish lifestyles of drug lords and illegal arms dealers testified to how hilariously easy it was to hide dirty money.

Normally Marvel wouldn't be involved in a case like this; for one thing he didn't have any specialist financial knowledge. Mostly he worked for prosecuting attorneys, tracking down witnesses for court cases, that sort of thing.

But the CEO of the company – a cautious guy who

had a reputation for being thorough – was an old Air Force buddy of Marvel's. They'd flown B-52s together back in the days when the world had worried more about full-scale nuclear strikes.

His buddy's name was Leigh Sampson. And Leigh was worried.

'We were starting to get suspicious,' he had said to Marvel when he'd met him in a bar in midtown because he wanted to keep Marvel's name out of the maelstrom of gossip and speculation that surged through the company. 'But he didn't know we were on to him. So why did he kill himself?'

'Somebody tipped him off?'

'Why not just go?'

'Maybe he had a partner. Partner got greedy.'

'Inside the company?'

Marvel shrugged.

'I want you to find out.'

'Find out what?'

'Anything that could be useful. Maybe the wife or sister knows something.'

'I'll look into it,' Marvel said, not sure whether he could be of any real help.

'Charge whatever you want,' Leigh said, waving his hand as if he was shooing a fly away. 'You got much else on?'

'Couple of things. This won't take long,' Marvel said.

There was no good without evil. No light without dark. Marvel was convinced that within every single person lay the possibility for both. It was all about your own personal tipping point. Which was why he was inclined not to judge Mitch Browning too harshly. They had different weaknesses; that was all. His was Sally. If anybody ever did anything to hurt her he knew that he would not be able to account for his actions.

Marvel finished his coffee and took a moment to savour the experience. In the old days he would have gulped down three or four, loaded with cream and sugar, and not even noticed what he was tasting. Now he took less of everything and enjoyed it more.

That done, he picked up Mitch's photo.

'Let's find out,' he said, flicking his index finger against the smiling face, 'what you were really up to, my friend.'

Fifteen

'Come on in.' Philip kissed Poppy and accepted the bottle of wine that she offered with a murmur of thanks. When he turned to lead her into the living-room, Poppy smoothed down her skirt and ran her fingers through her hair. She was nervous about this dinner party because she knew Grace was coming.

Philip peeled off to the kitchen and told Poppy to make herself at home. To her delight, Francesca was sitting in the living-room, chatting with Philip's father, William. She had run into Francesca a couple of times since Mitch's death because they belonged to the same gym and they had become friends.

William poured Poppy a glass of champagne. Poppy was raising the glass to her lips when she saw Grace coming out of the kitchen with a tray of cocktail snacks.

'Hello, Poppy,' Grace said. 'So nice to see you again.'

Poppy's hand jerked involuntarily and she spilled champagne on her skirt. What the hell was Grace Falco doing in her boyfriend's kitchen playing the hostess? Why wasn't she doing that job? She looked at William for a cue. He raised one eyebrow.

'Grace called when I was in the middle of dinner-party meltdown,' Philip said over his shoulder as he went to answer the doorbell. 'She was fantastic. She came over immediately and got everything sorted out.'

Poppy could think of a couple of biting things to say but she chose to keep them to herself. She dabbed at the champagne on her skirt with a cocktail napkin and was grateful for the opportunity it afforded to keep her head down.

Another couple arrived whom Philip introduced as Herb and Tiffany. Poppy knew Herb by reputation. He was an old high-school friend of Philip's who was developing the hotel that Philip was designing. Herb was a cheerful, round-faced guy with tousled dirty blond hair. Tiffany was tall and scary skinny and looked like she took private scowling lessons from Paris Hilton. A model, Poppy decided as she shook the bony hand, which felt cold and scaly. She wished quite suddenly that she had not come.

Dinner was announced. 'Don't sit next to the person you came with,' Philip said, and Poppy watched as Grace promptly sat down next to him.

'That means I get you, Poppy.' William pulled out the chair next to him on the opposite side of the table. Francesca slipped in the other side of her, squeezed her by the elbow.

'So, Grace,' William said after the first course had been cleared away and Philip was carving the roast lamb, 'tell us a little bit about yourself.'

'Not much to tell,' Grace said, taking the plate Philip passed to her and handing it on to Herb, who sat on her left.

'Where did you grow up?' William ignored her.

'Westchester.'

'Oh really? Whereabouts?'

Grace hesitated. 'It's not that interesting or glamorous.'

'Try me.'

'Dad, don't interrogate my guests,' Philip said, but Poppy looked on with interest and a small amount of satisfaction. William had no shame, God bless him.

'I grew up just outside Pleasantville.'

'Do your parents still live there?'

'Both my parents are dead.' Grace gave a wistful smile.

William didn't bother with the false expressions of sympathy. He pressed right on.

'And where did you go to college?'

'A little place in Oregon, nobody's ever heard of it.'

'I'm an academic,' William said with a broad, easy smile. Grace appealed to Philip for help, but he too was now looking at her with interest. 'Give it your best shot.'

'It's called St Agnes. It's a Catholic all-women's college.'

'Ohh, sounds like heaven,' Francesca murmured. Laughter rippled around the table and the thread of the conversation was broken.

Poppy didn't laugh. She was looking at Grace, who had turned to say something to Herb. Grace sensed that Poppy was looking at her and looked up. Their gaze met. Grace smiled her wistful, widow smile and Poppy raised her glass to her; her answering smile was friendly and uncomplicated.

'Are you having a good time?' she asked.

'Oh yes,' Grace said. 'It's so nice to be among friends.'

Poppy felt a little flutter of excitement – it was almost like falling in love.

A cop had once taught her this trick to gauge whether a person was lying. You asked a person a question that you knew the answer to, or one that they were likely to tell the truth about, and watched which way their eyes moved. For instance, if their eyes moved up to the left when they told the truth, they moved down to the right when they lied.

Grace's eyes had moved down and left when she had answered Poppy's rather inane question, differently from William's questions.

Had she lied about her background? Why would she do that?

Poppy piled a heap of vegetables on her plate and considered, with a little malice, that it might be interesting to find out.

Sixteen

Two weeks later

Francesca pulled her sunglasses from her forehead on to her nose and slipped the car into top gear. The Audi TT pulled ahead smoothly, overtaking some loser in a Dodge Durango. The car was new and it had cost a fortune, but what the hell – she was a single woman, no partner, no kids. No anybody any more. If being completely alone in the world was going to have its compensations, Francesca thought, precision German engineering would be one of them.

The car handled beautifully. For several miles Francesca allowed herself the luxury of just enjoying the familiar drive and not thinking about what lay ahead. It was lunchtime on a Saturday and the road was reasonably clear. She was making good time, so she stopped in at the Red Rooster in Brewster to grab a salad for lunch. She took her food to one of the outside picnic tables.

For the first time in months, she was going back to the house. She hadn't spent any time there since Mitch had gone.

I hate being the only one left, Francesca thought as she speared a tomato with her fork. *I feel like a freak. Why didn't I die young like the rest of them?*

She wished suddenly that she'd asked Poppy to come with her. Poppy would be an excellent buffer for all the psychic weirdness that was bound to come up. She had been nagging Francesca to take care of business, get all the clutter out, cleanse her energy channels. And she'd offered a million times to accompany her up to the house.

But no, Francesca thought. *I have to do it the hard way. What is that about? There are no prizes for being pigheaded.* She sighed, suddenly irritated and bored with herself and her stupid rules that only seemed to make life more difficult, then took out her cellphone and pressed Poppy's number.

'Hey, it's me,' she said. 'I just had a thought. If you jump on the train at Grand Central, I can pick you up at Wassaic . . . You still wanna do that? OK . . . Call me when you know which train you're on.'

She snapped the phone shut and tackled her salad with gusto. Poppy was coming. It was going to be OK.

Seventeen

So many memories. Francesca rolled over in bed and blinked. Sometimes when she woke in the house she had trouble not remembering *where* she was but *when.* The house had a disconcerting way of blurring and mixing events so that the present seemed like the past, and vice versa.

She was seven years old and it was Christmas. Mitch had woken her at three and they'd gone downstairs and opened all their presents in an orgiastic frenzy. Their parents, furious, had confiscated the presents and had only given them back after Francesca cried for two hours.

She was fifteen and in love (or so she thought) with Lenny Purcell, a geeky local kid whom nobody else liked. But he had sharp brains and a sly sense of humour and Francesca had always chosen brains over looks. It turned out that Lenny's sense of humour wasn't the only thing about him that was sly. Mitch had found out that he had another girlfriend and when he'd told her she'd hit her brother. Punched him right in the gut. Twenty years later Francesca could still feel the flush of shame – she had hit her brother, the person she loved most in the world.

The funny thing was that Mitch hadn't been cross with her. He had laughed. *You punch like a girl*, he'd said, before walking off, hitching his belt up with a slight swagger. Years later he had told her that the punch had hurt like hell.

And that morning in this house. She was eighteen when the police officer arrived and asked them both to sit down, as if a change of position could possibly lessen the horror of what he was about to say. *I'm dreadfully sorry*, and then the short sentence that brought the world as they knew it to an end. Francesca was often surprised that she had not ever fully recovered from the death of her parents. Everybody – the grief counsellors, her teachers, an ineffectual minister – had told her that she would, and she had believed them. But she'd realized after Mitch had gone that it was all lurking there, waiting to pounce so that she could begin to suffer all over again.

'Rise and shine.' Poppy came into the bedroom with a tray bearing coffee. 'It's a beautiful day.'

'God,' Francesca said, sitting up in shock. 'It's nine o'clock. I'm never awake at this hour.'

'Today you are.' Poppy was wearing running pants and shoes. Francesca squinted suspiciously at her.

'Don't tell me you've been out running,' she said.

'Just going. You have your coffee and when I get back I'll make us bacon and eggs.'

Francesca lay down and pulled the blankets over her head. 'I hate you.'

*

The air smelled of woodsmoke and grass. Thousands of feet above, two jet vapour trails sketched the cross of Saint Andrew against a pale blue sky.

Poppy began slowly jogging towards the gate. She looked carefully both ways before stepping out on to the road. A blue sedan had stopped at the intersection about fifty feet away and didn't seem in a hurry to move, even though there was no traffic approaching.

The joys of the country, Poppy thought as she started off in the other direction. There was no rush to be anywhere.

She couldn't honestly say she liked running, but she did enjoy the feeling of *having* run, a satisfactory cocktail of endorphins and smugness. Plus, this morning there was the benefit of being on unfamiliar territory. While she looked at elegant New England country homes and gardens she didn't have to concentrate so much on how her knees and her back creaked. In this way the time passed, so it was nearly an hour later when she arrived back at the house.

The blue car was still there.

She slowed to a stop in the driveway and pretended to do some stretches, trying to catch a look at the driver. Was he a weirdo who liked to stare at other people's houses? Or had he merely pulled over to have a nap or a cup of coffee?

She went into the house, kicking off her shoes at the front door. Francesca was sitting in the kitchen, two hands clasped around a coffee mug, listening to the radio.

'Hey,' she said. 'Get you a coffee?'

Poppy sat at the kitchen table, making sure she had a view out the window. The blue car had not moved. 'Sure.'

'Enjoy your run?' Francesca opened the cupboard door and selected a coffee cup.

'More or less.' Poppy took the cup from her. She decided not to mention the blue car to Francesca; she seemed edgy enough already.

'I always used to feel so peaceful here,' Francesca said, sitting down again. 'I don't feel like that any more. Mitch made the house over to me before he died. I wonder if I should just sell the place, buy some place where I don't have any history.'

'That's why Grace is hard up? She didn't get anything from Mitch?'

'Not to speak of. Mitch's lifestyle was largely an illusion. He had lots of debt. And I guess when he had made up his mind to check out he decided the house should stay in the family.' Francesca sighed. 'I should feel sorry for Grace. But I don't.'

Outside the window a tractor chugged by; the blue car remained where it was.

Marvel sat in the car with a cappuccino and a low-fat blueberry orange muffin that he'd bought at a café in Great Barrington. He had been tempted to stay and eat his breakfast in the café. Great Barrington was a good mix of weekenders and Massachusetts locals, those two tribes forever divided by footwear and attitude. It made for great rubbernecking.

But the big old house was calling to him. So he

had balanced the muffin on his lap, put the cup in one of the many 'beverage' containers that the rental car afforded the discerning drinker, put the car in gear and driven out there.

He had spent the previous day talking to the local cops and the medical examiner about Mitch Browning's suicide. He liked to be on the ground, you picked up things in person that were sometimes lost in a phone conversation. That was the way he worked, sifting, judging, looking at the things not said.

The cop was new in town, he said, and hadn't known Mitch personally, but the medical examiner, who was also the local doctor, had been friends of the family for years. Neither had any reason to believe that his death was anything other than what it appeared. Marvel had requested both the police and the autopsy reports.

The big white house had been empty the first time he'd driven by on Saturday morning. It was sheer instinct that had taken him back; he'd seen the fancy car parked in the driveway and, later, the redhead sprinting down the road, and figured that he might find out something interesting if he stuck around.

'So much stuff.' Francesca ran a hand over the jackets in Mitch's wardrobe. 'I should have done this ages ago.'

'It won't take long,' Poppy said. 'And you'll feel better when it's over.'

'Most of it will go to the Goodwill.' Francesca took an armful of sweaters off the shelf and scooped them into a black trash bag. 'Take anything you want, by the way. I want nothing hanging around.'

Poppy picked up a white shirt, held it against her chest and debated whether she should take it. She'd been wearing second-hand clothes all her life so she didn't have any qualms about wearing dead people's stuff.

'Doesn't Grace want any of this?'

'Grace?' Francesca fairly snorted. 'Please. Once she found out there wasn't any money she lost interest in Mitch's affairs.'

Poppy said nothing. She held the shirt in one hand, forefinger flicking the thumb of her other hand.

'Is it time to have the Grace talk?' Francesca asked, knowing what the answer was.

It came out in a dambreak of words. 'He's spending time with her and yet he says there's nothing going on. He refuses to talk about it. I feel like I'm being carved up, slowly and painfully and in utter silence. He didn't even used to like her. He used to tell me he couldn't see what Mitch saw in her.'

'Survivor's guilt. Think of all the firefighters who left their wives and married 9/11 widows. Dozens,' Francesca said. 'It's a documented phenomenon.'

'That's supposed to make me feel better?' Poppy put the white shirt in the to-go pile. She realized that she really didn't care for it.

'All I'm saying, sweetie, is it's not about you. Philip is dealing with this badly because that's who he is.

You know him, he's not exactly emotionally articulate.'

'That's no excuse!' Poppy said angrily.

'I'm being realistic,' Francesca said. 'Taking emotions out of the equation so you can see it for what it is. Grace is an Upper East Side gold-digger who gets her feminist manifesto from Candace Bushnell. All she wants is somebody to keep her, buy her new shoes and a place in the Hamptons. Once she figures out that Philip doesn't have access to those kinds of resources, she'll move on.'

'And I'm supposed to wait around till she does?'

'I didn't say that.' Francesca didn't even look at the clothes she was putting in the rubbish bags, she picked and scooped, picked and scooped. 'On the other hand, Philip's vulnerable too. He's lost his best friend. I've known Philip a long time. He's the original stand-up guy. Mr Utterly Correct in Every Situation.'

'He's not being correct with me.' Poppy flopped on to the bed, sighing.

'He's a guy. Guys don't like mess, they don't know how to deal with it.'

'I think that's a feeble excuse. Why are you taking his side?'

'I'm not. I'm laying it out. So you can see. For instance, have you had the talk?'

'Talk? What talk?'

'The talk about the future. Where the relationship is heading. Has he mentioned you moving in?'

'No.'

'Has he said he loves you?'

'No.'

'Then as far as he's concerned he's a free agent.'

Poppy groaned. 'Why does it have to be so hard?'

She sat up and Francesca laid a kindly hand on her shoulder. 'It is what it is, Young Skywalker. You can't change it, all you can figure out is how you want to respond. Now how about this? This looks like your style.'

Francesca held up an expensive-looking dark purple Patagonia windbreaker and Poppy was relieved to be diverted from the subject. 'This looks nice. I could use that.'

Francesca held it up so Poppy could put her arms into the sleeves.

'It was one of Mitch's favourites,' Francesca said. 'He used to wear it when he went out walking. He said it was very warm, even though it didn't look it. For some reason he was particularly proud of that fact.'

'It'd be useful for running.' Poppy zipped up the jacket, put her hands in the pockets and pulled out a small black Moleskine notebook, secured by an elastic band. She passed it to Francesca, who paged it briskly with her crimson-tipped fingers.

'Speak of the devil.'

Francesca passed Poppy the notebook. 'It's Mitch's handwriting. But then it would be. It was, after all, his jacket.'

The list was written in an untidy cursive, laid out like a shopping list.

Is G. lying?

Who is she really?

And then.

Talk to Philip.

Poppy looked at Francesca. 'Do you know what this is about?'

Francesca shook her head wearily. 'No. Communication in our dear little nuclear family was in scant supply in the last months. Another little gift from Grace to Mitch and me. She wanted him to raise some money on this house and I refused, so I wasn't his favourite person.'

Poppy shrugged the jacket off, throwing it on the to-go pile. It wasn't really her style after all.

Eighteen

Marvel knocked on the front door and stood waiting, moving from foot to foot.

'Yes?' The dark-haired woman who opened the front door was austerely beautiful. Or maybe she was just austere. She looked as if she hadn't smiled in years.

'Good morning.' Marvel handed her his card. 'I'm Frederick Marvel.'

The woman looked at the card. 'Shouldn't you be in a comic strip?'

The edges of Marvel's mouth twitched up. A formality. He'd heard all the lines before.

'What do you want, Mr Marvel?'

'I'm investigating your brother's death, Miss Browning.'

'On whose behalf?'

'His employer. There's some question of benefits.'

'I thought that had been straightened out.'

'We like to make absolutely sure,' Marvel said smoothly.

The door started to close. 'I really don't have the time,' she began. But a voice stopped her. Its owner had an accent; sounded English or something.

'C'mon, Franny, we might find out something.'

The door hovered between open and closed for a few seconds then swung back. He saw them standing side by side. But he really only noticed the redhead.

Trying his best not to gape, he almost didn't see that she had held out her hand. 'I'm Alexandra Adams,' she said with a professional smile, 'but most people call me Poppy. Why don't you come in?'

'Are you a cop?'

'No. I work for the same company as your late brother. I'm sorry for your loss,' Marvel said as he accepted the invitation to sit down. It was a beautiful room, made warm and welcoming by the morning sun. What a shame that Mitchell Browning had had to screw everything up so royally, Marvel thought. This wasn't a bad life, lots to like about it.

'You were parked outside the house,' Poppy said. 'I saw you this morning when I went for my run. What are you looking for?'

'I don't know,' Marvel said.

'Well, how will you know when you find it?'

'I'll know.'

'I need more coffee.' Francesca stood up. 'Anybody?'

'Please,' Poppy and Marvel said in unison.

She stared at him frankly when they were alone. Marvel was grateful that his gut was gone. He ran his hand through his hair, not too much grey. He looked all right, last time he'd checked in the mirror. He wasn't some young buck with no life experience, he'd been in the armed services, had a law degree from a good school.

She had a keen gaze. She was smart. She was smart enough to wait for Francesca to come back before she said anything of consequence. He listened to her as she chatted blandly about the countryside, the weather. It was a classic warm-up, he'd used it many, many times in the past.

Francesca came back with coffee and cookies on a tray. Marvel refused milk, sugar and calories.

'How can we help you?' Poppy asked pleasantly yet firmly.

Marvel took a sip of coffee before replying. 'There are a number of financial loose ends created by Mr Browning's death,' he said. 'The company has asked me to tie a few of them up.'

'What kind of loose ends?' Poppy asked.

Francesca glanced at Poppy before looking at Marvel. She hadn't touched her coffee and her arms were folded tightly over her chest. She's nervous, Marvel thought.

'I've left you a number of messages, Miss Browning,' he said, ignoring the question. 'Unfortunately you haven't been able to find the time to reply.'

'What is it that you want to know?' Francesca asked.

'Did you notice anything unusual about your brother in the time leading up to his death?'

'I didn't see much of him,' Francesca said. 'He got married.'

'But you spent time together. In this house.'

Poppy glanced at Francesca and Marvel took notice of that look.

'Any financial problems that you know of?'

'Well, obviously,' Francesca snapped. 'I'm not stupid. There was something. Had to be.'

'How do you know that?'

'Please,' Francesca sighed, reaching for her cigarettes, 'let's not insult each other's intelligence.' She lit the cigarette and breathed out. 'Why don't you tell us what's actually going on?'

Marvel looked from one woman to the other.

'Mitch appropriated some of his company's funds.'

Francesca drew a sharp breath and her whole body seemed to recede. Poppy reached out and gripped her hand.

'How much is some?'

'We don't know yet,' Marvel lied.

'Ballpark?' Francesca's voice was harsh and low.

'As far as we can tell, it's a significant amount.'

'Significant.'

'Yes.'

'And you're trying to find it?'

'That's right.'

'Where do you think it might be?' Poppy asked.

'I don't know.'

'Shall we look down the back of the sofa?'

'Be my guest. The reason I called you, Miss Browning, is that I'm interested in anything you might be able to tell me about the days leading up to your brother's death. Did he say or do anything unusual? Did he meet anybody?'

'You should be asking Grace these questions,' Francesca said. 'I talked to him on the phone the Wednesday before he died. He told me he was coming up to the house at the weekend. I planned to come up Saturday morning, but I changed my mind and drove up in the middle of the night.'

'Why?'

'I was at a party at the Cloisters,' Francesca said. 'It was pretty dull. I decided I'd rather be driving.'

'That your car outside?'

'No, it belongs to Hillary Clinton.'

'Nice wheels.'

Francesca nodded dismissively.

'What about you, Poppy?' Even the name sounded delightful on his tongue.

'I'm a friend of Francesca's,' Poppy said. 'I met her brother probably twice. I really can't help you.'

No point in wasting any more time. He got up and took two cards out of his wallet and handed one to each of them. 'If you think of anything at all, please contact me. I'd be happy to hear from you.'

He was pleased to note that while Francesca barely glanced at the card before she put it on the coffee table, Poppy studied it before putting it into her jeans pocket.

Nineteen

Philip sat at the bar watching Grace walk towards him. He felt a little tipsy. Grace had called to say she was feeling down, so he'd offered to take her out to dinner at a fancy new place that she'd said she would like to check out. It wasn't the kind the place he would normally have gone, he wasn't much into expensive restaurants. But it had made Grace happy to be there and watching her had made him feel better. It was, he told himself, the least he could do for Mitch.

'How's the job hunt going?' he asked as Grace resumed her seat. She was wearing shiny leather pants that looked expensive and new, although she said she'd got a great deal on them at a consignment store on Lexington Avenue.

'What?'

'How's the job hunt going?' Philip repeated. He really hoped he wasn't so drunk that he was slurring his words.

'Oh. Oh that. Fine. Lots of interviews but no solid leads.' Grace's smile was wistful. 'It's hard, you know? Hard to keep a positive attitude when you don't know how the rent is going to be paid. Sometimes I wonder whether I should just get a job waitressing or something.'

'That's counter-productive,' Philip said. 'Because you won't then have time to go on interviews. Job-hunting is a job, that's the way you have to treat it.'

'You're right.' Grace sipped from her water-glass and her eyes got a little teary.

'Everything OK?' His hand came out to cover hers.

'Of course. Everything's as fine as it can be.'

'Do you need help with the rent again?'

'Oh, that's very sweet of you, Philip. You're so kind to me but I couldn't.'

'Why not?'

'You've already done too much. Besides, I know I'll get a job any day now.' Grace paused and drew a breath. 'It's just a matter of hanging on and not losing my nerve. Something will turn up, it just has to.'

'Goddammit, Grace. Stop that!' Philip didn't actually slap his hand down on the bar but he felt like it. 'There are no medals for martyrs. I have the money and I want to help you. So let me write you a cheque. I can do it right now. I have my chequebook right here.'

Grace's eyes filled with tears properly this time. She hugged Philip and whispered her thanks in his ear.

'Eighteen hundred, right?' Philip began writing. The son of a Scottish school-teacher, he had been raised to be careful with his money. But since he had been getting to know Grace that had changed. He felt good spreading it around.

'Actually,' Grace cleared her throat, 'it's two thousand.'

'Oh, I thought you said eighteen hundred.'

'I told you a little white lie, so you wouldn't feel so bad for me.'

Philip dashed off the cheque. 'One of the joys of living in New York City,' he said. 'Paying too much money for not enough space.'

'You have a nice space,' Grace said as she took the cheque and made it disappear. 'Do you own your apartment?'

'Thanks to my mother. She left me a small inheritance when she died. I bought the apartment soon after I got out of grad school – mostly so I could have something to work on.'

'So nice to have that cushion.'

'I couldn't afford to buy it now, for sure,' Philip said, adding with a gallantry that had used to be foreign to his nature, 'and if it gives me the opportunity to help out a friend when she needs it, then I'm glad.'

'I feel like a kept woman,' Grace said and giggled. The giggle that used to annoy him.

'Well, you're not. You're just going through a bad patch and you have friends who can help you out. Just as you would do if the tables were reversed. So let's not hear any more about it, OK?'

'OK.' She leaned forward and at first he thought she was going to kiss him. But she stopped. A look of surprised alarm froze on her face.

'What's the matter?'

'Nothing.' She squeezed his arm.

A mirror ran behind the bar, making it look as though there were twice as many bottles and twice as many people having a rousing good time as there actually were. Grace had her back to it but Philip could see a man reflected there, regarding Grace with more than casual interest.

'You know what? I don't feel like being here any more,' she said. 'I read about this great new place on Third, let's go there.'

Philip looked at the man in the glass, who had transferred his gaze from Grace to him. There was a mocking look in his eye, a matched set with the mouth that curved in an ironic half smile. He was tall, as tall as Philip, and his snug-fitting shirt revealed that he most likely spent a lot of time at the gym.

'Grace Falco. As I live and breathe.'

He had a slightly nasal voice. Philip looked down at his shoes. He was wearing cowboy boots and the heels were worn away. His skin was very pale.

'Whitney.' Grace's voice was flat, without inflection.

'How are you?'

'We're leaving is how we are.' Grace tugged on Philip's sleeve.

But Philip remained where he was. He was curious.

'Philip Ross.' He held out his hand and delivered a professional, neutral smile. Grace shot him a sharp look. He had the feeling that she wanted to stamp her foot.

'Paul Whitney.'

'Nice to meet you, Paul. We were just ordering another round. What can I get you to drink?'

'Absolut martini, straight up with a twist.' He said it smooth, like a mantra.

Philip repeated the instruction to the bartender. 'Come here often?' he asked Whitney.

'Just got back into town.' Whitney's eyes slid across to Grace. She sat still on her stool, her arms crossed. 'Been away.'

The martini arrived. Whitney sipped it with a delicacy that belied his bulk. 'Thanks,' he said.

'My pleasure. How do you two know each other?' Philip hoped he wasn't overdoing the avuncular uncle.

'We go way back.' Whitney smiled at Grace. She looked at him without expression. 'College, wasn't it, sweetheart?'

'You know it wasn't, Whitney. Stop telling lies.'

'Earlier then. High school perhaps.' Whitney shrugged, lowered the level in his glass some more and directed his gaze to Philip. 'And how do you know Grace?'

'Mutual friends,' Philip said. If Whitney wasn't going to give anything away then neither was he.

'Mutual friends. That's nice.' Whitney bestowed his smile evenly between the two of them. His teeth weren't very good. His canines sloped forward, giving him a wolfish, snaggletooth look. Combine it with the goatee beard and the word trouble popped right up. 'How've you been, Grace?'

'I'm fine, Whitney.'

'You look fine. Look like you're doing well for yourself. Keeping your head above water.'

Grace smiled thinly. 'What's the alternative?'

'Alternative? Plenty. Especially in this great big country. Land of the free.' He laid a subtle emphasis on the last word.

Grace stood up. 'Philip, we really have to go. I have to be up early tomorrow for a job interview. Goodnight, Whitney.'

She grabbed Philip's arm in a surprisingly tight grip and he just had time to pick up his briefcase before she had herded him out the door.

'What was that about?' he asked as they stood on Park trying to hail a cab. 'You didn't tell me you had a job interview.'

'I don't. He's a creep and a loser. I knew him years ago and I didn't like him then either.'

'He seemed pleasant enough,' Philip said, enjoying the perverse sensation of penetrating Grace's façade. He didn't know nearly as much about her as he would like to.

'Well, he isn't.' A taxi drew up going uptown and Grace jumped in with a curt wave.

Philip intended to catch a cab going downtown but it was a mild evening and Park Avenue was holy ground for him, so he started walking. Even though he had seen the grand temples of Mies van der Rohe, Philip Johnson and McKim, Mead and White many, many times before, he could always allow himself to be seduced by them. It was safe here. Buildings weren't like people; they didn't stir up confusing emotions. A building was a building, either you liked it or you didn't. Over time you might grow to like something you had previously disliked, and vice versa, but the process was glacial. With buildings you didn't feel one thing about them one minute and another the next minute, or – even worse – both emotions at exactly the same time. You didn't feel quite so shaken up and out of control. That was why architecture had been more than just his profession these many years; it had also been his refuge.

He had been walking around for some time before he realized he was back outside the same bar that he'd just left and an idea occurred to him. Perhaps Paul Whitney was still there, working on his martini. Perhaps he would go in and sit down with him and have a talk, straight up. Talk about this woman called Grace Falco; deconstruct her. Try to figure her out. Find out something about her.

He had taken three steps inside when he realized why this was a bad idea. Paul Whitney was still there all right, sitting on the stool that Philip had vacated, another martini at his elbow, accessorized with an idle swirl of lemon peel.

And Grace Falco was sitting right beside him.

Twenty

I don't want to break up while eating soup dumplings, Poppy thought. Trouble was, she doubted she had a choice. Things had, as her mother was fond of saying, reached a pass. She sat a little straighter.

'Philip. Is everything OK?'

'I'm sorry?' Philip started as if he'd been spoken to by a stranger on the street. They were sitting in a busy Chinatown restaurant in front of plates of food. Philip had barely touched his, and Poppy's attempts at conversation had drawn unsatisfactory replies.

She carefully placed a dumpling on her spoon and bit a small hole so the hot, oily juices flowed out. She sipped. Magnificent. Then she picked up the tiny bowl of ginger and soy sauce and poured it over the dumpling. There was no way to do this elegantly and she had long ago given up trying.

'I'm sorry,' Philip repeated. 'What did you say? I was miles away.'

'Well then, it's funny that you should ask, because I said, what's on your mind?'

'Work,' Philip said after a short pause. 'Big hassles with the contractor. Looks like we might have to fire him. Herb is pitching a fit as his opening date gets pushed back further and further. It's a bit of a mess. How was your weekend in the Berkshires?'

'Not a laugh riot but as good as could be expected. Fran held it together pretty well. I made lots of coffee.'

'It was nice of you to offer to help,' Philip said automatically.

'Yeah, well, that's the kind of girl I am,' Poppy drawled to cover her dismay. Philip had the distant, formal manner of a child trapped into lunching with an elderly aunt.

Another plate of food arrived. Salt and pepper squid. They now officially had way too much food. *I always over-order when I'm nervous*, Poppy thought, reaching for the squid anyway and putting some in a neat pile on her plate.

'I took Grace out for dinner while you were away,' Philip said casually. 'She was feeling a bit down so we went to Lever House to cheer her up.'

Poppy nearly choked on her three-dollar dumplings. Lever House? Lever House was so deep in fat CEO expense account territory that you needed a native guide and a camel caravan to get there. He had never taken her to a place even remotely like it.

'And did it?' Poppy made what she thought was a pretty fine effort to keep her voice neutral. 'Cheer her up?'

'She seemed to like it.'

Maybe a soup dumpling joint *was* the ideal place to break up, Poppy thought as she smothered a sarcastic reply. She looked around the vast room. There were very few white people; most of the customers were either silently slurping down noodles or chattering loudly in large Chinese family parties. Nobody was looking at them or paying them any attention.

She put down her chopsticks. 'Philip,' she said. 'I think it's time we had a talk.'

Philip looked up from his food. For the first time that day he really looked at her. And not in a good way – it was as if he was a scientist examining a strange new insect.

'First off the bat, I need to know where I stand with you, and second I need to tell you something about Grace.'

'What about Grace?'

'Me first,' Poppy said firmly. 'Let me finish. I'm uncomfortable with the amount of time you're spending with her and the types of outings you're taking her on. It sounds a lot like dating to me. You may think you're doing the right thing for the widow of your friend, but I think that you've crossed the line. I'm unhappy with the fact that I hardly ever see you any more and every time I call you to arrange something you invariably have an excuse. You're treating me shabbily, Philip. It upsets and humiliates me.'

Philip made to say something but Poppy silenced him with a wave of her hand.

'I guess what I need to know is . . .' Poppy swallowed. She thought she might cry. How dreadful. 'I guess what I need to know is . . . whether you love me or not. Because if you love me . . .' she rushed on because she didn't like the mix of confusion and annoyance she saw reflected in his eyes ' . . . I can put up with Grace. I've got big shoulders, I'm not a jealous person, I can feel pity for orphans and widows. But if you're just stringing me along, then I need to know now. Before I begin to hate myself and you.'

Philip blanched as if a dumpling had lodged in his throat.

'Well, this is a surprise,' he said faintly.

God, in many ways he was so dense, she thought. If circumstances had been different she might have laughed.

'You don't mean that.'

Philip looked puzzled.

'A surprise? I followed you halfway around the world,' Poppy said. 'Didn't that give you just a tiny hint?'

Perhaps not.

'Never mind,' she said. 'Look. I get the message, OK? You don't love me, fine.'

'I didn't say that . . .'

'You didn't have to. I saw the way you reacted. It was like you'd got something stuck on your shoe.'

'I just . . . need some time to think about it.'

'No, Philip. If you loved me you wouldn't have to think about it. I don't have to think about loving you. I know. Even when I wake up in the morning in some crummy hotel and can't remember where I am, I know I love you. You're in my muscle memory, you're the first and last thing I think about every day. I can't help it. I wish I could.'

Philip just stared at her. It was the most painful thing that Poppy had ever had to endure. *I will remember this moment*, she thought. *It will be a very long time before I put myself in a situation like this again.*

'I'm going to make it really easy on you. I'm going to go now and I'm going to tell you that we are officially finished. I'm not your date. I'm not your girl. You no longer have to feel guilty about not calling – which should be a real load off your mind. Or not. You're free to do whatever you want with Grace.' Poppy paused. She saw his relief and her pain sprang up afresh. 'However, I do have something to say to you about Grace. And it's important.'

Poppy paused. This was her final act of love for Philip. There was no way she could do it without it sounding like sour grapes but what the hell. In a way it would be easier for her if he despised her. Any strong emotion was better than indifference.

'I don't need your advice, Poppy. Thanks all the same. To be honest, I resent the implication.'

Poppy was tempted to slap his smug face. 'Look, Philip. Listen to me. What is it that I do for a living?'

'You're a journalist.'

'No, what is it that I *do*?'

Philip looked upset and uncomfortable. Good, Poppy thought. Let him squirm.

'I talk to people,' she answered her own question. 'All day long. I listen to them and I write down what they say and I weigh it against what they've said in the past and against what they do and I try to figure out whether they're lying or not. I'm good at it, as a matter of fact.'

'What's this got to do with anything?' Philip's handsome face was pinched with annoyance.

'It's got to do with Grace.'

'Poppy, this is just embarrassing. Don't do this.

You've had two conversations with Grace in your life. You don't know anything about her.'

'And you are absolutely sure that you do?' Poppy pulled the small Moleskine notebook out of her bag and put it on the already cluttered table. 'See what your good friend had to say.'

Twenty-One

*It is not because things are difficult that we do not dare,
it is because we do not dare that they are difficult*
(Seneca).

Philip waited until Poppy had left the restaurant
before he picked the notebook out of a pool of soy
sauce and wiped it gently with a napkin. For as
long as he had known him Mitch had carried a notebook like this one, and he used it to record stray
thoughts and the to-do lists of life. This one was
new. Mitch had copied the words from Seneca from
memory, Philip knew, because it was one of his
favourite quotes. This was patently not what had riled
Poppy.

He turned the pages until he found the list.

Is G. lying?

Who is she really?

And then the final line.

Talk to Philip.

Philip closed the notebook and set it down on the
table, frowning as he remembered the conversation
he had had with Mitch at his birthday party. Something had been bothering him then; he had wanted to
tell him. Was it Grace? Or had he just been taking his

frustration out on her because they'd had a big argument over the party arrangements?

The notebook didn't mean anything, he decided. Poppy was jealous and wanted to hurt him. Well, he wasn't going to let that happen.

He really did feel bad about Poppy. He had let their relationship linger on past its expiry date and that hadn't been fair to her. He would apologize. He'd send a nice note and some flowers and express the wish that they could still be friends.

Friends. No, he couldn't do that. That was a cliché and it would make her despise him even more than she already did.

He paid the bill and walked north towards his office on Lafayette. In fact he wouldn't even bother with the flowers, at least not now. Perhaps in a month or so he'd send her a note, when she'd cooled down.

Perhaps he'd discuss it with Grace. She always knew what to do.

The thought, along with the walk, made him feel better, and as soon as he had stepped into the elevator in his building Poppy had slipped from his mind.

Poppy had just finished her morning run and collected a coffee and a low-fat muffin from the New World on her corner. It was an unseasonally warm sunny morning, the leaves were turning and the gracious buildings on the Upper West Side looked serenely cinematic. Poppy had run three miles around the reservoir in Central Park and was feeling good.

'Poppy.'

She stopped so suddenly that she almost spilled her coffee. Grace was standing in front of her. Ludicrously overdressed, carrying a handbag that loudly advertised the designer vision of somebody she'd never heard of.

Yep, life as an impoverished widow must be tough, Poppy thought. She felt her shoulders tensing up and forced herself to be calm.

'Hello, Grace. What brings you to this side of town?'

'Job interview. So I thought I'd walk across the park. It's such a beautiful day.'

Poppy looked down at Grace's shoes. They were laughably impractical. If she walked more than three steps before they fell apart she would be lucky.

'Well, *bonne chance* and all that,' Poppy said, moving off.

'Poppy, can we have a word?'

'Sure.' Poppy stopped. 'Which word would you like, Grace? *Man-stealer?*'

Grace smoothed her leather trousers. 'I was sorry to hear that Philip broke up with you.'

'Actually, it was the other way around.'

'Of course. Philip didn't talk much to me about it. I just implied from what he had said . . .'

Inferred, you smug bitch, Poppy thought. She said nothing. Grace's sharp features were a parody of shallow concern. Why was she doing this? She had won. There was no need to gloat.

'He also told me about the notebook.'

'Presumably he also told you where I live and that I go for a run at about the same time every day.'

Poppy widened her stance. The skinny cow was picking a fight? Excellent, that would really set her up for the day.

'I was very disappointed to hear what you had done,' Grace said softly, her long manicured fingernails stroking her 'It Girl' handbag. 'It was pretty sneaky, I thought.'

'What did you find sneaky about it?' Poppy adopted an exaggerated expression of nonchalance. 'I care about Philip and thought he should know what your own husband was saying about you. I have no loyalty to you. Why should I?'

'You have no idea what our marriage was like,' Grace hissed. 'None. And it's nothing to do with Philip, either.'

'Mitch didn't think so.'

'You didn't know my husband and you don't know me. What happened between us stays between us.'

'Well, we're just going to have to agree to disagree,' Poppy said, opening her paper bag and picking the muffin out. 'Because what happens to my friends IS my business.'

'He's not your friend any more. He's disgusted by what you did. It was really pathetic and bitchy.'

Poppy took a bite of muffin and shrugged. This was costing her but she couldn't let it show. She just couldn't. 'Funny, he didn't say anything of that kind to me. In fact, that kind of intemperate language doesn't sound like Philip at all. The Philip Ross I know, at least. Are you sure you didn't have a vicious little daydream?'

Poppy was delighted to notice that Grace was

becoming frustrated. Her face had flushed and she was gripping her hands in fists. Poppy fully expected her to stomp her foot. She hoped she would, she'd like to see anybody balance on those heels.

'All you did was make a laughing stock of yourself, Poppy. You achieved nothing and you alienated him even further.'

Poppy put the unfinished muffin back in the bag and screwed the paper tightly shut. 'I told you; I broke up with him. That's as alienated as you get. So good luck with shopkeeping work. You're going to need a lot more of it when Philip figures out that you're just another lightweight gold-digger.'

She turned away. She was halfway down the block before she heard Grace yell: 'He never loved you, you know. He told me that.'

The pain was unbearable. She thought the only thing that would relieve it would be to go back and pop that smug bitch right in her underfed stomach.

But she didn't.

There were other, better ways to get even with Grace Falco.

Twenty-Two

'I didn't expect to hear from you,' Marvel said, taking his feet off the desk. 'This is a pleasure and a surprise.'

Poppy took a seat without asking. She looked like her dog had just died, Marvel thought. Still, she was here. Suddenly the morning felt a little brighter.

'What can I do for you?'

'It's what *I* can do for *you*.'

'Let's start with coffee.' Marvel smiled. She did look rough, poor kid. Her eyes were smudged with dark circles. She looked as if she'd dropped a few pounds and her porcelain skin was paler and more fragile than last he had seen it. 'I was just about to order a latte. How about you?'

'Cappuccino,' Poppy said automatically.

'Fat, low-fat? Skim?'

'I don't give a shit.'

Marvel shrugged and picked up the phone. 'The place on the corner delivers for free,' he said, just for something to say. 'I've got a deal going with them.'

Poppy nodded distractedly.

Marvel ordered, set the phone down, crossed his hands and looked at Poppy. She was wearing very old faded jeans with a hole in the knee and a little white

T-shirt that was so thin he could see the outline of her sports bra. She was older than he had first assumed, more like her early to mid thirties. Her glorious hair was tied back in a ponytail and she wore no make-up. If he was any judge, she hadn't slept well in a while.

'This your daughter?' Poppy picked up the photo that sat on his desk.

'Sally.'

'She looks lovely,' Poppy replaced the frame on the desk.

'She is. She's more than I hoped for and better than I deserve.'

'I'm sure that's not true. You seem like a decent enough chap.'

The subtle implication was that some other 'chap' had not been so decent.

'How old is she?'

'Twenty.'

'You don't look old enough to have a kid that age.'

'I was a child bride.'

'And still happily married? Amazing.'

'Maddie and I are still happy, we're just not married.'

'That's an achievement too.'

'Well, neither of us had done anything to make the other really angry and we had a third person to think about.'

Poppy sat silent with a look of panic on her face, as if she had forgotten what she had come here for.

'Forgive me for making an assumption but you look as if you're going through a rough patch,' Marvel said gently.

'I'm not going through it,' Poppy corrected. 'I'm stuck in the middle of it. I need to get out. And I thought you might be able to help.' She rifled around in her large leather handbag for a few minutes and pulled out a photocopied sheet of A4 paper. 'I don't know if this is relevant to you at all, but Francesca and I found this when we were clearing out Mitch's things up at the house. It was written in a notebook.'

Marvel read.

'Where's the original?'

Poppy looked embarrassed. 'I gave it to Philip Ross. Since it mentioned him, I thought he might be curious to see it. I left it with him.'

'How do you think it's relevant to Mitch Browning's death?' he asked neutrally.

'Francesca said Grace Falco was always on at Mitch to spend more money. She tried to get him to mortgage the house in the Berkshires so they could buy a place in the Hamptons. Apparently she didn't like being stuck in the country. She talked him into it but she couldn't push it through because Francesca also owns the house. And in any event, she spent all this money on various things and Mitch was getting very worried about the expenditure. Philip told me that.'

'Who's Philip?' Marvel asked, although he knew.

Poppy swallowed. 'He was Mitch's best friend. I used to be friends with him.'

The coffees arrived. Marvel pushed more money across the table than they were worth and murmured his thanks to the delivery guy.

'So you think . . .?'

127

'Two things,' Poppy said crisply after sipping her coffee and seeming to derive some vim from it. 'Actually, three. I have no proof for any of this,' she added, and Marvel thought he saw her brush a tear from her eye.

'We'll call it a working hypothesis,' Marvel said encouragingly. He just wanted to listen to the sound of her voice.

'First off is obviously the issue of identity. Is she who she says she is? Second is, did she drive Mitch to steal money from his company? I mean, what if she was banging on night and day about how they needed a place in the Hamptons and fancy parties and what-have-you and he finally gave in and started thinking about ways to find that money? I went to his birthday party this summer and it was pretty extravagant. Apparently he always had the same party every year and it was simple. This year suddenly there's servants, a marquee, a band, the whole nine yards.'

'What's the third thing?'

'The third thing that occurred to me is, what if she knew he was stealing, she figured it out somehow, and what if he gave her money to shut her up?'

'You have a very low opinion of their marriage.'

'I saw that woman a week ago and she is dressed pretty well for a widow who cries poor. The bag and shoes alone were worth more than a thousand dollars.'

'Perhaps she'd had them for a while?'

Poppy shook her head. 'They're the very latest. I read *InStyle* magazine. You know what they call the shoes she was wearing? "The celebrity must-have for the season."'

'What does that mean?' Marvel asked, genuinely puzzled.

'It means there are lots of twits out there who only buy something if Britney Spears thinks it's a good idea,' Poppy said wearily. 'Got any sugar?'

Marvel opened the top right-hand drawer and pulled out two sachets that had been sitting there from the bad old days. He felt a tiny tug of desire for them as he handed them over to Poppy. *I'm over that*, he told himself firmly.

'And what's the fourth thing?'

'I didn't say there were four things.'

'No, but I observe human nature for a living, so I know there is something else you want to tell me,' Marvel said kindly. 'And you're going to feel a whole lot better if you get it off your chest.'

Twenty-Three

It was eleven thirty, time for a Heineken.

Whitney had spent what felt like years that morning with his parole officer, a humourless woman called Juanita Ortez. Probably gay. Whitney was used to getting his way with women and it irritated him that Ms Ortez didn't laugh at his jokes and had insisted on spending their time together exploring his prospects for work.

Work. That was the only downside of being a free man. No longer was the taxpayer picking up the bill for his room and board.

Working in a warehouse, for instance. Carrying boxes from point-fucking-A to point-fucking-B. On the scale of meaningful existence it didn't rate.

As a recently freed convict he knew that society paid only the barest lip service to the notion that he had 'paid his debt' to it and that this unforgiving attitude limited his prospects for immediate advancement. Even so, Whitney still did not relish the idea of working in a warehouse, or a factory, or flipping burgers.

Whitney believed that he had been blessed with a good brain and a deeply philosophical outlook on life.

He believed that his rare gift, unlike the drones who went eagerly to work each day to enrich the bank accounts of others, enabled him to see more clearly the big picture, which was that life was a short and precious thing. It was a miracle that we were here at all, the product of natural selection that had given our ancestors the wit and strength to survive, breed and gift their genes to future generations. It was incredible when you thought about it. What were the odds?

No, life was short, and that was, for the foreseeable future, a fact. Unless some scientist came up with the cure for death, or, at the very least, old age, pretty soon, Whitney had his lifespan reckoned at about seventy-five years, judging from how long the majority of his worthless relatives had lingered, sucking up perfectly good oxygen, taking up perfectly good space and steadfastly refusing to contribute one whit to the good of mankind.

Whitney didn't have much in common with his relatives but he did share their DNA, and that, according to all that he had read, was a fair indicator of longevity, barring a real bummer from left field like cancer or an accident.

Using that rationale, Whitney figured he was exactly at the halfway mark, give or take a year or two.

In other words, there was no time to lose. He had to figure out the best way to make the best use of his allotted span. And he had to do it quickly.

It was a good omen that he'd found Grace Falco. He had not thought he would ever meet her again, but he'd got lucky. Sometimes God just came right out and told you that he loved you; finding Grace Falco was excellent proof of that.

She had looked right at home there with her new boyfriend and his tortoiseshell glasses and expensive suit. What was his name? Philip Ross. Philip Ross looked like he knew lots of things, but Whitney was fairly sure he could educate him on a couple of points.

He had, to coin a business phrase, leverage. And he was about to get more.

Grace had offered him joke money to go away quietly. Two thousand dollars!

Whitney was generally a fan of money. He rarely turned it down. However, this time he had; even though he could have done with a few spare bucks, he had said no. He wasn't stupid. This time he would wait, assemble his cards and play the hardest game of his life.

Grace Falco owed him. And she had only just begun to understand how much.

Whitney was thinking deeply along these lines as he walked south on Ninth Avenue. Hell's Kitchen, his old nabe. He was so concerned with plotting his new career that he didn't notice, until he was right at the door of his old regular bar, that it had gone completely. In its place stood a Thai restaurant filled with suspiciously well-dressed chattering men. Whitney reeled in surprise and disgust.

Fucking prison had really put him off faggots.

Twenty-Four

'I can't believe I'm telling you this,' Poppy said as Marvel handed her the tissue box yet again. 'You must think I'm nuts.'

Marvel smiled. He got the confession thing a lot. People trusted him, even when they didn't know him. Especially when they didn't know him. So he regularly heard things that people swore they'd told to not a single other living soul.

It was a gift and a curse.

'I don't think you're nuts.'

'I had to drag it out of him. God!' Poppy threw the Kleenex into the bin, which Marvel had moved closer for her convenience. 'It was awful! Right there in a crowded restaurant. I couldn't stop myself.'

'You have nothing to be ashamed of,' Marvel said firmly. 'It sounds like you did pretty good.'

Poppy grabbed another Kleenex and screwed it into her eyes. 'I suppose there's no point in talking about blame. I was the one who made a bad judgement call. I came all this way – with no encouragement or promises of any kind from him. And now I'm all alone.'

'You're not alone, ' Marvel said. 'You know me.

You know Francesca. And anyway, you're a New Yorker now. So stiffen up. Whatever this city deals out, you can handle.'

Poppy lifted her eyes from the tissues and smiled a thin, watery smile.

'That's better,' Marvel said. 'You're going to be just fine. I know that for sure. In a couple of months you won't even remember what he looks like. You'll find somebody else who adores you and treats you the way you deserve to be treated and you'll remember that New York is the greatest town in the world and you'll be right back on top.'

'You're very kind,' Poppy said. 'I'm glad I met you.'

'It's entirely my pleasure. My door is always open to beautiful young women,' Marvel said gallantly, thinking, *My God, I'm flirting. I never flirt.*

He decided that after Poppy left he would call Madelaine and tell her what a foolish old goat he had been for having a crush on a woman more than ten years his junior. She would laugh with him, tell him that yes he was a foolish old goat, and the feeling would go away. Madelaine was good for that.

Poppy began to make leaving noises, hunting for her handbag, which had fallen to the floor. She picked it up and shouldered it. Marvel checked his watch. He had a meeting with a lawyer on another job in half an hour and after that was due to spend the afternoon in court.

'I'm sorry we kind of got off track,' she said and to his delight reached up and kissed him on both cheeks.

'I'm not. Come back any time. I mean that.'

As soon as the door had closed behind her he picked up the phone to call Madelaine.

'Something weird's just happened,' he said. And told her about Poppy's visit. 'Tell me I'm being a foolish old goat.'

'You're being a foolish old goat,' Madelaine said automatically. 'Hang on a minute, my tea has just boiled. Can you wait?'

'Sure.'

'That's better.' She came back on the phone and Marvel could picture her curled up in the window-seat of her new garden apartment in Cobble Hill, with the mug between both hands and the phone propped between her ear and her shoulder.

'So how old is Lolita?'

'Thirties.'

'Then you're not a foolish old goat. Good heavens, Marvel, the guy I'm seeing is twenty-nine.'

'You're seeing a twenty-nine-year-old?'

'Didn't I mention it? He's my yoga instructor.'

'Isn't there a law against that?'

'I swapped classes after we started going out. And don't change the subject, Marvel. You've got a lot to offer. Think about it. You're fully employed. You're in great shape, you have all your hair, you're a witty conversationalist.'

'I don't feel very witty when I'm around her. Anyway I'm forty-five.'

'It doesn't matter any more. The forties are the new thirties.'

'That makes the thirties the new twenties, which makes Poppy about as old as Sally.'

'You're twisting my words.' Madelaine paused. 'You didn't call to get my blessing, did you?'

'Did you call me to get my blessing to start doing downward dog with some kindergarten pupil?'

'Absolutely not, and that is precisely my point. We're not married any more, so start acting like it. Do not call to ask my permission for anything, ever again. Go forth and have fun because we'll be in our graves soon enough.'

'I guess you're right.'

'I am right. You're gorgeous. You're a catch. As soon as you stop thinking of yourself as an old geezer, women will too. Now, I'd love to stay and chat but I've gotta get back to work. Ciao, sweetie.'

Marvel murmured his goodbyes, hung up the phone and grabbed his suit jacket. If he didn't hurry he'd be late for his meeting.

As he walked the two blocks to his client's office he thought about Poppy. Why exactly was he attracted to her? The red hair definitely helped. And he was a terrible sucker for an accent. Actually, he was a sucker for anything exotic. Was he just a sad, pathetic middle-aged divorced man who went for any single woman who crossed his path? No, that wasn't true. He was feeling pretty good these days, all things considered.

As he thought about this for a little longer, imagining himself calling her, asking her out to dinner – there was a little French place just around the corner from his apartment that he thought looked like fun for dinner *à deux* – he realized that he didn't have her phone number. He had given her his card but she had not reciprocated.

So there was no way to contact her unless she called him again. Well, there was, but that would involve methods that right-thinking civilians would find creepy, so he did not intend to use them. Anyway, she hadn't given him her card for a reason. And that reason was she didn't want to see him again.

So that was that.

Twenty-Five

Damn Philip Ross, Poppy thought as she logged on. *I'm not normally like this.*

She had spent a restless morning, padding around her office, going out for coffee she didn't need, staring out the window. Usually she was a disciplined worker. She didn't get sidetracked bidding for unnecessary bargains on eBay or waste hours playing computer games. Poppy liked her work and normally she brought her complete attention to it.

Not today though. Not for many days, in fact.

Even Mick Davis, her editor and a scratchy individual who as a matter of highest personal principle never had a kind word for anybody, had called to enquire, gruffly, if she was OK.

'Silence from Poppy simply isn't natural,' he growled over the phone. 'In all the years I've been working with you I've become used to that irritating little stream of thoughts and story ideas. And this past week or so, nothing.'

'I'm working on a big story,' Poppy said.

'Pants on fire.'

'I am,' Poppy insisted, 'it's just not one that can be printed in the paper.'

'Doll, forgive me for what may seem to you to be an unreasonable bias, but I'm only interested in stories that can be printed in our paper. You see where I'm going with this one?'

'Sure, thanks for the reminder.'

'It's not a reminder. As the managing editor of this venerable institution reminded me just this very day, we're paying an enormous amount of money to keep you in New York City and all he expects in return is to see your work every now and then. He specifically asked me to stress to you that it is not too much to ask, all things considered.'

'Thanks, Mick. I'll come up with something. Promise.'

'Sure you will. Something sexy and fun, just to let us know you're still alive. And by the end of the week. I mean that.'

Poppy put down the phone and picked up the *New York Times* to look for some story ideas. She hadn't read the papers for over a week and they sat in a reproachful pile in the corner of her office.

This must be what depression feels like, she thought as she put down the paper and paced her tiny office for the umpteenth time. She felt listless and dull, as though she had a low-level chill. Her attention span was shattered. She didn't even feel like going to the gym. Francesca had called a couple of times to commiserate, but Poppy had declined her invitation to go out and 'trawl seedy bars for questionable men'.

She sat back down. Took a sip of her jumbo cappuccino, broke off a piece of poppy-seed bagel and stared at the computer screen, which displayed only the logo of the company that had made its owner the world's richest man.

Bloody Philip Ross. I should have better things to think about.

But try as she might, she could not coax her brain off the subject, it kept running back to it like a puppy. She replayed her conversation with Grace. All her conversations with Grace. She remembered her conversation with Philip, the look of pity on his face when she had revealed her feelings.

Bloody Grace Falco, this is all her fault, Poppy thought fiercely.

She pushed her coffee aside – it had gone cold anyway – and logged on to her computer. She typed the name Grace Falco into her favourite search engine but didn't come up with anything relevant. A lawyer in Cincinnati, a marathon runner in Florida, someone who had hyphenated herself to a chap in LA called Ruffingham. None of these looked promising but it was a common enough name in this country, Poppy guessed, with all those southern Italian immigrants.

Then she remembered the dinner party at Philip's house. Grace had talked about going to college somewhere out west. What was the name of the place again?

Poppy leaned back in her chair, willing herself to relax. Ironic that she had replayed this conversation many, many times and yet the most pertinent piece of information was not forthcoming.

She hummed a few bars of 'Stairway to Heaven'. That usually did the trick.

St Agnes!

Poppy whistled jauntily as she typed the name into the search engine and pulled up the number of the dean of St Agnes College in Eugene, Oregon.

'Hello,' she said, trying to sound like her mother, who had an American accent. 'My name is Alexandra Adams, and I work in Human Resources for *Time* magazine. A former student of yours has applied for a position at our company and I'd like to speak to somebody who can verify her academic credentials, please.'

'Just a minute, please.' The woman's voice was light and sing-songy. 'What year did she graduate?'

'You know, I think she accidentally left off the date on her résumé,' Poppy said smoothly. 'It says here that she has a Bachelor's degree but it doesn't name the year.'

'Don't worry. I should be able to find that out. If you'll just hold for one moment please.'

The woman put Poppy on hold and she listened to Fleetwood Mac for a couple of minutes. Fleetwood Mac stopped and Stevie Wonder started. She held the phone away from her ear and took a sip of coffee. Still cold.

'Hello, Ms Adams? Our records show that Grace Falco was an English major, correct?'

'Yes,' she said. The website had described St Agnes as an exclusive women's-only liberal arts college, so it seemed like a safe assumption.

'And that she graduated in 1994?'

141

Poppy did a mental calculation. Grace was probably about the same age as her, which would put her in her early to mid thirties. 1994 was kind of late to be graduating, if that was the case. But then she remembered that an American undergraduate degree takes four years and Grace may not have gone directly from high school. She might have taken a year or two off.

'That sounds about right.'

'She graduated with a degree in English literature,' the woman on the phone said. 'That's all I can really tell you. I have only been here three years, so I didn't know her.'

'Is there anybody there who might remember her?'

'Why?' The woman's tone sharpened. 'Surely she has provided references that you yourself can telephone?'

That was a good point.

'I'm sorry, that is true, of course,' Poppy said. 'But this is my first week at this job and I'm trying to be as thorough as I can.'

A brief silence and then: 'Excuse me just one moment, I'll see if I can find one of her teachers.'

Poppy listened to Bill Withers.

'Ms Adams?' The voice was deep and confident. 'I'm Anne Lasswell. How may I help you?'

Poppy repeated the story she had told the woman in the dean's office.

'Grace Falco,' Anne Lasswell said. 'Yes, I knew her. A girl who didn't quite live up to her promise.'

'How do you mean?'

'She came to us with extremely high SAT scores.

But she had trouble with college, despite the fact that she worked extremely hard. What kind of work is she applying for?'

'A position as a researcher at *Time* magazine,' Poppy said.

'You might encourage her to become a little more involved in our alumni affairs. We do like to keep in touch with our girls and Grace Falco is one of the few who has displayed little inclination to pursue an ongoing relationship with St Agnes. It's a great pity.'

'Did she have many friends?'

'I wouldn't say friends. Grace didn't really mix well with the other girls. She kept to herself.'

'Can you think of any of her classmates who might remember her?'

'I scarcely think that one's college friends are relevant to a job application.'

'This is a very desirable position – the successful applicant will be working within an extremely tight-knit group. We at *Time* magazine need to be absolutely assured that Ms Falco can handle the inevitable pressures that will arise.'

There was silence on the long-distance line for a moment.

'Actually now that I think about it she did have one close friend. It was a strange friendship. The two girls were not in the least alike. This woman was everything that Grace was not. She certainly had brains – otherwise she would never have been accepted at St Agnes – however, she never applied herself. It was as if she had expended all her energy in getting here and had decided that that was all the work she needed to do. She left in fact without taking her final exams. Let me think what her name was . . . Eliot, that's it. Marie Eliot. But where on earth you would find her, I have no idea.'

Poppy thanked the teacher, put down the phone and looked at the untidy shorthand notes. Her depression had lifted, her thinking was crisp and clear. She went back on line and ordered a copy of the 1994 St Agnes alumni magazine sent express post.

Twenty-Six

Francesca was on her second margarita by the time Poppy arrived. She had one elbow on the bar, hand up, as if holding an invisible cigarette, and pretended to survey the talent on display. *I'm doing a pretty good job of holding it together*, she thought, *considering I'm all on my own here.* And she cursed her younger brother, as she did regularly these days. She hadn't asked for much out of life, she had done well in her career almost by default, because she *didn't* care about fashion, in fact she openly despised most of her colleagues' concerns and interests. She refused to be a 'yes' woman and from the beginning, even when she'd been an editorial assistant, had told her boss exactly what she thought. To her surprise this had not been taken as sedition but a sign of Francesca's daring and original thought. Thus she had risen through the ranks, modelling her behaviour more on Patsy from *Absolutely Fabulous* than on any of the famous fashion editors of yore. To her bemusement she was now at the top of a pile that she could not even remember having set out to climb. Life was like that, she supposed. If one wasn't paying the closest attention, one ended up miles from where one had intended to be.

Here she was at thirty-seven, well-paid, well-dressed and missing the only thing in her life that held any meaning for her.

In all of the different ways she had seen her life turning out, the only constant, the one that she had not even questioned, was that Mitch would be around. They were family. They had started together and the certainty that they would finish together was knitted into her bone.

But he had broken their unsaid agreement and had left her absolutely alone.

Panic squeezed her lungs so tight she couldn't breathe, and she had the strongest urge to pick up her glass and smash it on the floor.

I can't do it, she thought. *I can't go on.*

She forced herself to breathe, pushing her stomach out, relaxing her shoulders. Her shrink was urging her to go on anti-anxiety medication but, for a reason she had not been able to articulate until now, Francesca, who was no stranger to the benefits of pharmacology, had resisted. As she loosened her grip on the glass she realized why she'd said no. There was a part of her that wanted to really feel how shitty and awful her life was now, because if she did that then perhaps there would be a time when it wouldn't be so bad and she would feel that she had made some progress.

In the meantime, there was day by awful day to be endured.

To her relief she could see Poppy pause at the door; she held up her hand and Poppy waved back as she squeezed through the crowd and berthed at the bar.

'Good news,' Francesca said, kissing her on both cheeks, although what she really wanted to do was hug her. 'The wait is only a millennium or two.'

Café Habana was always full.

Poppy ordered a margarita. She looked better, Francesca decided. She too had lost some weight. In different ways these days had been hard on both of them.

'Glad to see there's a light in your eye, chica.' Francesca squeezed her arm.

The overworked maitre d' jostled her way through the tightly packed crowd of patrons to tell Francesca that they would be seated in a few minutes.

'I'm feeling good,' Poppy said. 'I had this thought today that perhaps I'd never really loved Philip. After all, you can't love somebody when all you see is their façade. Perhaps I was just in love with the idea of Philip.'

'Entirely possible. Sillier acts have been committed, even by sensible, absolutely gorgeous people such as ourselves.'

'And now that I think about it I realize how much hard work it was being in a relationship with him, especially if you were seeking any kind of emotional validation.'

'He certainly doesn't give anything away,' Francesca said. 'So tell me what's put the light in your eye.'

'Nothing. I just decided he's not worth it.'

'Poppy, my dear,' Francesca said. 'We really cannot continue to be friends if you are going to assume that I'm an idiot. It's simply too tiresome. So tell me what's actually going on.'

'It really doesn't matter.'

'No, it really does.'

'I've been checking up on Grace. We met in the street and she was all gloating and smug about the fact that she had Philip and I didn't and I thought, why not just find out if she's telling the truth about college and everything? You know, to set my mind at rest.'

'Ah, a vendetta, my favourite kind of emotional transaction.'

'I just want to know,' Poppy said stubbornly.

'And then what? You'll go running to Philip with stop-the-press news that she lied on her résumé or that she really had a lucrative career as a white slave trafficker? Wake up, dear girl. It's not going to bring him back. All it will do is to make you look foolish.'

'I'm not going to go running to Philip,' Poppy said. 'That would be stupid. I know he's not coming back. I'm doing it for my own sake.'

'You won't be able to help yourself going to Philip. I can see it now. Just like you did with the notebook. It won't be pretty. He'll despise you.'

'Look, can we talk about something else?'

'We can.' Francesca was surprised to find herself relieved. 'But let me just say, you will do yourself no favours if you pursue this. None at all. Forget it and walk away. Otherwise you will regret the day that you ever met them. Trust me, Auntie Francesca knows best.'

*

Philip sat on the balcony of his apartment with a cup of espresso in his hand. The view was of the rooftops of the flower district. Nothing special, but it soothed him with its familiarity. It was early in the morning and the sounds of the street floated upwards. A copy of the *New York Times* metro section was folded on the table that sat next to his chair, but he hadn't even glanced at it yet.

Grace was in the bedroom getting dressed. He could hear her humming a Springsteen song. Before he'd met Grace he'd never thought much of Springsteen. She was introducing him to lots of things that he would otherwise never have considered. It was as if she had enabled him to take a vacation from himself. He was seeing the world as a child might – in all its possibilities. His senses were sharpened; he took pleasure in the smallest things.

Take the break-up with Poppy. When he thought about the scene she had created in the restaurant he was always surprised at how little it had affected him. The old Philip Ross would have mulled over that for weeks, reliving each discomforting moment, examining it from every possible angle to extract the most embarrassment and shame. He had shared the details with Grace, who'd dismissed it with two words – forget it.

Surprisingly, he had. And as time passed, on the rare occasion that it did cross his mind he was able to take a more sanguine view; it had actually been beneficial for both Poppy and him because it had stripped their relationship, such as it was, down to its specifics, like a bushfire that prepares the forest for the growth of the coming season.

Poppy had always been good like that, he reflected with a smile. She thought clearly. She was like a terrier, always diving straight for the truth and seizing it without fear.

And in ending their relationship that way she had done him a huge, huge favour. Who knew how long he otherwise might have lingered, torn between passion and duty? Perhaps driving himself to cheat on Poppy because he couldn't resist Grace. No, a short, sharp cut was a far, far better thing.

He had realized what he must do after seeing Poppy that day, which was not wait one minute longer to be with the woman that he loved wildly and without reservation.

He had called Grace immediately and told her. To his delight she had said she felt the same. That was it.

They had agreed she would move in when the lease on her apartment expired in a few weeks. In the meantime she was staying over several times a week. Simple. Just like his dad said; just like breathing.

Love was a foreign country for him. A delightful place of silly 'when-did-you-first-know?' conversations and long walks through the city that he felt he was seeing for the first time. Love made him feel young and vulnerable and at one with the world – he even gave change to panhandlers on the subway.

Philip looked at his watch. Grace was running late, her job interview was in less than an hour. As if to emphasize this, she hopped into view.

'I can't find my other shoe,' she called through the French doors. 'Oh God, I haven't cleaned my teeth. And my earrings!'

'Your earrings need to be cleaned?'

'Idiot.' She dropped to her knees, groped under the couch and retrieved the shoe with a small cry of triumph.

'I'll get the earrings. Where are they?'

'I think they're in my bag, in the side pocket.'

Philip picked up her bag. 'What do they look like?'

'Small and gold. Star-shaped.'

Her handbag was a tangle of things that Philip would not have thought necessary to carry around on a daily basis. As Grace dashed into the bathroom to clean her teeth, he picked through the contents. The first earring was tucked inside Grace's cosmetics bag. But the second one eluded him. He dug deeper. Nothing. He tipped the bag upside down and spilled its contents on to the table, sorted through them and still failed to find the earring. He ran his hands around the lining of the bag and discovered that a piece of folded white paper had become wedged into the seam. He teased it out, feeling as he did so a small hard object that might well be the missing earring tucked inside.

He unfolded the paper and hardly noticed that the earring dropped on to the table because his attention was diverted to the writing on the page. It was a receipt from a very expensive Madison Avenue designer.

The words 'black leather pants' were scrawled in

black ink and the figure on the same line read two
thousand dollars.

Philip checked the date. The pants had been
bought less than a month ago, at a time when Grace
had told him that she was particularly hard up and
he'd written her a rent cheque to tide her over. A
cheque for two thousand dollars.

She'd also told him that she'd picked up the pants
second-hand at a consignment store for fifty dollars.

A steal, she said.

'Darling? Having trouble finding them?' Grace
emerged from the bathroom, wiping toothpaste foam
from around her mouth.

'No, they're right here,' Philip said, sliding the
paper back into the handbag. 'I had to excavate down
to the Pleistocene era to find them, but I found them.'

He held the earrings out to Grace. She covered his
hand with both of hers. 'You have such beautiful
hands,' she said.

Two thousand dollars for a pair of pants that would
be out of fashion by the time the season had changed.

Had Grace lied when she said she needed money
to pay the rent?

Who is she really? Mitch's words came back to him.
He could almost hear his old friend saying them out
loud.

Grace caught sight of his watch, squealed and
began frantically re-stuffing her purse. It seemed like
an impossible task. Laughing, Philip tried to help her
but they ended up spilling more stuff on to the floor.

This is what I want, he thought. *This woman, as
she is right now. Forever.*

152

He would ask Grace about the pants later. There was plenty of time to sort out what must surely be a simple misunderstanding. And now that he had found her he didn't want anything as silly as money to come between them. Besides, he already knew he wanted to marry her. There was plenty of time to iron out the wrinkles.

Twenty-Seven

The St Agnes year book arrived a couple of days later as Poppy was running out of the door to catch the train to Washington DC to cover a story. Her editor had given up waiting for her to suggest ideas and had thrown her a few of his own. Poppy was grateful. Although she wasn't feeling so despondent now that she had decided on her mission to expose Grace Falco, she was still having trouble fully concentrating on her work. Getting out of town would help her to concentrate.

'Be careful,' Mick had told her as they discussed the stories. 'There's not much room for error in this job. Lots of other hungry little fishies would love to take it off you.'

Polly signed for the package, thanked the UPS guy and stuffed it into her computer bag, then slung the bag on to her back and dashed downstairs to hail a taxi.

Penn Station was a zoo as usual, and when Poppy saw the line to buy tickets she groaned – her train was leaving in ten minutes and she would certainly not have time to get any breakfast before she boarded. Yet by some miracle the line moved quickly and she

154

was seated on the Acela with a coffee and an egg and bacon roll a full one minute before the train began moving out of the station.

The last couple of days had been busy. She had spoken to Marvel a couple of times; she found she liked to chat with him on the phone. It was a good way of discussing Philip, if even in a roundabout way.

'Why did Mitch kill himself?' Poppy asked. It was the question that had bothered her ever since Marvel had first told her about the money. 'If he had all that money why didn't he just take off for Brazil?'

'Don't know. Maybe the story's a little more complicated than we think.'

'Or maybe it's simpler than we think. Perhaps he didn't have the moxy to go through with it. It sounds from what Philip told me that he wasn't a bad man. Maybe he just lost his nerve. Some people value their good name.'

'If they value their good name they don't steal.'

'We don't know what kind of pressure he was under. I spent ten minutes with Grace Falco a few days back and I was entertaining murder.'

'How're you going with finding Marie Eliot?'

'Still looking. There's lots of Marie Eliots.'

'Let me see if I can help,' Marvel said. He had a freelance guy he had been wanting to try out, a law student, the son of a friend, who was looking for extra work to get him through university. He'd give the job to him, a simple job to see if he liked the way he worked. His business was going well, it was time to take on some extra help.

'You ever see that movie with William Hurt and

Kathleen Turner? And she had swapped identities with a friend who looked just like her? I bet that's what Grace Falco did. I bet she didn't really go to that college at all.'

'I thought that movie was rather contrived,' Marvel said. 'Convenient, don't you think? She just happens to have swapped identities years before?'

'Maybe she always knew she'd commit a clever crime.'

'Why did the friend go along with it? Explain that to me.'

'I don't care, it was clever.'

'And pick the one guy who had the dodgy history that made him the perfect patsy and even more conveniently he falls in love with her?'

'Marvel, it was Kathleen Turner!'

'All I'm saying is the plot creaked a bit in places.'

Poppy laughed. 'You're not very bright, are you? I like that in a man.'

'Yeah, yeah,' said Marvel. 'I'm going to hang up the phone now, OK? Have a good time in DC. Hopefully I'll have some news for you about the elusive Miss Eliot by the time you get back.'

The train moved out of the tunnel and into the bright day of New Jersey. It was full of people whose interpretation of business casual meant a blue blazer and chinos. Everybody looked serious, tapping into computers and thumbing Blackberries and talking on phones. Poppy was the only person in the compartment wearing jeans.

She opened the yearbook. It was heavy and unwieldy, about the size of a coffee table art book.

Poppy flipped through the pages describing the students' various achievements. She stopped when she came to the graduating class photos. Marie Eliot wasn't there, of course, because according to Anne Passwell she hadn't graduated.

Grace Falco was. A small out-of-focus photo of a woman who wore spectacles and was carrying a little more weight than she did now and had an unflattering bowl-styled haircut. But there was no doubt it was Grace Falco.

'Oh no,' Poppy groaned, out loud.

'Is everything OK?' Her neighbour looked up from his Blackberry. 'Are you all right?'

'I'm fine, thank you.'

'Looking at your college photos? I wouldn't, it's too depressing. Either you've gained thirty pounds and forgotten what it felt like to run the length of a football field, or you're forced to remember that you once found paisley kaftans cool.' The guy was about her age, with a buzz cut, a friendly open face and a wide grin.

'Yeah,' Poppy said politely. 'It's a bitch all right.' She closed the yearbook and reached automatically for her coffee. *Marvel will get a laugh out of it, that's for sure*, she thought uncomfortably, wishing she didn't have to tell him. Not to mention Francesca. She could hear the 'I told you so's' ringing throughout the land.

The train came out of the tunnel into New Jersey. The sky was a high, hard blue and free of clouds. It was a beautiful day. Normally travelling by train cheered her up. Today she just felt embarrassed and depressed.

It was time to admit it: she was jealous and she wanted revenge. She wanted Poppy Adams to be right and Grace Falco to be irrevocably wrong. She had wanted to expose her as a cheat and a fraud. Instead all she'd done was make a fool of herself.

'Bugger,' Poppy said out loud. 'Bugger, bugger, bugger.'

Twenty-Eight

'Marie Eliot?'

'Who are you?'

Marvel smiled and flashed a card as he put a foot in the door. 'Frederick Marvel. Wanted to ask you a few questions, if you have a moment,' he said genially, while managing to sound at the same time as if she didn't have a choice.

In the background a television studio audience applauded.

'What about?'

'A woman called Grace Falco.'

'From college?' Marie Eliot's face, which up till then had been creased with suspicion, cleared momentarily in genuine puzzlement. She shifted her weight and opened the door further.

Marie Eliot ran blue-painted fingernails through her tangled blonde hair. She was barefoot and the polish on her toes matched the colour on her hands. Marvel could see the tight cigarette pants that had fitted her well about fifteen pounds ago.

'May I come in?'

'What's in this for me?'

'A hundred bucks.' Technically, he shouldn't have come here – the freelancer could have done it.

Marvel didn't want to admit to himself that he wanted to see the look in Poppy's eye when he found something interesting about Grace Falco.

'To talk about somebody I knew years ago?'

'It's important,' Marvel said, thinking how much easier it had been to get inside strangers' homes when he was fat. Nobody really believed that fat men were capable of sexual predation.

'Let me see your ID again.'

Marvel handed over his card.

'Private investigation. Like Magnum.'

'Exactly like that. Except without the Ferrari. Or the moustache.'

'I guess you might as well come in then,' Marie Eliot said, as if it had been her idea all along. She opened the door wide and stood back, allowing Marvel to enter the hallway. 'Sorry about the mess, I wasn't expecting any company. Just go down the hall and the living-room's to your right.'

The living-room wasn't messy at all, but Marvel hadn't expected it to be. People always apologized for 'the mess' when they asked an uninvited person to step across their threshold. It was automatic, like crossing yourself when you entered a church.

'Take a seat.' Marie pointed to an overstuffed velour sofa that was much too large for the dimensions of the room. 'Get you anything? A soda?'

'No thank you.' Marvel sat down gingerly. On the very large flat screen television Montel was counselling a woman whose marriage had been ruined because of her husband's sexual deviancy.

Marie Eliot used the remote to kill the sound and disappeared into another room. Marvel could hear the sound of a refrigerator door opening, ice falling into a cup and the door closing.

'So what do you want to know?' Marie Eliot returned to the living-room carrying a 14oz bottle of Diet Coke in one hand and a large plastic cup in the other. She sat in a chair that matched the sofa and poured. Her eyes moved automatically towards the television.

Marvel knew from the freelance researcher, whose work he was impressed with so far, that Marie Eliot had put one marriage behind her and was currently unemployed but receiving an alimony settlement from her ex. She had had a variety of careers in marketing and sales and had briefly moved to LA. Now she was back where she had started, in one of the less salubrious corners of Westchester County.

'You were friends in college with a woman called Grace Falco?'

'Yeah. What's she done?'

On the drive up to Westchester, Marvel had considered making up a story. Lost investment funds was always a plausible cover, as it was a fact that millions of dollars in investments went unclaimed all the time. However, now that he had met Marie he decided that probably wouldn't do.

'I'm not sure yet,' he said. 'I'm hoping you might be able to help me.'

'Tough luck. I haven't spoken to her since I left college.'

'But you were close in college?'

Marie took a sip from the cup. It was so huge that it almost obscured her face. It matched everything in the room, Marvel thought, in that it was too big for its circumstances. Perhaps it all indicated that Marie Eliot had oversized plans for her life. If so, they hadn't amounted to much yet.

'Haven't seen her? Haven't gone to any college reunions?'

'They weren't the best years of my life,' Marie said. 'I didn't even buy the monogrammed coffee mug.'

'You didn't enjoy college.'

'I didn't enjoy *that* college. It was boring and pointless. Maybe if I'd gone somewhere more fun.'

'Why did you go?'

Marie looked at Marvel as if he was stupid. 'Obviously, since I didn't own a crystal ball I didn't realize it would be boring and pointless before I went there. What did I know? I was the first person in my family to even think about college. So I had no clue. Would have been much better off at SUNY.'

'What do you remember about Grace?'

'God, I barely *can* remember her. Who dwells on this stuff?'

'Humour me, it's my dime.' She was hedging, Marvel thought. He wondered why. Just a natural distrust of authority? Or something else?

The mention of money did have the effect of unsettling the sediment of Marie's memory. 'Well, to begin with I thought she was an uptight stiff, just like all the rest of them. But then in our junior year I found out we came from similar backgrounds. At first she wasn't so happy to talk about that. She was always pretty ambitious, so she was kind of secretive about her past. I guess it was understandable, there weren't too many students there whose fathers weren't lawyers and doctors, that kind of thing. You wanted to blend in. Not that anybody made a big deal of it, they were much too PC for that.' Marie held up one finger and frowned then began picking lightly at a cuticle.

'How did you find out you were from the same place?'

'In a weird way. I was on the phone to my friend complaining about the fact that the only New Yorker at the school didn't want to talk to me and it turned out that my friend knew her name. Some high-school friend of hers had a friend who had dated her before college, I forget the details now, but it was something like that.'

'Can you remember his name?'

'God, after all these years? Of course not. Grace couldn't remember him at the time and she was the one who'd dated him.'

'What about your friend who told you about her?'

'She moved down to the Jersey shore. I haven't heard from her in a while, but her name's Kathy Holtz. She's near Asbury Park, or someplace.'

'How long were you friends with Grace?'

'I wouldn't say we were friends. We hung out. She wasn't like a bosom buddy.' Marie's attention strayed to the television set. The Montel credits were rolling.

'I don't know, halfway through freshman year till I left. About eighteen months all up.'

'What was your impression of her?'

Marie's eyes came to rest on Marvel and he could see she was actually giving the matter some thought. For the first time Marvel could see glimpses of the intelligence that had got her into a good school.

'On the surface, she was fine. She was pleasant. Once she found out that I knew about the old boy-friend she was quite nice to me. We hung out. But despite that, I never thought that I knew the real Grace Falco. In fact, there was something about her niceness that was brittle and a bit off. And there were times when you looked into her eyes and saw real anger. Never for long, just a flash of it.'

'What was she angry at, do you think?'

Marie shrugged. 'I have no idea. What is anybody ever angry at? Everything and nothing. Life, the guy who cut you off on the road this morning.' Marie placed the plastic cup on the side table and leaned forward towards Marvel. 'I'll tell you one thing; there were times when she scared me with that look.'

Twenty-Nine

Kathy Holtz popped the third teaspoon of sugar into her coffee cup. Marvel, Pavlov-like, began to salivate.

They were sitting in a coffee shop in Penn Station. Kathy Holtz commuted into the city three days a week to work at a corporate law office in midtown. She had agreed to meet Marvel after work and before she got on her train. It suited Marvel just fine. Poppy was coming home today and he had decided to meet her train. He had pretended it was because he had lots of news, but it was mostly because he wanted to see her.

Kathy Holtz was saying something and Marvel refocused his attention. She was a comfortably plump woman with soft brown eyes and fluffy blonde hair. She had a kind smile, Marvel decided.

'It might seem like a long way but it's actually pretty do-able. The train takes an hour from Red Bank and my office isn't that far from here, so I walk. It gives me some exercise. After I broke up with my husband I felt like I needed a fresh start. I really had to get out of the city. Jersey isn't so bad, it's really quite pretty.'

Marvel agreed that there was nothing at all wrong

with New Jersey. He in fact had been born there and was quite partial to it.

'But I'm rambling. You wanted to talk about Marie. I don't know if I can help you. I haven't kept in touch with many people from high school.'

'I actually wanted to talk about a woman called Grace Falco.'

Kathy's smooth forehead puckered in a tiny frown.

'She was at college with Marie and you knew her because she'd dated a friend of a friend of yours.'

'Gosh, that's long ago now.' Kathy massaged her temples in tiny circles with her index fingers. 'Do you know what the friend of a friend was called?'

Marvel shook his head. 'That's all the information I have.'

'Hmm.' Kathy frowned. 'Let me think about this for a minute. Gosh, there was that one summer, a group of us. We used to go to the beach. I was thinner than I am now, I looked pretty good in a bikini. Now what was his name? I'm usually good with names . . . Brad, Brian, something like that. I can even see him. Dark hair, kind of skinny, he had a moustache to hide his hair lip. Had surgery on it but it was always just a little off. His father was a mechanic; he ran the local garage. He always had great cars.'

'Did you ever meet Grace Falco?'

Kathy Holtz shook her head regretfully. 'You know what? I may have done. But I really don't remember. You know how it is when you're a teenager, you hang around in this huge crowd. She may have been at some parties that I went to, but jeez. Sorry.'

'What else do you remember about that time?'

Marvel hoped that Kathy's memory might be prompted by association.

'Grace Falco wasn't really one of us, at least how we understood the term,' Kathy said. 'I remember the feeling being that she was out of his league. We were pretty ordinary blue-collar kids. I don't even know how Brad or Brian or whatever his name was knew her. Hmm, what *was* his name? This is so frustrating. Memory is so fickle, you know there are some things that are so clear in my mind that I think they must have happened but when I think about it rationally, they can't have. Where does that stuff come from, I wonder?'

Kathy continued in this vein for a few more minutes and Marvel checked his watch. Poppy's train was arriving soon and he had a plan. He had told her he would meet her at the station (because he happened to be in the neighbourhood) and he'd update her on the meeting with Kathy. Then, at the end of it, he'd casually invite Poppy out to dinner, as if it was the most natural thing in the world.

He'd even picked out the restaurant, a great little seafood place in the Village that served an excellent lobster roll.

'Bill Brady.' Kathy Holtz slapped her pale, plump hand down on the table. 'Brady. That was his name. Father owned the garage. God, I haven't spoken to or even thought about him for years and years.'

'Any idea where he is now?'

Kathy Holtz shrugged. 'Somewhere in the tri-state area. He was cute, but not that bright and he didn't have much of what you'd call drive. I can't imagine he's gone too far. I'd try the garage. It was called Brady Motors.'

'The Marvel you see before you today is a sliver of his former self. I was pretty gross.'

'I can't imagine that.'

'Picture this: I ate chocolate cake for breakfast. And lunch. And dinner. And a chocolate snack before I went to bed. And that's not including all the fries and burgers and shakes.'

They were sitting in the same coffee shop in Penn Station where Marvel had sat with Kathy Holtz. Poppy needed caffeine. She had offered to buy him cake and he'd turned it down.

'What made you stop eating like that?'

'I don't know. I just got tired of who I was, I suppose. And after my wife and I split up and my kid went to college I had more time on my hands. Had to fill it somehow, so I started running and found I enjoyed getting out around the city. Then my wife got me into yoga and I liked it better than eating. Besides, I think if you're reasonably sensible, you get to the point in your life where you realize you're never going to change unless you start pretending to be the person you want to be.'

'I'll drink to that.' Poppy held up her cappuccino and Marvel noticed that her bag, which sat open beside her on the floor, contained the college year book that she had ordered.

'So I haven't been sitting around since you've been gone.'

'That's good,' she said, grinning. 'I'd hate to think you were pining.'

Marvel was so unsettled by the thought that she might be flirting with him that he launched into an account of what he'd been doing while she was away. *It doesn't sound right*, he thought as he listened to himself blurting the words, and wondered what had happened to the seasoned, unflappable investigator. He sounded defensive, too eager, like he'd been called into the principal's office.

When he'd finished he anxiously scanned Poppy's face for any hint that he had betrayed himself.

'That's interesting.'

'You don't sound like you mean that.'

Poppy shrugged one shoulder. 'I've been giving it some thought in DC. Actually, I've been giving it a lot of thought. And I kind of decided that it's a bit pathetic to be chasing around after my ex's new girlfriend. I've got a life to live, I should just get on with it. I thought she was lying about college, she wasn't. I made a value call and I was wrong. Time to stop embarrassing myself even further.'

'Right,' Marvel said, a little surprised by her change of direction.

'The photo proved it.' Poppy pulled the book out of her bag. 'I was way off beam.' She opened it to the correct page and turned the book around so that Marvel could see.

'Definitely her,' Marvel conceded. 'No switcheroo.'

'No switcheroo. Just me making a big fat arse of myself.'

Poppy was right of course, it was a bizarre thing

for her to be doing. And he was encouraging her because he had a personal agenda all of his own, which was, in its own way, just as fucked up. Why couldn't he simply come out and say that he liked her and wanted to see more of her instead of playing these games? He didn't honestly believe that there was much chance Grace Falco's background would hold any clues to where her husband hid the money that he stole.

'Stopping is probably the most sensible thing to do,' Marvel said after a short pause. 'For you I mean,' he added hastily. 'Me, I still got a job to do.'

'It absolutely is. I mean, really. What do I care? I made a hideous mistake with Philip. It's time to stop, before I turn into a mad-eyed stalker.' Poppy drained her cup and checked her watch. Marvel shelved his plan to ask her out to dinner. She looked like she had to be somewhere.

'You're right, you're absolutely right,' he said automatically.

'I mean, you must have thought I was a bit crazy, right?'

'Not the craziest I've seen, not by a long shot.'

'But still . . . a sandwich short of a picnic.'

'No. You were right to think the way you did. She did steal your boyfriend when it comes right down to it.'

'You're very kind,' Poppy said, and Marvel felt it like a knife in his gut. Kind. The kiss of death. 'Look, I gotta go. Thanks for the coffee.'

'You're very welcome,' Marvel said, standing up.

Watching her heft her bags on to her shoulders. She was used to being on the move.

'I'll walk you to your taxi,' he said.

The line for cars was long. *Good*, Marvel thought. *We'll have a mini date, right here on Eighth Avenue.*

'Where are you from?'

'I'm not from anywhere,' Poppy said. 'I was born in Thailand and I've lived all over the world – Hong Kong, Russia, China for a while. I spent some time in high school in Canberra and went to university in London.'

'Army?' Marvel asked, although he was thinking CIA.

Poppy shook her head. 'My father's in the same line of work as me. Or I should say I'm in the same line of work as him. He's been with the AP for years. He and my mother live in London. I have two younger brothers who live there too. My mother's very proud of the fact that her children were all born in different countries.'

'And you write for a British newspaper?'

'Australian. I hooked up with them when I was freelancing in Timor a few years ago. One thing led to another.'

'Your parents must be proud of you.' Marvel regretted the words the instant he said them. They were patronizing and, worse, they made him sound like an old fart.

'Proud? I guess. It's not something they would ever say. They're pretty eccentric. They don't go around boasting about what their kids do. They don't care about status.'

'What do they care for?'

'Hard to say. It's not something they would ever articulate. Their dinner parties are pretty wild. All sorts of crazy people turn up. Lots of drinking, lots of arguing. Politics mostly. They're kind of relics, actually, from another time. I guess it's because they've lived all their lives as expats, so they've had to create their own world wherever they go.'

'They sound like fun.'

'That's what everybody says.' Poppy grinned. 'Fun and mad in equally infuriating doses.'

To Marvel's disappointment a bunch of taxis appeared.

'Well, thanks for everything,' Poppy said as he put her bags in the trunk. 'Now that this is all over maybe we should get together some time. For like a drink or something.'

'Terrific,' he said, trying to sound like he believed that she meant it. 'That'd be really great.'

'Great. See you around.' She kissed him on the cheek so briefly that he didn't even feel it and got into the cab.

Marvel headed back underground to catch the subway.

Thirty

Marvel didn't turn on any lights. He opened the French doors out on to the terrace, poured himself a glass of Scotch and sat down in the semi-darkness to meditate on the city skyline.

The view normally soothed him. His apartment normally soothed him. Sipping finely crafted alcohol normally soothed him. But not tonight.

Why hadn't he just said to her, 'How about we make a date?' Simple words, easy to say. She would have said yes or no and he would have known exactly where he stood.

But what if she'd said no?

Absently Marvel stroked at his stomach. *Forget the thirty-four-inch waist*, he thought, *I'm still a land whale on the inside.*

The hands of the Williamsburg Savings Bank Tower showed that it was two a.m. but Marvel disregarded it – the clock had four faces and it was very rare that any one of them showed the right time and almost never were they in complete agreement.

His Tag said it was eleven thirty. He'd stayed late at the office catching up on paperwork from his other cases. He'd very nearly gone to that little seafood place in the West Village on his own, eaten at the bar. But that would have been sad. Instead he had chose to be sadder – ordering in Chinese and eating it at his desk.

He wanted to talk to somebody but it was much too late to call Madelaine, who was a very early riser. Even if it wasn't, she might be with her new boy-friend, the infant yogi.

Marvel imagined the boyfriend for a moment and then wondered why he didn't feel the slightest bit jealous that his partner for most of his adult life was sleeping with somebody else. And a twenty-nine-year-old somebody else at that.

Fact was, he didn't really care.

He wondered what Poppy was doing. Did she have a date? He didn't want to think about that.

Get over it, he told himself crossly. *She's not interested, you just have to get used to that.*

Bill Brady had the face of a man who'd spent a lot of time outdoors. Squint lines fanned out from his milky blue eyes and his skin was the colour of basted leather. A pale white line, the surgical scar that had corrected his cleft palate, divided his moustache at a drunken angle.

'Help you?' he asked, wiping his greasy hands on an equally dirty rag.

'Frederick Marvel.' Marvel handed over his card.

Bill Brady looked at the card, handed it back.

'I'm interested in Grace Falco.'

The creases around Bill Brady's eyes deepened

while he considered this information. 'You're not an investigator, you're an archaeologist,' he said. 'That's history.'

'I'm interested in history.'

'You'd better come inside.'

It was a cool day and Marvel was grateful for the offer. The garage had a lone pump out front but it was clear from the carcasses of cars that lay strewn about the forecourt that the business at hand was motors, not dispensing gasoline. Marvel wondered if Brady was any good; his ancient Saab was extremely temperamental and he'd never been able to match it up with a mechanic who fully understood its needs.

A pot of stale coffee perfumed the tiny, overcrowded office. Bill Brady cleared a stack of papers off one chair and invited Marvel to sit down. He wedged himself behind the desk. He was as slender as a teenage boy.

'It's not very good.' Bill Brady handed Marvel a cup, not seeming to doubt that he'd accept it anyway. He's got me pegged, Marvel thought, taking the cup.

Bill Brady poured a second cup and flung himself into a chair.

'What's this about?'

'A distant relative of Grace Falco's has died, leaving her a bequest. I'm trying to find her to settle the bequest.'

Bill Brady sipped his coffee thoughtfully.

'Right.'

'I'm interested in anything you can tell me,' Marvel said. 'Anything at all that you remember.'

'Why would I know where she is?'

'I don't know. I'm following up every angle I can.'

Bill Brady stared at Marvel silently. His look said he didn't believe him but Marvel pressed on.

'How did you meet her?'

'I met her here.' Bill Brady gestured around. 'She came in one day, she'd run out of gas. My father gave me the job of walking back with the gas can along the highway and filling up her car. I was smitten. So I asked her out. She said yes.'

So that's how it's done, Marvel thought. *I should take lessons.*

'How long did you go out with her?'

'A month or so.'

'And what happened?'

'She just stopped calling one day. I was pissed. Then I heard a couple of weeks later that her mother had died so I tried to call her but when I rang her number I got a female relative who told me Grace wasn't seeing anybody at the moment.'

'Does this look like the woman you knew?' Marvel took from his briefcase a photo of Grace Falco that he'd snapped the day before. She had been leaving Philip Ross's apartment at 9 a.m. It was information that he wouldn't be sharing with Poppy.

Bill Brady squinted and frowned at the photo. 'I guess,' he said. 'It's been a few years. Her hair wasn't that dark but, yeah. That's her.'

'But you're not sure.'

'I'm sure. She just looks a bit different, that's all.'

'Did she have any distinguishing characteristics?'

Bill Brady looked at Marvel blankly.

'Like moles or tattoos.'

'She wasn't into stuff like that. She was pretty straight.'

'Anything else at all you can tell me about her?'

'She was fun,' Bill Brady said after a short pause.

'What were her interests? What did she tell you about herself?'

'We didn't talk much about stuff. She was burned out from high school, she was one of those people who worked real hard and had plans for her life. Her father was dead and her mother wanted all kinds of things for her, good college, good career. And she wanted that too. But she was tired. I think that's why she took to me. I didn't care too much about talking. Overrated, I used to say. Talking changes nothing. What's the point in wasting your breath?'

'Especially when you're a teenager,' Marvel said. 'Much more important things to be doing.'

'Damn straight,' Bill Brady said, deadpan. And then he grinned. Hare lip or not he would still be pulling in the girls with that routine, Marvel thought. Sometimes there was nothing to beat an easy-going attitude and six-pack abs.

'What'd you do together?'

'Nothing much. We hung out with my crowd mostly. I didn't meet any of her friends, she wasn't too keen on introducing me to her life. Son of a mechanic with no plans for his life, I guess Mom wouldn't have been too pleased. So we did the typical summer stuff, drank beer and went to the beach.'

'Sounds like fun,' Marvel said, meaning it. 'Any places that you remember in particular?'

'One place.' Bill Brady's smile became gentler as he recalled the memory. 'We got in my car – my father had just given me a new Mustang, well, it was new for me. A bunch of us and we drove up to northern Connecticut. We went to this waterfall on the Houstatonic River, the place was called Falls Village, you ever heard of it?'

Marvel shook his head.

'No reason why you would, I guess. A buddy of mine used to live there, that was how he knew about it. It was a blistering day in August and we drove up to the waterfall. It was maybe a thirty-foot drop but you could also jump off a large boulder into the pool below. That was about twenty feet. So all us guys had to do it. You wouldn't see me doing it now but when you're twenty-five you think you'll live for ever.'

Marvel couldn't remember feeling like that at twenty-five but he could see how Bill Brady would.

'We were having a great time and Grace had had a couple of beers and she decided she was going to do the jump. We all tried to talk her out of it but she insisted. She said that if she didn't start taking chances her life would be worth nothing. So she clambered up on to the rock. There wasn't really a proper place to stand, you just had to scrabble around while you plucked up your courage, there were a couple of weeds to hang on to but that was about it. And then you jumped.

'By the time she got up there, all the other guys were right into it, so they were shouting, "Jump, jump," and you could see she was having second thoughts but of course by then it was too late to back down. It was impossible to scramble down the rock face again; it was too sheer. There was no way out.'

'So what happened?'

'She jumped,' Bill Brady said, as if surprised by the question. 'What else was she going to do?'

'And she was OK?'

'OK? She did a backwards swallow dive.' Bill Brady laughed and slapped his knee. 'Turned out she'd been a high-diving and swimming champion in high school. The stuff before, leading up to it? It was all just an act.'

Thirty-One

It was all just an act. Marvel thought about Bill Brady's story as he drove back to the city. It was a funny story, and Brady had told it well. Probably embellished it over the years. Still, it had emphasized the opinion that Marvel was starting to form about Grace Falco: that here was a person who presented her life fully packaged to an audience.

Marvel looked at his watch; he had a living to make. He put his foot down and rounded a corner. As he did so he could see that the traffic coming the other way had been halted by an accident. Two cars lay strewn across the road as if deposited there by a careless and very large child. Two cop cars' lights blinked blindingly and Marvel could hear an ambulance siren becoming more irritating as it got closer.

Rubberneckers had slowed traffic on his side of the highway to a standstill. Marvel got out his road map. Brady had told him the town where Grace Falco had lived was not too far. If he turned off the highway now he could be there in minutes.

Occupational hazard, Marvel thought as he eased his car through the left lanes to the exit. Hard to pull back once you've started.

The small Westchester town where the Falcos had lived had been blessed with good bones. The buildings on Main Street were all mid-century or earlier. Well-designed, single-storey structures that had adapted easily as the town's fortunes had risen and butchers and hardware stores had been replaced by gourmet coffee shops, classy delis and boutiques that sold ten-dollar bars of hand-milled French soap. The angled parking spaces were taken up with shiny and large late-model vehicles and Marvel's shabby Saab stood out. He had been meaning to get it spray-painted ever since the time some wally in a Chevrolet had scraped the paintwork on the driver's side about eight months ago, but he couldn't decide on the colour.

The offices of the local newspaper were glass-fronted and drenched in sun. Behind a single desk and underneath a large replica of the paper's mast-head sat a middle-aged woman with a fierce perm. Marvel was directed to the paper's microfiche archives and spent the next half hour or so squinting over the film as he remembered that he had cancelled an appointment to have his eyes checked.

The story about Grace Falco's parents, as told in their obituaries, had been a local tragedy. George Falco had fallen dead of a heart attack while out jogging one morning. Two years later his wife Diana had succumbed to cancer.

There was no photo of the daughter, who had been eighteen at the time of her mother's death and preparing to go away to college. Relatives had whisked her away to somewhere further north (the small-town boosterism, even in the midst of tragedy, shone through and the paper managed to imply that this relocation, to a less salubrious town, had merely heaped more trouble on the unfortunate Miss Falco). Marvel looked at the photos of the Falcos. Clear-eyed and happy, they looked like a couple who were content with their lives. He had died at forty-six, one year older than Marvel was now. She had been forty-three. The death numbers are getting closer all the time, Marvel thought.

'The reporter who wrote this story,' Marvel asked the receptionist. 'He still live here?'

The receptionist glanced at the stories. 'I don't think so, hon,' she said. 'I don't recognize that name. Course I've only been here myself for five years.'

'Anybody else here on staff who might know anything about the Falcos?'

'There's just me and Charlie the editor these days. And he's in Queens today visiting his sister who's sick.'

Marvel ordered a hard copy of the stories, paid his money, had a quick discussion with the receptionist about suitable places to eat lunch, and ambled out into a day that had become much warmer.

Judging by the menu, the diner was owned by Greeks. Marvel ordered the salad and a Reuben. The waitress was about the same age as the woman in the newspaper office and she had the same perm.

The food was good but when Marvel told her so she looked at him suspiciously, as if she feared a trap. There must be lots of places like this in the county, Marvel thought, where people watched in dismay as their family homes became teardowns and people with dollar signs in their eyes moved in with talk of increased square footage that was just as incomprehensible as the prices their homes now commanded. Marvel's father, who lived in a newly ritzy town in New Jersey, was facing this very situation. Every time Marvel spoke to him he had some new story about a bond trader wanting to buy his Victorian home for a laughable sum of money just to tear it down and put up something that Marvel senior thought ran contrary to the laws of good taste, God and nature.

'Get you something else?'

'More coffee, please.'

'Do you remember the Falco family?' he asked when the woman returned.

'Sure,' she said. 'Everybody who lived here remembers that.'

'Well, I'm trying to track down the family who took the daughter after the mother died. See, I work for an insurance company. Turns out that Grace Falco's due for some money from an insurance policy that got forgotten.'

The waitress looked as if she didn't believe a word that came out of his lying mouth. *I must be losing it*, Marvel thought. *I used to be so much better at this.*

But it seemed that a suspicious sneer was the waitress's conversational tic. For in a moment she nodded her head once.

'She left town. Went to live with relatives.'

'I heard that. Any idea where?'

'I don't remember,' she said. 'It was in the paper.'

'The paper didn't name the town. Or the relatives.'

'She left soon after. Didn't come back. Nobody blamed her.'

'Do you know anybody who might know where she is? Did she have any friends here?'

'Marv?' The woman's bellow made Marvel jump and at first he thought she was addressing him. But a minute later a bald, grumpy-looking man stuck his head out of the kitchen door.

'Whaddyawant?'

'The Falcos. What happened to the girl?'

'Some relative,' he mumbled. 'Came one day. Uncle. Took her away. Last we saw.'

'See?' said the waitress, as if Marvel had been trying to catch her out in a lie.

'But where? Who was the relative?'

'The wife's brother,' Marv said. 'Never met him, don't know his name.'

Thirty-Two

Philip studied himself in the mirror and frowned.

'You look terrific.' Grace came up behind him and put her hands over his eyes. 'Stop staring like that.'

'I look like an ass.'

'C'mere, I've got something for you.' Grace pulled him down on to the bed and handed him a small box, Tiffany blue.

'What's this?'

'Open it.'

Philip pushed the lid up. Inside was a set of cufflinks. Sapphires set in gold.

'Don't you love them?' Grace's voice became squeaky when she got excited. 'Aren't they just the best? If you're going to be John Travolta for the night you've got to have a little bling.'

'Sapphires?'

'C'mon, don't look like that. It's fun. It completes the outfit.'

He took the cufflinks out of their velvet prison and allowed Grace to fasten them to his shirt. He hated costume parties. He'd been trying to talk Herb out of having one but had not succeeded.

'There,' she finished with a pat on the arm, 'very Bay Ridge. Admit it, you look great.'

He turned his wrist to view the cuffs and felt uncomfortable. He hated spending money on frivolous things.

'Tiffany. How much did they cost?'

'Don't be silly. It's only money.'

'But where did you . . .?'

'I sold my body on the street of course, darling. What else would you expect? I got something for me too.' Grace pulled out a larger box, the same blue. 'Here, help me.'

Philip fastened the diamond choker around her neck. Grace was Madonna as material girl.

'You see?' She pulled Philip up so that they could both look in the mirror. 'What a perfect pair we make. What's the matter? You don't like it?'

'Where did you get them?'

'I told you. Turning tricks on 14th and Ninth.' Grace grinned at both of their reflections in the mirror. 'Philip, Jesus Christ. You know it's paste, right?'

'Paste?' he said blankly.

'I had a couple of boxes from stuff Mitch bought me,' Grace said. 'I just put these in them.'

'Mitch.' Philip said the name uncertainly. Was she implying that Mitch bought her jewels and he didn't?

'Philip, it's a little joke, sweetie. C'mon. We have to get in the party mood with a little bling. I bought the stuff for twenty dollars at that consignment shop on Lexington.'

But that's what she'd said about the leather pants. And he'd found the receipt. He examined the cufflink more closely. It was fake, of course it was. Nothing at all to worry about. He was too jittery these days. And there was absolutely no reason.

It was Herb's birthday party and he intended to celebrate as if business was going well, which it was. The hotel had opened to rave reviews and full bookings. The restaurant had been favourably written up in the *New York Times* and Philip had just that week been flagged as a young architect to watch.

As a special treat for himself, Herb had promised an excitingly vulgar event and delivered it without reservation. The theme was twentieth-century bad taste and Philip thought it interesting just how many people had interpreted this to mean the eighties.

The dance floor was crowded with Boy Georges, Simon Le Bons and Cindi Laupers. Madonna in almost all her permutations was everywhere. Some enterprising person had come as Tiananmen Square, although he or she was finding it difficult to dance. There were at least two men dressed as Margaret Thatcher.

Frankie Goes to Hollywood. Queen. Talking Heads. The Bee Gees. The music was loud and danceable. Everybody knew the tunes. Everybody was having fun and either drunk or on the way to being drunk.

Philip had been preparing to hate this night for weeks but he discovered that it had its own alchemical mix. The costumes made it easy to strike up a conversation with a complete stranger, especially if they had interpreted the theme in a similar way. Philip's costume seemed positively restrained compared to the outfits around him, and he permitted himself a moment of regret that he hadn't given a little more thought to his own choice.

Philip had also expected the party guests to be a little more from Herb's 'smart' set, but all Herb's family and friends were there, including some guys Philip hadn't seen since high school. Sitting in the corner, plates piled high with food, were a couple of Herb's aunts. The decorative painter Philip worked with had been invited, plus almost all of the construction crew who were working on renovating Herb's town house. Perhaps in the interests of saving the cost of at least one costume, they had come as the Village People.

'Happy birthday to me.' Herb thrust a drink into Philip's hand.

'Happy birthday to you.'

'Where's Poppy? I thought you'd bring her. I like her.'

'We broke up,' Philip said.

'Hang on, hang on.' Herb put his free hand on Philip's arm. 'Too much information. How come I never heard this? You broke up? With Poppy? Why, for God's sake?'

'She broke up with me.'

'Oh, well, that explains it.'

'Yeah, I thought it would.'

'She finally saw through you.'

'You could say that.'

'I'm sorry, man. You must be upset.'

'Actually, I'm here with Grace.'

'Right. Saw she was here. She came with you, did she?'

Philip had been meaning to tell Herb about his relationship with Grace but every time he had met him recently they'd had hotel business to discuss. The last couple of weeks had been just frantic.

But now was his chance.

He was just about to make his announcement when Grace chose that minute to wave to Philip from the dance floor. She was dancing with Herb's girl-friend Tiffany, who looked surreal as David Byrne in a big white suit.

'Remember when I was in graduate school at Rutgers? Used to go to that strip bar? The Silver Stiletto?' Herb said.

'What does that have to do with anything?'

Herb glanced at Grace, who was doing a rather good impersonation of early Madonna for Tiffany. 'I thought she looked familiar, the first time I met her at your place. And now I remember why. She's a dead ringer for this woman who used to dance there.'

Thirty-Three

'She used to wear a wig, a blonde one, and a tiny silver bikini,' Herb said. 'And she had an itty bitty tattoo of a ram's head on her hip. The other girls were always hit and miss but Katalina, she always gave a hundred and ten, you know what I'm saying?'

'You're a sad creature,' Philip said, putting his arm around Herb. 'You know that, don't you? You're rich and successful, you've got a great girlfriend and a terrific family, and here you are, on your birthday, reminiscing about a New Jersey stripper.'

'I didn't say she was *from* New Jersey,' Herb protested, 'I said that's where I saw her. She could have been from anywhere.'

'I'm going to forget I ever heard you say that,' Philip said. 'Because it's just stupid, OK? Grace is not and never has been a stripper.'

'I didn't say she was a stripper. I said she reminded me of one. And it's not like there's anything wrong with stripping,' Herb insisted. 'A couple of women in my graduate programme said they'd toyed with the idea because it paid a helluva lot better than waitressing. Look, here she comes, why don't we tell her? She'll get a laugh out of it.'

'No!' Philip's arm tightened around his friend. 'You've had too much to drink.'

'I haven't had too much to drink.' Herb disentangled himself from Philip's grasp. 'Why do you care anyway?'

'I'm seeing Grace now.'

Herb's mouth fell open. 'Sorry, man. You know I didn't mean . . . would never have said anything if . . . Jesus, why didn't you tell me?'

'I meant to. It's been busy.'

'I think I need that drink now,' Herb said.

Later that night when Philip was making love to Grace, Herb's words came back to him. He watched her underneath him, listening to her sighs, her unguarded murmurs. Her eyes were closed and her hair was fanned out on the pillow. And Philip had a thought. What if Herb hadn't been mistaken?

Ridiculous. Grace was the last person in the world to be a stripper. She was too modest for one thing. The idea of her taking her clothes off in front of a bunch of strange men was simply inconceivable.

Afterwards, they lay close together, their fingers entwined. Then Grace rolled away and Philip noticed a small scar on her right hip.

His stomach flipped.

'What's this?' he asked, running his thumb over the roughened ridge about the size of a dollar coin. He wondered that he hadn't noticed it before.

'Oh, that?' She hesitated before replying and in that fraction of a second Philip was struck, forcibly, by the feeling that he was about to be lied to. 'That's the result of youthful indiscretion.'

'A tattoo?' he asked, jokingly casual.

Another glance, another infinitesimal silence. 'Nothing so exciting. I spent too much time in the sun and got a melanoma.'

'Of course,' he said, 'of course.'

'Of course what?' Grace teased, running her fingers through his hair. 'You don't think I'm the kind of girl that could have a tattoo? Would that shock you?'

'No,' Philip said indignantly, although the truth was he had never understood why tattoos were considered cool, they always looked a bit trashy to him.

'Well, maybe I should get one then.' Grace's fingers moved down, tracing his collar bone. 'Perhaps a little something witty right here.' She moved her hand to her left breast. 'Would that make you love me more?'

'There's nothing you could do to make me love you more,' he said, drawing her to him, kissing her, feeling her soft, soft body and feeling relief because he knew that nothing else mattered except that he and Grace were together.

After Marvel found out that the Westchester county reporter had moved to Long Island he made an excuse to go out there.

Eugene Marchetti was selling real estate in a suburban town about an hour's drive from the city and doing well at it, if the Lexus he drove was an indication.

'I got divorced,' Eugene said to explain his change

in career. They were sitting at a Dunkin' Donuts in the town that Marvel had already forgotten the name of. 'You need tons of money when you get divorced. And journalism was never going to do it. So I had a pal out here with his own business and he asked me to come out and set up with him. It was slow for a bit but it's working all right now.' He shot his cuffs, affording Marvel a glimpse of the gold links. *Wasted at Dunkin' Donuts*, Marvel thought. He was having black coffee and Eugene was having three donuts. The soft skin of what had formerly been his waist pushed against his well-made shirt. A sharp memory hit Marvel, the memory of how uncomfortable it was to be fat. You were always forced to think about your gut because it was always attempting to colonize yet more space that your trousers didn't have.

'I wanted to ask you about the Falco story. You remember it?'

'Of course.' Eugene Marchetti crammed the remains of the first donut into his mouth, leaving a sprinkle of white powder on his nose. 'Sure. Damn tragedy. A genuine happy family and God goes and punishes them like that.'

'Did you know them?'

'Not well, to say hi to in the street, that sort of thing. I had my own problems at that time; my marriage was breaking up. My wife and I were . . . well, let's just say my situation was taking up all of my thoughts.'

'Can you tell me about the girl?'

'Grace? From all accounts she was a bright kid, applied herself at school. Everybody agreed she had a future. Got into a good college and had plans to be a writer or something. I talked to her a couple times about coming in to the paper to intern over the summer. She was keen but then her mother died and she left town. Never saw her back there again. Too many unhappy associations, I guess.' To Marvel's relief Marchetti finally wiped his nose clean of sugar.

'Do you remember the name of the family who took Grace? I heard it was her wife's brother.'

'I don't know his name. Somebody pointed him out to me at the funeral, standing all alone. He was a scrawny-looking guy, like a rat on two legs. It was weird.'

'How do you mean?'

'Well, I never got to talk to the guy and I only knew Diana Falco in passing, but I heard that they were twins. And I've never seen two people less alike in my entire life. She was open and friendly and beautiful and he looked twenty years older, all worn and haggard, somebody you'd probably avoid on a dark street. Apparently they hadn't spoken in years. You could see why. Didn't look like they had much in common except genes. Rumour had it that he was only sniffing around because there was money to be had. George Falco had built a pretty respectable pile of cash with all those rugs he sold.'

Where there's money there're lawyers.

Marvel should have thought of it before. The family retainer would know exactly what had happened to Grace Falco after her mother died.

He called directory assistance while he was stuck in a traffic jam on the Long Island Expressway and got the number of the law firm that Eugene Marchetti had told him handled the Falco affairs.

And then, because he was still motionless, he called, spoke to the receptionist and to his surprise was put straight through to the firm's senior partner, Nelson Thomas.

'How can I help you?' The voice was wavery with age and rich with the cadence of New England's privileged class.

'I'm told you represented the estate of George and Diana Falco,' he said. 'I'm a private investigator working in New York on a fraud case and I'm trying to talk to Grace Falco in connection with it.'

There was a silence so long that Marvel thought his phone connection had been lost.

'Hello? Are you still there?'

'Yes,' the voice said. 'Yes, I'm here. Pardon me; I must seem very rude. I haven't heard anybody mention Grace Falco in more than ten years.'

'I'm trying to find out where she went after her parents died.'

'She went to live with her uncle. It was just for a short period of time before she went off to college.'

'Do you remember the name of the uncle?'

'John O'Reilly,' Nelson Thomas said promptly. 'He was Diana's twin brother. At that point he was her only living relative. George had been an only child and both his parents had died years before.'

Marvel wrote the name John O'Reilly down on the back of a carwash flyer. 'Where did he live?'

'Upstate. Pawling, I think. I can check, I've probably got it in a file somewhere.'

Marvel wrote Pawling on the back of the flyer.

'I wouldn't count on him being there still. He moved around a lot.'

'What contact did you have with Grace after her parents' death?'

'None once the estate was settled. She went away out west to school and I never saw her again. As far as I know she has never even been back to visit their graves.'

'Did they leave her a lot of money?'

'Why should I tell you that without a court order?'

'I think something might have happened to Grace Falco because of it.'

The silence wavered and Marvel thought the connection had been lost.

'There was no money,' the lawyer finally said. 'A small trust to pay for her education and that was it. George Falco was a gambler, a bad one. He got involved in junk bonds and silliness like that. After he died there was almost nothing left after his debts had been settled.'

'Except the money to send Grace to school.'

'That was Diana's victory. She would not let him touch that money.'

'Did you find it odd that Grace never came back?'

'What was there for her to come back for?'

The traffic started to loosen; Marvel had the distinct sensation that he was going backwards as the cars in the lanes on both sides of his moved forward.

'Grace's boyfriend back then mentioned that when

he called the house after the accident he spoke to a female relative. Do you have any idea who that might have been?'

Nelson Thomas paused again and when he spoke his voice was as crisp and dry as New England leaves in fall. 'John O'Reilly had a daughter,' he said. 'She was about Grace's age.'

Thirty-Four

'This is ridiculous,' Grace said. 'You know I don't have it.'

Whitney just smiled, his slow, infuriating smile that seemed to gradually increase until it took over his whole face. Grace had the strongest urge to punch him in the mouth.

'I know you,' he said, massaging her shoulder. Grace shrugged it out of his reach. 'I know that you can always find a way to get it.'

'I'm broke. How many times do I have to say it? I have no money, I have no job, I can barely pay my rent.'

'Grace, Grace. I know you. You're always working on something.'

'I'm not.'

'This architect guy must have bucks, why else would you have hooked up with him?'

'You ever heard of love?'

'I've heard of it but I've also heard of UFOs and I don't believe in them either.' Whitney leaned back and regarded Grace, his right hand cupping his chin as if he was studying a painting. 'You wish I'd just go away, don't you?'

'Must I say it?'

Whitney put both hands on Grace's shoulder and this time she made no move to escape. 'Well, I'm not going to. I'm going to be an inconvenient fact in your life for a long, long time. It's harsh, but it's real. So I suggest that we figure out a relationship that takes this into account. Because you know how I can be when I get angry.'

Grace looked down at the floor. Whitney's breath smelled of wintergreen gum. She had never hated him more than at this very minute.

'I've changed my mind. I don't wish you would go away. I wish you were dead.'

Whitney laughed at this but at least he dropped his grip on her. Grace massaged the place where his hands had been.

'I ain't dead.' Whitney slapped his hand to his heart as if to provide evidence. 'In fact I never felt better in my whole life. But the fact is that I'm gonna need some money and I'm gonna need it soon. You will see to it, won't you? Good girl.' He stood up and threw a couple of bucks on the table to pay for his coffee. 'Let me know when you've seen to it. And don't make it too long.'

Poppy had just put her bags down when the phone rang. It was Francesca.

'Where the hell have you been?' she demanded. 'I've been calling you all day.'

'I was flying back from Utah,' Poppy said. 'I was on assignment. What's the matter?'

'Thank God you're here.' Francesca broke off to cough.

'Are you OK, Fran? You don't sound well.'

'Fine, fine, just smoking too much. God, I simply cannot believe this.'

'Believe what?'

'Grace, that bitch.'

'What's she done?'

'What's she done? The little bitch is suing me for half of the house. She doesn't even like the fucking house. She's trying to force me to sell it so she can get her greedy little hands on a big pile of cash.'

'Jesus,' Poppy said, sitting down and flipping off her trainers. 'Can she do that?'

'Poppy, I just don't know what to do.' Down the phone line Poppy heard a rasping, hacking sound that was Francesca crying. 'That house is my only connection to normal life. That house is my family.'

'Can you mortgage the place and pay her some money?'

'I'm not doing that,' Francesca snapped. 'It's my home. Mitch signed it over to me before he died. She has no right to it. None. No matter how much she whines about being hard up.'

Philip was sitting very still on the Mies van der Rohe daybed when Grace arrived in the apartment.

'You're in the dark,' she said.

'How was the job search?'

'Not great. Not even a nibble. I wonder why they

bothered to call me in for the interview at all. Can I fix you a drink?'

'No thanks.'

'Everything OK?' Grace sat down beside him and put her arm around his shoulders.

'Francesca called me. She told me about the house.'

'Oh, right.' Grace removed her arm from Philip's shoulders and stood up. 'I'm going to fix myself a drink, if that's OK.'

'Why are you doing this, Grace?'

'Why shouldn't I? I was married to Mitch. He left me absolutely stranded. Why shouldn't I get a little help?'

'You could have just talked to Francesca instead of going straight in with the lawyers.'

'She can't stand me, Philip.'

'That's not true.'

'Trust me.' Grace poured her glass of wine and sat down opposite Philip. 'It's true.'

'Is that why you're doing this? To get even with her?'

'No, Philip. I don't give a shit about what Francesca thinks about me. Really. I just need a little space to be able to think and money will provide it. There's no mortgage on that house so Francesca can easily raise the money. She's acting like it's some grand drama. It isn't. It's a perfectly reasonable request. The house did belong half to Mitch, after all, who was my husband. Why shouldn't I have some of it?'

'Do you feel so exposed?'

'Yes, I do. I feel very exposed. I don't know how I'm going to survive. I'm not getting anywhere with job-hunting. The little money I do have is draining away. I'm desperate and I don't know what to do.'

Philip took both of Grace's hands in his. They were cold. He chafed them slightly.

'I know what you can do,' he said softly. 'I know exactly what you can do. You can marry me.'

John O'Reilly's old hang wasn't what you would call a high-rent neighbourhood. Diners and car repair shops bumped along with bars and no-name fast food outlets. Double-wide trailers had gathered most of the accoutrements of lower-class country life around them. Weeds and rusting automobiles competed to be the most outstanding feature of garden design.

Nelson Thomas had come through with the last known address and Marvel had forgone a poker night with a few old buddies to check it out.

The road looked even spookier at night – there were few street lamps and the smell of cow manure hovered in the air. Marvel parked the car and walked a little way and stood outside one of the homes. Inside he could see the blue light of a television flashing.

'Got something I can help you with?' A woman came out of the trailer with a Doberman straining on the leash. She was skinny in tight jeans and a sleeveless shirt. Tattoos covered her shoulders.

'Just looking for a friend of mine who used to live on this street.'

'Funny time to come calling.'

'I happened to be passing,' Marvel said, eyeing the dog, which looked as if his whole life would be a miserable failure if he couldn't take a chunk out of a passing private investigator. The woman yanked on the chain and the tattoos bulged in the thin white light that came from indoors. 'His name was John O'Reilly. Do you remember him?'

'Who wants to know?' The dog lunged in Marvel's direction and the woman leaned back on the lead, knees bent as if she was water ski-ing.

Marvel told her his name. Then he took a smart step back. He didn't like attack dogs much.

'That's old business,' the woman said. 'He hasn't lived here in years. I don't know where he lives now. And we got nothing to do with him, OK?'

A night mist had come in and Marvel decided that it was official, the place creeped him out. He thought about the snarling, slobbering dog and the fact that he wasn't on anybody's dime except his own. Time to go perhaps. Then he saw the figure coming from around the back of the trailer, holding something that looked like an axe in his hands.

Thirty-Five

His hands were large and flat and looked right at
home carrying that axe. His arms were clad in
checked flannel. He wore workman's boots and a
baseball hat, which bore a farm equipment brand that
hipsters in Brooklyn thought droll and ironic. Marvel
was fairly convinced there was nothing droll or ironic
about this guy.

'Asking about John O'Reilly,' the woman said.

'You a friend of his?'

'No.'

'What do you want?'

'I want some information about him.'

'You looking for money?'

'No.' Marvel hoped he sounded sufficiently grim
as he covertly measured him up. They were about the
same height – five eleven, six foot, something like
that. But the guy had thirty pounds on him and it was
hard muscle. It suddenly occurred to Marvel what a
pathetic concept 'gym fit' was.

'You don't want money?'

'I'm trying to find out about his niece.'

'You don't want money?'

Marvel shook his head.

The axe moved gently up and down in the guy's hands as he flexed his muscles.

'You'd better come in. Doreen, get that damn dog out back.'

The trailer was cluttered but neat. A large flat-screen television dominated the small living area and a fake leather reclining rocker sat in front of it. Beside that was a chipped wooden table with a can of Yuengling beer.

'Beer?'

'Sure,' Marvel said, hoping to build on the sliver of rapport that he hoped he had established outdoors.

His host pulled two beers from a below-counter refrigerator in the galley kitchen and put them on the bar. Marvel sat.

The woman came in from stowing the dog and sat on the sofa, picking up a nail-file. The television was on but the sound was down. She stared at it anyway.

'I'm Ralph,' said the guy, holding out a well-muscled arm. 'And that's Doreen.' He nodded at the woman, who looked at Marvel briefly before her eyes swivelled back to the television set. She hit the remote so the sound jumped up a couple of notches.

'Turn that damn thing down,' Ralph shouted at Doreen. With a guilty look she obliged.

'Stuck in front of that idiot box twenty hours a day,' Ralph muttered to him. 'You'd think there was nothing else to life.'

Marvel nodded sympathetically.

'John O'Reilly,' Ralph said in a tone that suggested

I would know what he was talking about. 'Used to live here. We had some problems because of that. That's why my welcome wasn't as friendly as it could have been. For a while there people turned up at odd hours, wanting their money.'

'I don't want any money,' Marvel said hastily to distinguish himself from other angry night callers.

Ralph looked at Marvel and shrugged. 'Hey, I can see you're not the kind of person who'd be stupid enough to get involved with O'Reilly. We bought this place fair and square. Got it cheap on account of his forfeiting on the mortgage and everything. That was eight years ago now. Trouble was, news hadn't got around. Every week it seemed like somebody was turning up here, or wanting a piece of O'Reilly. Some of them wouldn't believe that I didn't have anything to do with him. I got these companies trying to take my home away because of debts he owed. It was rough,' Ralph said simply. 'Had to hire myself a lawyer to get it all sorted out. Like I don't have enough things already to spend my money on.'

'*Our* money,' Doreen said from the sofa.

Ralph shot her a fond glance and Marvel felt a twang of envy for their easy familiarity.

'I'm trying to find out about his family. He had a daughter and his niece came to live with him the summer before she went to college.'

'Not much help to you there.' Ralph shook his head. 'Like I said, we came after. Bought the place in good faith. My life's savings.'

'Our life's savings,' Maureen corrected.

'You never heard where O'Reilly went? Where he lives now?'

Ralph shook his head. 'This ain't Mayberry,' he said. 'People come and go. Nobody pays too much attention. People mind their own business, keep themselves to themselves. If I was John O'Reilly I wouldn't want anybody to know where I was either.'

Marvel pulled Grace Falco's photograph from his pocket. 'Does this woman look familiar to you?'

Ralph shook his head and got up and passed it to Doreen. She took the photo with long fingernails, squinted at it and then rummaged on a side table, picked up a pair of glasses and put them on. They made her look surprisingly prim.

'Jesus Christ,' she said, demolishing prim. 'I have seen her.'

Ralph took the photo again, squinted. 'Nope,' he said. 'Not me.'

'Yes, you.' Doreen jumped up and headed out the back. 'Yes, we did. Remember when we did over the spare room and pulled up the carpet?'

'Sure,' Ralph grumbled good-naturedly. 'I did most of the grunt work, didn't I?'

'We found those photos, must've slipped down behind the dresser, 'cos the old carpet was newer in that corner?'

'So?'

'The photo, it was this girl. It's the same person, Ralphie.'

'Grace Falco,' Marvel said.

'Yeah, yeah, that was the name. It was written on

the side. One of those things you send out for Christmas. Like we did a couple of years ago with Frank.'

'Damn dog,' Ralph muttered. 'Posing with the damn dog wearing reindeer horns. Made me a laughing stock.'

'Did you keep the photo?' Marvel asked.

'No, hon,' Doreen said. 'I couldn't see that it would be of any use to me.'

Doreen and Ralph walked Marvel to his car. The dog started barking. Marvel jumped.

'He's a good watchdog,' Ralph said. 'Sometimes you never know what you're going to get out here. All sorts of stuff goes on.'

'Right.' Marvel opened the door and slid into the car.

Doreen handed him the photograph, Grace's photo.

'You forgot this.'

Marvel heard a coyote howl and he was suddenly anxious to get away. He handed Doreen his card. 'If you think of anything else, give me a call,' he said out of habit.

He planned to call Poppy from his office the next afternoon. He would be in court for a couple of hours and his evening was free. He had everything worked out. He'd rehearsed it. He'd say he'd called to check up, see how she was getting on. And then say something casual like, 'There's this great new place that just opened near me and I've been dying to try it. How about you join me? My treat.' Or something like that.

When he was leaving court his cellphone rang. It was Poppy.

'Philip's getting married,' Poppy said. 'He's fucking getting married.'

Marvel stood completely still for a moment. 'Where are you?' he said. And then: 'I'll be there in ten minutes.'

Thirty-Six

Poppy opened the door. She was wearing sweat pants and a paint-stained T-shirt. She had been crying. The shock and pain on her face made her look as if she had been punched.

'How could he?' Poppy wailed. 'How *could* he? When we were together he wouldn't even stay over at my house. That woman turns up and . . .' Her train of thought was distracted by sobbing. Marvel hesitated a second after closing the door before taking her in his arms.

'It's OK,' Marvel said quietly, as he would have done to his daughter, 'it's OK.' He could feel Poppy's tears soaking through his newly laundered shirt. It was a good feeling.

'Oh God, I wish I was dead.'

Marvel said nothing. He held her and waited. Eventually, Poppy asked for Kleenex. The box was sitting on the coffee table. He guided her to the sofa, handed it to her and she sat back, blew her nose, wiped her eyes and rearranged her hair.

'I'm sorry,' she said, 'you must think I'm a twit.'

'I don't think you're a twit.'

'Ever happened to you?'

'Not in exactly that way, but yeah. Same tune, different words.'

Poppy blew her nose again. 'God, I must look a mess.'

She didn't. She really, really didn't. Marvel told her so and Poppy grimaced with embarrassment and looked down at her feet. She wasn't used to receiving compliments, he realized, and wondered just how emotionally stunted Philip Ross had been.

What did he care? He had a clear path to Poppy now, and time to figure out how to be everything Philip Ross had not been.

The trick was to ensure that he wasn't just the rebound guy.

'Let me make you some tea,' he said, getting up. 'I understand that tea is the cure for everything.'

He made a pot and they drank it together, a big effort for him. Poppy liked strong English tea and Marvel felt his throat become furry with tannin. *I won't sleep for weeks*, he thought and decided he didn't care.

After the tea he cleared up, washed the dishes and put them in the rack to dry. Dinner seemed like a very natural suggestion; he was sure he could bring it up, perhaps with the pretext of not wanting Poppy to be alone. Nothing more desperate than takeout in your apartment the same day you've found out your ex is tying the knot.

'You fancy some dinner?' Marvel said. 'I know a great little place.'

'Thanks, but I'm meeting Francesca at a bar in

Hell's Kitchen in an hour. We plan to get me very drunk and say some very rude things about Philip and Grace, in the time-honoured dumpee tradition.'

'That's a good plan,' Marvel said. 'Want me to stop by later and make sure you get home?'

'You are sweet.'

'People say that. But usually they just mean sucker. They say sweet but they really don't mean that.'

'I mean it.' Poppy reached up on tiptoe and kissed him on the cheek. She kept her balance by putting one hand on his arm. 'Thank you.'

'Don't mention it,' Marvel said. Time to go, welcomes were in danger of being overstayed.

Poppy walked him to the door and turned back. She unlatched the lock, paused a moment, and then said, 'Look, I can't promise I'll be brilliant company but why don't you join us?'

The bar was a dive. It was dimly lit and the furniture was falling apart, right along with most of the patrons. Charlie Parker was on the jukebox. Francesca was already sitting regally on a stool with a martini in front of her. She managed to look magnificently out of place and completely at home.

Marvel nodded at the bartender, who recognized him.

When Marvel reintroduced himself Francesca regarded him warily. 'To what do we owe the pleasure?' she said icily as Marvel settled himself on to the wobbly stool on the other side of Poppy.

'I happened to be in the neighbourhood.'

He ordered a Heineken and Poppy ordered the same, with a shot of Jack. The barman poured and placed. Marvel gave him a twenty. If he couldn't buy Poppy dinner then a few cheap beers would have to do.

'Holding steady?' Francesca asked Poppy.

'Will be soon.' Poppy knocked back the shot.

Marvel said nothing. He enjoyed his beer and the tunes and sitting next to Poppy.

'Does this mean she's going to drop the legal action?' Poppy asked.

'We'll see.' Francesca polished off her martini and nudged the empty glass across the bar. 'I think I told you that Mitch put the house in my name right before he died.'

'Why?' Marvel chipped in.

Francesca took his measure a second or two before answering. 'Hmm, let me see, I don't know exactly because he didn't tell me he was doing it but at a rough guess I'd say so that greedy little witch couldn't get her hands on it.'

'Grace asked Francesca for money, from the house,' Poppy told Marvel. 'She thought she should have half of what it was worth.'

'She started on me the way she started on Mitch,' Francesca said. 'Constant. Like water on rock. Some nerve.'

'Strange person,' Poppy said. 'And I can say that because I'm about to be drunk and she stole my boyfriend.'

'I found out some things about her. Grace Falco

had a few troubles. Her father died of a heart attack when she was a teenager and a couple of years later her mother died of cancer.' Marvel worried the label on his beer with his thumb. 'After that she went to live with her uncle and her cousin in a trailer in Pawling.' He wasn't making much sense, he realized. In fact, he was babbling. He couldn't remember the last time a woman had made him babble.

'Trailer?' Francesca snorted. 'Grace Falco lived in a trailer? That must have been a shock.'

'Why did she do that?' Poppy asked.

'It was only for a month or so, before she went to college. And her mother's will stipulated it. Besides, as far as I can tell, John O'Reilly was Diana Falco's only living adult relative.'

'And he was her brother, after all,' Francesca said. 'These little distinctions do mean something, darling. When it came right down to it, he was family.' She shuddered lightly. 'Shared DNA and everything.'

Shared DNA. Marvel forgot his barfly slouch and sat up straight, causing the chair to wobble. He put his hand on the bar for support. Big mistake. It was sticky with the residue of thousands of drinks.

Shared DNA.

'What?' Poppy asked.

'Nothing.'

'What?' Poppy asked. 'What?'

'Really, it's nothing,' Marvel said, standing up. 'I remembered something I forgot to do. Gotta make a call. I'll be right back.'

*

He joined the smokers outside the bar and put a call through to his freelance researcher. Told him to find the daughter of John O'Reilly. The kid, delighted with the prospect of more work, said he'd get right on it.

Thirty-Seven

The evening progressed in a stately manner from semi-inebriation to complete drunkenness. They went to a Thai place for dinner and from there to another couple of bars for a nightcap and then on to another place to have one for the road.

Marvel enjoyed every minute of it. At two a.m. they were standing on Broadway looking for cabs; he was helping both of them stay upright and was carrying Francesca's designer bag looped over his shoulder. Times Square was as tacky and as bright as midday.

I fucking love this town, Marvel thought.

Francesca caught a cab. Marvel handed over her bag, made sure the taxi driver was clear on the address and that she had enough cash for the fare.

He and Poppy were left standing on the street.

'You're fucking brilliant, Marvel,' Poppy said.

'Yes I am.'

'Fucking marvellous Marvel.' Poppy was swaying now. 'I think I'm going to kiss you. I think I really am.'

A cab came by and Marvel deflected her drunken advance by flagging it down. 'Let's get you home.'

He went through the same routine as he had done

with Francesca. As she was driven off he watched the
taxi fade into the relative gloom of uptown and stood
for a moment or two, breathing in, breathing out. Glad
to be alive. Glad to be forty-five and thirty pounds
lighter than at thirty-five. Glad that a red-headed lass
called Poppy had said she wanted to kiss him, even
though she was drunk.

Francesca sat in her office with a cup of coffee in one
hand and a pencil in the other. The fact that she had
a hangover was appropriate. The crescendo of pain in
her head matched her heart. Her circumstances. Her
life.

Damn, she hated Mitch. If she could have him
back for an hour she'd use that hour to beat the shit
out of him.

'It's a perfectly reasonable request,' Grace Falco
was saying.

Francesca brought her full attention to the situation at hand: coercion.

'I'm entitled to something.'

Francesca was seized by the strongest desire to
crawl across the desk, rip Grace's throat out and leave
it on the radiator to dry. A good thing she was hung-
over or she might well have done it.

'You're entitled to nothing, sweetie. So be a good
girl and run along. Before I call the fashion police and
have you and that tacky little outfit thrown out on the
street.'

Grace Falco's fists clenched, giving lie to the smile
on her face.

'See, here's the thing. I know what Mitch was up to. Believe me, I am not stupid. I knew that there was something going on. Something illegal. And there are things those investigators don't know about him that I do. Things that I could tell them.'

Francesca held her eye for a second or two. Neither blinked.

'I wasn't going to use it but the game has changed and I really need to lay my hands on some money. I could go to the media. Tell everything I know; all my suspicions.'

Francesca sat very, very still. Her headache had vanished. Her concentration was totally focused on Grace, whose voice was getting softer.

'You know how the media works. They follow each other, they don't check facts. Lies become truths faster than you can say morning talk show. It's a disinformation circus.'

'Mitch is dead. You can't hurt him. Besides, the story is old. Journalists have the attention span of fruitflies.'

'Mitch is dead but you aren't. And you have a high-profile, highly political job. I know how sensitive these things can be. I'm sure there's ten or twenty people probably in this very office that would love to stomp all over you with their Jimmy Choos on the way to this nice office.'

Modern furniture, Turkmeni rugs, modern art. View of Fifth Avenue. Francesca was attached to her office, however much she pretended not to be.

'I thought Philip was going to take care of all your

problems,' she said, allowing bitterness to creep into her voice and knowing that she should not be showing any sign of weakness. But where Mitch was concerned she had always been weak.

'This is business,' Grace Falco said with an insulting artificial smile. 'Nothing to do with Philip. Besides, you wouldn't want me to start my new life with him on an unequal basis, would you?'

'I thought I had made myself clear. I don't give a shit about you,' Francesca said bitterly, although she knew she had lost.

Grace knew it too. 'Terrific,' she said. 'I'll look forward to hearing from you. You've got a week.'

Grace Falco left Francesca's office. Her legs were shaking and she could hardly breathe. She felt ill. Her knees were wobbly.

It was nearly lunchtime and Fifth Avenue was crowded. Grace began walking south, briskly.

A sexy red overcoat was displayed in Saks' window. It had a sixties feel, with a round collar and chunky buttons. Cute.

Any other day she would have gone in and at least tried the coat on. It was definitely calling her name. But today she had more important things to think about. It was crucial that she remained focused; there was too much at stake.

She turned her back on the coat and dialled Whitney's number. He answered almost immediately.

'It's me,' she said. 'It's all arranged.'

'Knew you'd come through.'

'A thank you would be nice,' Grace snapped irritably.

Whitney just chuckled. 'Want to get together for a drink? To celebrate?'

'What do you think?'

'I think you're dying to see me.'

'Think again. Besides, I've got a wedding dress to buy.'

'Ah, the wedding. Funny my invite hasn't arrived. I guess the mail is slow.'

'Yeah. That's the reason.'

'When's the happy day?'

'Two weeks time.'

'You want to hook him before he finds out?'

'Are you blackmailing me?'

'A rhetorical question.'

'I'll call you when I have the money.'

Grace shut down her phone. God, she really wanted to go shopping. She yearned for expensive clothes the way other people yearned for caffeine. All the bright, pretty stores of Fifth Avenue were lined up, waiting for her. And if she didn't like anything that she saw in any of them, she could walk a block to Madison. It was all so very easy.

She looked at her watch. She had a dress fitting in an hour. There was a little time; she would slip into Saks and just have a look.

Marvel had a meeting with a prospective client in Brooklyn Heights at ten and so he didn't get to his office till nearly midday. There were two messages waiting for him. The first was from Doreen, in Pawling.

'Hey, hon,' she said in her cigarette-roughened voice. 'I was talking to my friend Annie, works down at the beauty parlour. She knew O'Reilly. Or at least she was around when he was living in these parts. She can tell you about his daughter, who worked for her. So listen, hon, here's her number. I told her you might call, so why don't you just go ahead and do that?'

The second message was from his freelancer. Marvel called him back.

'John O'Reilly's daughter was called Sarah Jane O'Reilly, born January 1970 in the Bronx. She lived with her father, mostly upstate, for the first twenty years of her life,' he said, pausing, 'and then her life gets really interesting. When she's twenty years old she simply disappears.'

Thirty-Eight

'DNA.' Poppy's voice on the phone was thick with alcoholic regret.

'And a good afternoon to you, Miss Adams. How are you feeling?' She'd obviously forgotten that she'd tried to kiss him, Marvel thought. Good. He didn't want her to feel embarrassed.

'It's partly the booze, but partly that I couldn't sleep,' Poppy said. 'I was thinking about DNA. Diana Falco and John O'Reilly were twins. Twins are genetic clones. So what are their chances of having daughters who look alike?'

'How do you know O'Reilly had a daughter?'

'You said Grace had a cousin. Fifty-fifty chance it's going to be a girl.'

'Sarah O'Reilly,' Marvel said, thinking how wonderful it felt to be on the same wavelength as another person. 'And guess what? She disappeared about twenty years ago.'

'Why didn't you tell me this last night?'

'I didn't know last night. How's your head?'

'Terrible. And don't change the subject.'

'I'm not changing the subject. I'm asking if you want to take a trip to the country. To get some fresh air. I hear that fresh air is excellent for a hangover.'

Philip had a meeting with a prospective client in New Brunswick. He could have taken the train but he decided that the car needed a run.

He left the tunnel behind and headed west through the mosaic of dirty metal belching smoke that gives New Jersey a bad name. It was a great day to be barrelling down the highway, even if the highway in question was the New Jersey Turnpike. He liked driving; it relaxed him and gave him a chance to think.

In a couple of weeks he would be a married man. Every time he thought about it, it still gave him a little shock. He had never thought he would meet someone whom he'd want to share his life with and yet Grace and he had found each other.

He had always thought himself privileged, with his happy home, with a supportive father. He was privileged too to be making a living in architecture on his own terms. After the great impression that the hotel had made, his phone was ringing. And now there was Grace to top it all.

There was no doubt that he was a lucky guy.

The meeting lasted nearly three hours and Philip judged that it went well. The client was young and open-minded about design. A first-generation immigrant, he was planning to take his Brazilian-themed restaurant and build it into a national chain and the first step was to build a second restaurant in New Brunswick. Philip ate lunch with the client at the first restaurant (the food was excellent), then drove out to the site of the second, where they talked for about another hour and Philip made notes and sketched. He felt very excited about this project and he liked the client's energy and vision.

The two men parted with warm handshakes and Philip felt confident that he had made a good personal impression. He decided he had Grace to thank for that. She had loosened him up. Since he had met her he had begun to care less about his job and therefore he did it better.

The site of the new restaurant was an abandoned warehouse on the east side of town. The client had to rush off to another meeting but he had given Philip directions on how to get back to the turnpike.

Before too long he was quite lost.

And then he saw the Silver Stiletto.

It was wedged in between two roads on which the traffic travelled fast, as if it couldn't wait to get away from the place. The building was squat and brick, with small, high windows that were as grubby as the rest of the exterior. A large neon sign on the roof depicting the eponymous shoe lunged tipsily to one side.

An invisible hand seemed to guide Philip into the parking lot, alongside the pickup trucks with bumper stickers that conflated the virtues of gun ownership and patriotism.

He pushed his way into the gloom of the bar. About ten people sat around small tables, their eyes fixed on a woman with enormous breasts and a purple wig who swayed idly from side to side. The only thing that appeared to be keeping her upright was her grip on the pole. Philip sat at the bar and ordered a weak beer. It tasted soapy.

The strip bar wasn't what he expected. He had imagined it would be raunchy, the air fizzing with male libido, but instead everybody seemed tired and bored. Even the patrons, although they would occasionally move to put their glasses to their mouths or to show their monetary approval of the dancer's moves, didn't display any expression other than a glazed ennui. The dancer could have been doing advanced calculus judging by the faraway look in her eye.

Now that he was here, Philip was not sure what to do.

A large man sat down two stools over from him. He looked Philip over. Once up, once down. He was fat. More than fat, he was morbidly obese. His stomach sagged to his knees. But the eyes, almost hidden between doughy folds of flesh, were sharp.

'Hey,' he said. 'Nice day for it.'

'Sure.'

'You look like you're from out of town.'

'New York.'

'What brings you across the river?'

'I'm looking for my sister,' Philip said, amazed at the words even as they left his own mouth. 'I haven't spoken to her in some time and last I heard she used to work here. Our mother's sick. I need to get in touch.'

'What's her name?'

'Grace Falco.'

The fat guy shrugged. 'What she look like?'

Philip remembered that he had a photo of Grace in his wallet. He took it out and pushed it across the bar.

He took one look and shook his head.

'Nah,' he said. 'Never seen her.'

The barman slid a shot of whisky to his boss, who looked at the glass but didn't drink from it.

'When?' the barman asked Philip.

'When what?'

'When did she work here?'

Philip thought back. When was Herb in grad school?

'Ten, twelve years ago,' he said. 'Something like that.'

'Neither of us,' the barman nodded at the boss, 'worked here then.'

'It's a high turnover industry,' the boss said, as though he was talking about arbitrage or air traffic control. 'People burn out fast.' He flicked the snapshot. 'MoMa Queens,' he said, referring to the logo on Grace's T-shirt. 'Kinda recent photo for somebody you haven't see for years.'

The barman and the manager exchanged glances. 'Your sister, eh?' the manager said.

'My mother has cancer,' Philip said. 'Liver cancer. It's imperative that I find Grace. She sent me this photo but I lost her address. My mother wants to see her before she dies.'

The manager shrugged. He didn't believe a word, but the shrug said, too, that he didn't care.

'What about Lennie?' the barman said. 'He's been here a while. He'd remember.'

'Lennie.' The manager nodded his head. 'Yeah.'

'How can I speak to him?' Philip wanted to know. 'Is he here?'

'Shift starts at six.'

It was five. Philip didn't fancy lingering.

'If you give me his number, I'll call him. Maybe go by his house.'

'Relax,' the boss said. 'He'll be here. Have another drink. It's on the house.'

He pushed himself off the barstool and walked slowly into the back where he disappeared in the darkness.

'What'll it be?' asked the bartender brightly.

Lennie arrived at ten to six. He was a lean and tall black man with a mild expression. He wore faded jeans and a T-shirt and had a suit carrier hooked over his shoulder. His leather shoes were clean and highly polished. He was in superb shape – ex-military or maybe a moonlighting cop. The barman, whose name Philip had discovered was Jon and who aspired to be a screenwriter, introduced them. Philip was relieved to have somebody else to talk to. The previous hour had dragged, as Jon had imparted far too much information about his life and his ambition to become a screenwriter and live in Hollywood in a house with a big pool.

Lennie sat down next to Philip, draping one leg over the stool as if he was poised to spring up and quell any disturbance among the strip club clientele. It seemed unlikely that any action of the kind would be required – over the last hour the crowd had become, if it was possible, even more soporific.

The barman put a glass of seltzer water in front of Lennie.

'How can I help you?' he asked, his tone polite and disinterested.

'I'm trying to find out if a woman called Grace Falco ever worked here.' Philip placed the photo on the bar. Lennie took the photo and squared it up neatly in front of him on the bar. It was a photo Philip had taken of Grace about three weeks ago. She was sitting at an outdoor café with a mug of tea in front of her. Philip's heart squeezed tight when he looked at her smile.

'Why do you want to know?'

There was something about Lennie's placidity that encouraged the truth. He looked as if he absorbed life and was impervious to people's secret shames.

'I'm getting married,' Philip said. 'In two weeks.'

'That's nice.'

'Somebody told me that she used to . . . I mean, they thought she might have . . .'

'Stripped?'

Philip nodded.

'Lots of people do. Doesn't make them whores. Just trying to get by. Support kids, pay school bills, whatever.'

'Sure,' Philip said. 'Sure. I just want to know, that's all. Somebody said . . .'

Lennie studied the photo some more. Hunched

over it like a scientist at his microscope. Then he sat up and turned his calm face towards Philip. His voice was soft and low. 'They were wrong,' he said. 'I've never seen her before. And I never forget a face.'

'Are you sure?'

'Go home and get married,' Lennie said. 'Have lots of babies. Be happy. She didn't work here.'

Thirty-Nine

Philip took the turnpike as far north as it would go. Nyack was a little out of his way but he was seized by a strong desire to see his father.

'You're here.' His father was standing on the porch with a mug of tea in his hand. Mitzi the Maltese terrier sat at his feet. 'I'm cooking up steak and potatoes and as long as you promise not to tell my doctor you can have some too.'

Philip followed his father inside.

'How does sautéd green beans sound? To give it an overall patina of respectability?'

'Sounds great,' Philip said shortly, sitting at the kitchen table and staring around at the familiar blue and white décor. The kitchen had last been renovated in the sixties. Periodically his father talked about having Philip put in something modern but he never got around to it. Philip was glad that he hadn't. Not all change is good – sometimes it's better just to let things be. He scratched Mitzi the Maltese behind the ears.

'You look funny.' His father took two huge steaks out of the fridge and began slicing garlic.

'Been in New Jersey interviewing for a commission.'

'How'd it go?'

'Fine, I think. You never know until you know but I think it went OK.'

'Business good then?'

His father stripped some leaves off a rosemary plant and banged them with the knife a couple of times. He laid the steak in a grill pan and scattered the garlic and rosemary over the top.

'There's lots of interest. The hotel is creating buzz so I'm getting a couple of calls a week. I'm going up to the Berkshires in a few days. Near Mitch's. Some guy up there heard about me. Wants a weekend place with pizzazz.'

'Pizzazz? Does anybody still use that word?'

'Apparently.'

'Excited about the wedding?'

'Yes,' Philip said. 'I can't wait.'

His father began peeling potatoes.

'Want a hand?'

'No, sit. Relax.'

'What do you think of Grace?' Philip asked after a short silence.

'She seems perfectly nice.'

'Does it bother you that I'm doing this? Getting married?'

'Why would it? I think marriage is a good thing and your choice of partner is yours, not mine.'

'I want you to like her.'

'I will, as soon as I get to know her.'

'You're a saint, you know that.'

'I know,' his father said placidly.

When the potatoes were peeled he put them in a

saucepan and turned the gas to high. He put the steak in the oven. 'Let's have a glass of wine,' he said. 'There're some things I want to talk to you about.'

They sat on the furniture for a few minutes in silence. Through the large bay windows Philip could see a tanker sliding past on the ebb flow of the Hudson.

'I love this place,' his father said. 'There's not a day goes by when I don't think that. I've been very, very happy here.'

The tanker disappeared from view.

'So. What's on your mind?'

'How do you know there's something on my mind?'

'There's always something on your mind. You came out of the womb with a worried frown.'

'A strange thing happened to me today,' Philip said. And he told his father all about the strip club and what Herb had said about Grace.

His father held his glass of wine up to the gentle evening light and said nothing.

'So what do you think?'

'About what?'

'Dad! What should I do?'

'Want do you want to do?'

'I want to marry her.'

'Well, there you go then,' William said. 'Go ahead and do that.'

'But what if Lennie was lying?'

'Why would he do that?'

'I don't know.'

'You're over-thinking this,' William said. 'If you love her it really doesn't matter.'

Philip said nothing.

'Not everybody's had your advantages, Philip. You've lived a sheltered life, your mother and I worked hard to give you that. You've never had to make difficult choices because of lack of money. You really have had the best of everything. And I'm damn proud of the way you've turned out. But many people don't live in that world. And sometimes when you don't have the luxury of choice your life becomes messy. You get trapped. It just happens, it's not a moral failing.'

'You think I'm too judgemental?'

'All I'm saying is if you love her, it shouldn't matter. Look at her now, judge her on how you find her now. Not on something she may or may not have done. Besides, I think you're reading too much into the morality of a strip club bouncer. Why would he lie?'

'To spare my feelings?'

'What does he care?' William jumped up. 'I've got to check on the steak.'

They ate in the kitchen as they had done many times when Philip was a child. It was a good meal, in every way. He and his father talked about nothing in particular. For long stretches they didn't talk at all.

Afterwards, Philip helped his father wash up and he took comfort in the familiar routine, the smell of dish detergent and his father's witty small talk. Then he got in his car and drove south.

It wasn't until he was crossing the George Washington Bridge that he remembered he hadn't asked his father what it was he'd wanted to discuss with him.

Forty

Time had ceased to exist in the beauty parlour somewhere around the mid-1970s. Even the potted plants
looked old. The faded, yellowing posters on the wall
testified to a hairstyle last seen when *Charlie's Angels*
was a television programme, not a blockbuster chick
flick.

The room smelled of spray and overheated hair.
Two women sat under huge hooded dryers thumbing
through magazines. A girl with preposterously long
fingernails leaned against a sink, watching Marvel and
Poppy.

Lizzie was a bustler. She had busy movements and a
quick, light step.

'So sorry to keep you waiting,' she said when she
arrived about ten minutes later. 'I have an elderly
customer who can't come to me any more so I see
her at her home. She can't get by without her weekly
shampoo and set.' Lizzie flicked her own long, carefully blonded hair over her shoulder. Her jeans were
tight, her heels high, her neckline low. Two tiny
blow-dryers hung from her earlobes and she wore an

enormous diamond ring on her wedding finger. It was so large that Marvel decided it had to be fake.

'So nice to meet you,' Poppy said shaking her by the hand. 'This is a lovely place. You must work very hard.'

It was the right thing to say. Lizzie grimaced but Marvel could tell that she was pleased. 'Every hour that the good Lord sends,' she said. 'I started working here when I was Tiffany's age.' She nodded at the girl at the washstands. 'Worked my way up. Bought the place when I turned thirty. I spent the next ten years without a minute to call my own. Lost one marriage over it. Fingers crossed the next one don't go the same way.' She crossed the fingers of the hand which testified to the fact that she was now off the market.

'Congratulations,' Marvel said.

'Oh, thank you. Aren't you sweet, but I'm gonna shut up about me now because you didn't come all this way up here for idle chatter. You want to know about Sarah O'Reilly. Let's go back to my office, we'll all be more comfortable there.'

The office was small and cluttered. Posters advertising hair products were pinned to the walls. A coffee machine stood atop a tall filing cabinet. It smelled freshly brewed.

Coffee was served, seats were allocated and Lizzie sat behind her big desk, her fingers steepled.

'Perhaps we could start with this.' Marvel put Grace Falco's photo on the desk.

Lizzie swivelled it around. 'Nice cut,' she said. 'That cut cost money.' She studied it in silence for a few minutes before saying, 'I think that's Sarah.'

'But you're not sure?'

Lizzie tilted the photo on an angle and pursed her lips. 'It's been such a long time,' she said. 'I couldn't say for sure.'

Marvel took the photo back.

'What can you tell us about her?'

'I met her the day after she moved to town with her father. She came in looking for a job. She sat exactly where you are now and told me to hire her. And I did. It worked out fine. She was a good worker, she swept and cleaned and after a while I let her do the shampooing. That worked out OK too.'

'What did she tell you about herself?' Poppy asked.

'She lived with her father out on a trailer near Katalina Lake. They'd come from somewhere upstate. She said her father got work on building sites. They moved around a lot, that's what she said.'

'Any friends, boyfriends?'

'She started seeing this guy, Jake Connor. Used to pick her up outside here on Saturdays. Rough-looking guy, at least he looked that way. There were some stories about him, he wasn't quite on the level but Sarah liked him well enough. I think she was pretty serious about him. Too young in my opinion and I told her so. Gave her the benefit of my experience.' Lizzie took a reflective sip of coffee. 'But that's the thing about experience, once you've got it, nobody gives a damn about hearing from you.'

'Did you ever meet her cousin, Grace Falco?'

Lizzie shook her head. 'I didn't meet anybody called that. I didn't even meet her father. Used to see Jake often enough though. Too much for my liking.'

'Why?'

'She used to come in with bruises. Nowhere obvious, not on the face, but I would see them from time to time, her arms, on her legs. They were talking about moving in together. I tried to tell her that it wouldn't be any different once she did that but she wouldn't listen. Denied it was even happening. For a smart girl she made some damn fool choices.'

'Where's Jake now?'

Lizzie shook her head. 'He died in a fishing accident. Went out one night on the lake when he'd had too much too drink. He fell in and drowned. At least that's the official version.' Lizzie looked straight at Marvel and raised one carefully plucked eyebrow.

'What do you think happened?'

'Sarah came in with a terrible black eye the next morning. Said she'd slipped in the shower.' Lizzie paused for dramatic effect. 'It seemed kind of a coincidence.'

'You think Jake Connor's death wasn't an accident?' Poppy prompted.

'All I'm saying is that people who abuse women sometimes get what's coming to them, that's all. I've got no proof. But I wonder if he didn't punch her one time too many.'

'But you didn't say anything to the cops?'

'I didn't exactly have hard evidence. So she looked rotten the next morning, so what? That's not evidence of guilt. And besides, like I said, nobody asked me. And you know what? From the bruises I saw no court in the land would've convicted her.'

'What happened then?' Marvel asked.

'She stuck around here for a week longer and then one day she came in and said she was going away. I paid her what I owed her and I never saw her after that.'

'Did she say where she was going?'

'No. She said she was going to start over. Who could blame her?'

'That's an old story.' Sergeant John Roden's skin had the dark, burnished quality of an outdoor sportsman. Marvel noticed nicotine stains on his right hand.

'I'd just arrived in town. Transferred from Mamaroneck. Wife wanted to live in the country. I was there when they fished him out of the lake.'

'Anything about it strike you as odd?'

'Not at the time. His blood alcohol level was off the scale. He liked to drink, everybody seemed to agree on that. And he liked to drink out in his boat. There was no indication that anybody was in the boat with him. His girlfriend had an alibi – she was home watching television with her father all night. There were no witnesses, at least none that we could find.'

'But you said nothing bothered you at the time. What bothered you afterwards?'

'About a year later, we booked a junkie and he was anxious to share all that he knew for a lighter sentence. He said that Jake Connor had done a drug deal the night he died, small-time stuff, but our informant said that he should have had about thirty thousand dollars on him.'

'You didn't know he was a dealer before that?'

John Roden shook his head. 'Apparently he'd hooked up with these Mexican guys from Texas. They offered him the chance to buy some quality marijuana. The night he died he'd sold it on to a guy from Albany. Least, that's what the informant said.'

'And you never found the money?'

'Never did. By the time we even knew Connor had had it, it was long gone.'

Forty-One

Marvel met Leigh Sampson for breakfast near his townhouse on the Upper East Side.

'Do you think her background's relevant to our concerns?' his old friend asked after he'd heard the story. 'It was hardly Grace Falco's fault that she had to go live with that family and there's nothing to suggest that she was involved in this guy's death.'

'I'm sure you're right but it might be useful as leverage,' he said. 'She's getting married to an uptight . . .' Marvel nearly said 'prick' '. . . guy. And this is a tacky situation. I wouldn't want that if I was trying to put my best foot forward.'

'Blackmail?' Leigh Sampson said. He looked older, tired, Marvel thought. This scandal was riding him hard.

'I'm thinking of applying a little confident persuasion,' Marvel said, sipping his coffee. 'I'll tell her what we know, and see what she does.'

'I don't have time to talk to you,' Grace Falco said. 'I've spoken to a million people from FirstVenture, I've told you everything I know and I have a wedding dress fitting.'

She was walking fast along Lexington Avenue, arm up looking for a taxi. Marvel had to hustle to keep up with her. 'Another wedding,' he said. 'You must like getting married.'

Grace's look was pure venom. 'There's no law against getting married. Not that it's any of your business.'

Marvel wondered why anybody would prefer Grace over Poppy. Philip Ross must be out of his mind.

'I wondered what you could tell me about Sarah O'Reilly?'

Grace's taxi arm came down and it was a long time before she answered. 'What does she have to do with anything?'

'I don't know. That's what I'm trying to find out.'

'Look.' Grace Falco moved into Marvel's personal space, an index finger like a punctuation mark between their faces. 'I'm not stupid. I know Mitch was up to something illegal. I figured that out from all the interest the company has shown in his financial records and the fact that his pension seems to have gone into permanent limbo. But I don't know anything about it. I had nothing to do with it, so go away and leave me alone.'

'I need to know what happened to Sarah O'Reilly,' Marvel said, ignoring Grace's finger. 'And either you can tell me nicely or it could get awkward.'

Their eyes locked but it was Grace who looked away.

'Drugs. The murder of Jake Connor. Two girls who look alike enough to pass as twins. It's a little messy. Easy to get pertinent details mixed up.'

Grace's face went white. 'You're scum,' she hissed. 'You're no better than all the rest.'

'Never said I was,' Marvel said cheerily.

'Jake Connor was the deadbeat boyfriend my foolish cousin happened to be dating when he did the world a favour by taking himself out of the gene pool.'

'What were you doing the night he died?'

'Same thing I did every night I was in that dump. In my room, trying to read.'

'Hear or see anything unusual?'

'No.'

'And Sarah never left the trailer?'

'She might have done. I don't know. Like I said, I stayed in my room.'

'You ever see her boyfriend beating her?'

'No.'

'But you knew that he did.'

'Didn't stop her from wanting to move in with him,' Grace snorted.

'Did you ever talk to her about it?'

'We weren't close. She resented me being there and I resented having to be there. It wasn't a sure-fire recipe for happy families.'

'Did she talk about the fact that Jake Connor was planning a drug deal?'

Grace's mouth stretched into a mocking smile. 'I'm sure she found the details of her sordid little life endlessly fascinating but I think she sensed that I wouldn't share her enthusiasm for it. So no, we didn't share. Now if you'll excuse me, I have an appointment to keep.'

Forty-Two

She had been here before; the old Russian guy on 47th Street knew her.

Diamonds are forever. Ha-de-fucking-ha.

She took the ring that Mitch had given her to celebrate their engagement and placed it on the counter in front of him. Mitch had gone all out on the ring and she loved it. But she couldn't wear it any more. She was marrying another man. She was marrying Philip Ross, who thought diamonds were tacky and had designed their own wedding rings out of white gold.

Besides, she needed the money.

Grace Falco didn't think diamonds were tacky. She loved the looks that other women had given her when they had seen the ring. How the green monster fairly darted from their eyes. How they would cover up their envy with false exclamations of joy.

No way white gold was going to do that, no matter how artfully designed.

The jeweller plugged an eyepiece into his left eye and pulled the ring towards him; he examined it for a few minutes and then named a sum far lower that Grace knew the ring was worth.

She bartered with him for a few minutes, barely moving the price up.

It didn't matter, she told herself as she left the shop, the piper had to be paid. And she had to concentrate on getting married tomorrow.

Forty-Three

One week later

William Ross awoke at six, his normal rising time. It was a gift of a day and he felt perky and bright and ready for his morning run.

He thought about Philip as he pulled on his running clothes. The wedding had been tastefully low-key. A brief civil service at City Hall and then a small reception in Philip's apartment. There had been no more than twenty guests.

William wasn't entirely sure about the wisdom of the match – he personally would have preferred his new daughter-in-law to be Poppy rather than Grace – but it was not in his nature to tell Philip what to do, just as it wasn't in Philip's nature to accept advice. Even as a little boy Philip had always gone his own way. William Ross had learned to respect that.

Suited up, he considered whether to slurp a quick coffee before he went out to run but decided not to. Pleasure deferred, he reminded himself. That coffee would taste even better after he'd pushed his old pegs a mile or two.

The sun was up and the air was crisp and tangy as the first bite of a fall apple. He could smell salt in the air because at Nyack the Hudson River was still technically a tidal estuary.

William stretched his calves and hamstrings against the porch. He helicoptered his arms one direction and then the other. Hands on hips, he swivelled, humming a few bars of 'Hound Dog'. Feeling particularly nimble, he touched his toes. Not too bad. A few years left in the old goat yet.

He broke into a gentle jog and headed for Broadway. Past the bookshop, the coffee store, the trendy new Asian fusion place. He hadn't eaten there yet but he had been meaning to. Past the real estate agent's office. He had an appointment with the agent later in the day. He'd seen a little place that he liked the look of and was considering making an offer. It'd be a good rental, low maintenance.

Everything hurts for the first twenty minutes. No matter how many years he'd been doing this, it was always the same. Hot nails of pain in his ankles and knees, a mysterious ache in his right shoulder, hips that jarred and creaked.

He passed a neighbour driving south. Waved. Seeing him reminded William of the community meeting next week, another probably futile step in the seemingly never-ending struggle to prevent a proposal to widen the Tappan Zee Bridge from completely destroying their town.

He reached his halfway point and turned. Normally he stopped here for a second to catch his breath, but he felt good today so he didn't. The pains vanished, his lungs expanded and he picked up speed. It was no longer toil; it was joy.

He got back to his street and felt so good that he kept going, turning left down towards the pier. He had plenty of time, he'd take a few minutes to watch the river.

A kid was fishing on the pier. William recognized his face but didn't know his name. He nodded 'Hi' and sat down. God, he loved this time of day. People who didn't rise early missed the best part of life. The kid baited his line and tossed it into the water. He had sure, quick movements. William remembered Philip at that age. He'd tried to teach him to fish but the concept had both revolted and puzzled him. Why get your hands messy with smelly old bait when fish were available in the stores? William couldn't persuade him otherwise, so the fishing poles went up into the attic and stayed there. Perhaps when Philip had kids, William would bring them down and try the same thing with the next generation. He was sure he'd be a good grandfather, like one of those you see on mutual fund ads – debonair and avuncular at the same time.

The sun was gaining in strength. He was sweating now. He peeled off his sweatshirt and wiped his face. He decided to go over to the kid and ask him his name. It was silly not knowing, in a town this size.

He stood up. No, that wasn't right. He sat down again, fighting dizziness. It really was hot. Had he exerted himself too much this morning? It hadn't felt like it.

He tried again. Hand gripping the bench, he pushed himself to stand, but more slowly this time. That was it. Easy does it. Not a young man any more, however great you feel.

Two feet. Standing. The dizziness cleared. He could focus. He took his hand off the bench and just stood. It was OK. There was nothing wrong with him. He put one foot out. Tested his weight. Everything was fine. He was still sweating like a demon but everything was fine. Another step. He raised his hand. Called to the kid. Hey kid, my name's William, what's yours?

The dock seemed spongy, like walking on a trampoline. Or maybe it was just his legs. Tired old legs, tired from all that exercise, and somehow he couldn't get his knees to lock. It was a bit like being drunk. Except for the pain in his chest. A deep, vicious pain.

The kid turned, his mouth shaped by surprise. And the last thing William Ross saw was the fishing-line clatter to the dock. Almost gratefully, he fell down with it. He was glad something had given him that idea. It seemed easier than trying to go on.

Forty-Four

'I'm so sorry, Philip.' Gabe Mendez, the family lawyer, was an old friend of Philip's father. They had been in the army together as young men and remained close, so Gabe looked as bad as Philip felt. Philip and he hugged, Grace's hand was shaken and they were ushered into his office.

'A helluva way to begin married life.'

Philip nodded dumbly. He had buried his father, seen his coffin go into the ground, thrown some dirt on it, but still he could not seem to make sense of it. He couldn't fit the words 'massive coronary' and his father together.

'There wasn't a single sign,' he said. 'Not one.'

'It happens,' Gabe said sadly. 'It just happens.'

'He had the heart of three people,' Philip said. 'He had the biggest heart in the world.'

Gabe's assistant brought coffee and cookies on a tray. Philip didn't touch them. He hadn't eaten much in the past week. He hadn't slept much either. The doctor had prescribed pills. He took them gratefully. He'd never needed pills to help him sleep before.

Grace squeezed his hand and offered to pour some

coffee. Philip shook his head but kept gripping her hand.

Gabe seated himself behind his desk and opened a folder.

The folder, Philip knew, contained his father's will. That's why they were here.

Gabe cleared his throat. He looked at the words in front of him and then looked at Philip and at Grace.

'I know you've had a helluva lot to deal with this past week,' he said, 'and I'm afraid there is one more surprise in store.' He paused, cleared his throat and laid his plump hand with its large pinky ring on the desk. 'You are now a wealthy man, Philip.'

In a week of shocks, this was not what Philip had been expecting. The proceeds from the sale of the house, maybe. Perhaps a small annuity from his father's university pension, just as he'd got from his mother.

'His estate is valued at more than five million dollars,' Gabe went on. 'Most of it's going to you.'

Grace gave a strangled cry.

'Five million dollars? How? He was a school-teacher, for heaven's sake!'

Gabe rustled through some papers. 'Compound interest,' he said. 'Albert Einstein called it the most powerful force in the universe.'

'I'm sorry.' Philip shook his head. 'But what does this have to do with Dad?'

'He bought stocks, Philip. And when those stocks made money he bought more stocks. He bought Microsoft in the days when everybody thought it was a joke. He bought and he never sold. And then he started branching out, buying property. In case you feel like moving from the city, you are now the owner of two houses in Nyack, each valued at around half a million. You'll laugh when you see how little he paid for them.' Gabe pushed some papers towards Philip, who read blankly about mutual funds and bonds. Saw a deed for some land in the Berkshires. Ten acres on a lake, quite near Mitch and Francesca's house.

'Why didn't he tell me?'

'He didn't like to talk about money. He was going to tell you but I guess he didn't get the chance.'

Philip remembered his impromptu visit to Nyack. His father saying he wanted to have a chat. And how they hadn't had that chat.

Five million dollars!

In a way it seemed like a silly joke. He wished his dad had been around so he could share the joke with him, sitting on the porch with a bottle of wine and a plate of his terrible cocktail snacks. He missed him. It seemed impossible that he could no longer pick up the phone and ask him to recommend a book, or to meet for dinner. He could no longer drive to Nyack on a Saturday afternoon and take a walk along the river and be entertained by his stories.

'You don't have anything stronger than coffee?' he croaked.

Gabe opened a cupboard well-stocked with expensive liquor and poured him a generous shot of single malt whisky. He offered one to Grace but she shook her head.

'I thought I'd have to borrow money to pay for the funeral.'

'That won't be necessary,' Gabe said crisply, pouring himself a drink. 'He even made provision for that. You could have chosen a nicer coffin, by the way.'

'When I think about how much he complained about the cost of my school fees,' Philip said. 'To hear him say it, I had ruined him forever by going to graduate school. And yet he insisted on paying.'

'He was a perverse old buzzard,' Gabe said. 'You know better than I how he didn't like to part with it. But you're going to get him a nice headstone, right?'

Grace and Philip stood on the sidewalk outside Gabe's midtown office. It was a foggy day. Everything seemed sombre and low. Grace was paying one last visit to her old apartment uptown and although rivers of cabs flowed by, none had its vacant light on.

'You really had no idea?' she asked as yet another sailed by.

'None.'

'He didn't drop any hints?'

'No. In fact he hated people who bored on about their portfolio. He thought it was crass and bourgeois. I always assumed it was because he was jealous that he didn't have one. He was funny about money.'

'Lucky for you,' Grace said. 'Now you've got a windfall.'

Philip looked shocked.

'My father's dead, Grace. That's not a windfall.'

'Of course not, but I mean . . .'

'It's not a windfall.'

A cab pulled up and Philip put his wife in it.

252

Afterwards he stood in the middle of the street, allowing himself to be buffeted by pedestrians who had a firmer sense of purpose at that moment than he did. What to do now? He couldn't think of a single thing that would make the pain go away. He'd never felt more alone in his life.

Forty-Five

Poppy was in Marvel's office, feet tucked under her, a shorthand notebook balanced on her knee.

'What do we have here? Really?' Marvel said. 'Two women who look kind of alike – maybe not identical but close enough. One has the nice, middle-class upbringing, good education, la-di-la, everything going marvellously until one day her mother dies. The other doesn't have it quite so smooth. Money problems, father moves around, boyfriend beats her, dead-end job. Maybe her father beats her too, maybe that's how she developed such good judgement in men.

'And then middle-class Grace is forced to go and live with working-class Sarah and her father. Not so great for her but not the end of the world, either. It's only a couple of months then off to her fancy women's college out west. A completely new start for Grace Falco.

'Sarah O'Reilly sees Grace Falco up close maybe for the first time and she is struck by the unfairness of it all. Here they are, they could be sisters except Grace has a future and Sarah has a lot of bruises. Chances are, they don't get on. And maybe she gets to thinking. Why didn't I have a life like that? Why isn't it me going off to a nice college with everything all squared away with a trust fund?

'Then she finds out that the boyfriend is planning something big. He likes to drink so maybe he lets something slip. And she starts to wonder if she can't make a few positive changes in her life. And she starts to imagine what it'd be like if she had a clear shot at her boyfriend's drug money . . . and a ready-made place to go hide out.'

'What about Sarah's father?' Poppy asked. 'Surely he would wonder what had happened to his niece? And if Sarah killed Grace, what did she do with the body? Bodies are hard to hide. Anyway, why did she have to kill Grace? She could have made a fresh start with the boyfriend's money.'

'Maybe the father was in on it. Maybe Grace found out what Sarah had done to the boyfriend and threatened to go to the cops so Sarah killed her too. It would have seemed simple, because "Grace" doesn't die. Sarah just drops off the map.'

'Marvel, you're assuming the woman we know as Grace Falco is Sarah O'Reilly. And there's no evidence of that. Doreen positively identified her. So did Bill Brady,' Poppy said.

'True, but Lizzie the hairdresser wasn't sure. And Lizzie probably saw more of her than the other two. Remember, all Doreen saw was a photo of somebody she didn't know. You ever been to a line-up? Witnesses choose the wrong suspect all the time.'

'And what about Bill Brady? They were dating. Presumably he had a good look at her.'

Marvel chewed the corner of his lip. 'I'm reserving my judgement about Bill Brady's testimony,' he said.

'Why?'

'A feeling.'

'I still say it might just be as simple as it seems. Perhaps Sarah really did just go away. People do that for all sorts of different reasons.'

'There's money,' Marvel said. 'That means the solution can never be simple. Money makes everything complicated.'

'Or maybe when the money went missing. Perhaps she had nothing to do with it but somebody else started to hassle her about it. Somebody else who knew what happened that night.'

'Perhaps Sarah had nothing to do with her boyfriend's death and the disappearance of the money, but somebody else thought she did and started to hassle her about it. Somebody else who knew – or thinks they knew – what happened that night. Perhaps they even threatened her and she ran because she didn't know what else to do.'

'Like who?'

'I don't know.'

'All right, assuming for a minute that you're right, how would we even begin to go about proving something like this?' Poppy asked. Marvel grinned. He liked the sound of that 'we'.

'Don't know yet. But I do know one thing. I'll come up with something if I think about it for long enough.'

Forty-Six

Philip did not believe in life after death. He had been raised without the benefit of a religious education, and the behaviour he had seen from the people who claimed an intimate relationship with a higher being had not tempted him to examine the matter more closely. Where others turned to the Almighty, he took comfort from the scientific fact that matter can neither be created nor destroyed and that, when it was his time to go, the collection of atoms that was Philip Ross would eventually break down and rearrange themselves into some other thing that would, in its own unique way, assume a useful place in the universe. And that, as far as he was concerned, was enough.

But after his father died, his views began to change. He started to feel that William was still with him. He would find himself in a situation, usually having to make a decision, and his first thought would be, 'What do you think, Dad?' And then the answer would come to him. In some ways he felt closer to his father than before he had died.

*

Death eats into the time of the living and Philip's days were busier than ever. He had several meetings with Gabe about his father's estate. It was complicated, and Philip realized that managing money actually took up time and that he was going to have to carve out more of his week to make sure his affairs didn't get out of control. He also had to draw up a will. He had never had a will before and it seemed like a strangely adult and foreign thing to do.

He decided to leave everything to Grace.

On top of everything he'd had another prospective work offer. Peter Rivkind, a film director who specialized in schlocky horror films, wanted an extension on his holiday home in Litchfield County, Connecticut.

Twelve days after his father's funeral, Philip drove out of the city.

He found his prospective new client friendly and down to earth. He had not had time to rent any of Peter Rivkind's movies before the meeting; the posters around the house conveyed an air of cheerful, splattery irreverence. Peter walked him around and explained his ideas, which included extra space for a screening-room, a Pilates studio and an indoor/outdoor swimming-pool. Afterwards they ate lunch in the kitchen.

It felt less like a client meeting than a casual lunch with a friend, and Philip thought, with sadness, of the two friends he had lost.

'Everything OK?' Peter asked. 'You look like the food isn't up to scratch.'

'I'm sorry. I spaced out for a moment.'

'Sure you're all right? Want some water or something?'

'Do you believe in life after death?'

If Peter was surprised by the segue, it didn't show. 'Absolutely. I've built a very lucrative career out of it,' Peter said, topping up their wineglasses. 'It's a pretty tightly guarded secret, but you know near the end of the third act where the monster dies? Well, he's not really dead. He's just waiting for another opportunity to say, "Surprise!"'

Philip smiled.

'In real life, I'm not sure. I guess you could call me cheerfully agnostic. I believe you should give this go-round the best shot you got, because what if those religious fuckers are wrong? What if you don't get another chance?'

'I've had a couple of bereavements lately; my best friend and my father have died in the last few months.' Philip had no idea why he was telling a complete stranger this, but Peter Rivkind did not seem to mind.

'I'm sorry to hear that,' he said. 'My long-time companion, as the press so delicately put it, died in the World Trade Center and it still shocks me sometimes when I think that he's not around, even all these years later. I find it fascinating that we are constantly surprised by death – the one and only thing in life that we can absolutely be sure of.'

'Do you talk to him?'

'Jon? God yes, he helps me with all my important decisions. Even what to wear on the bad days.'

'My father's started doing that too. Even though he knows nothing about architecture.'

'That's OK, Jon knows nothing about fashion. Seriously. Why not?' Peter stabbed an olive and popped it into his mouth, 'Nobody's proved there's life after death, but nobody's proved there isn't. Talk away, I say. If it helps you – and I know it helps me – what the hell does it matter?'

He had not intended to call at Mitch's house, but after he left Peter Rivkind the car just seemed to end up there. When he got there he knew that he wanted to talk to Mitch about Grace and try to explain what had happened between them.

Then Mitch, he felt sure, would understand.

The house looked forlorn. Philip parked his car in his usual spot, located the spare key under a log in the lawnmower shed and went inside.

It smelled like nobody had been there for a while. A couple of *Vogue* magazines lay on the coffee table in the living-room but they were out of date. The milk in the fridge was off. Philip tipped it down the sink and rinsed out the carton. A pile of clean laundry sat neatly folded in the laundry-room.

Upstairs was quiet and still. Philip looked in all the bedrooms, just out of habit. In the master bedroom hung a painting that Mitch had done of the house when he was at college. He had taken painting classes in his first year and dropped them in his second because he said that he found his lack of talent depressing.

It didn't look like anybody had used Mitch's bedroom; either that or Francesca hadn't cleared everything out. Philip thumbed through the books sitting on the side of his bed. Political biographies mostly, a couple of spy novels.

Philip went downstairs and stood on the lawn.

He walked over to the garage where Mitch had died. It was a big old red barn, nothing special, hundreds of them in Berkshire County. The doors were padlocked. Philip knew where the key was. It wouldn't be difficult to take a look inside. He felt that he should look. Explain everything to Mitch right there.

Philip took the key out to the barn and stood in front of the lock. He sniffed the air, expecting, irrationally, to smell exhaust fumes. There were none.

He put the key in the lock and it opened sluggishly. All of his weight went into sliding the doors back. The tracks were rusted and the door had warped from disuse.

Incredibly, the car that Mitch had turned into his coffin was still there. It was surrounded by the bones of a hammock, plastic pool toys, old bikes, all blunted with dust.

Philip closed his eyes and tried to imagine the despair that Mitch must have felt that night. The process could not have been quick. Not like pulling a trigger or throwing oneself off a bridge. He had to hook up the hose to the exhaust pipe, feed it around to the front window. And then he had to sit there and wait for death. How long did it take? Half an hour? Longer? What went through his mind during that time? Had he thought about changing his mind?

Philip opened the driver's door and sat in the car. Mitch and he had been the same height, so his feet reached the pedals comfortably. He settled back into the seat. The leather was cold and stiff.

He heard footsteps. He glanced into the side mirrors. The mirrors were wrong. All of them. Weird, he thought. Mitch had been the last person to drive the car and he and Philip were the same height. He should be able to see who was behind him.

He got out of the car. The handyman, Pike, was standing in the doorway. Pike had been taking care of the place for years, mowing the lawns, making sure that repairs got done. He and his mother lived about a mile down the road in a little house with a listing white picket fence. He'd been brain-damaged at birth and his conversation was slow.

'Hello, Pike,' Philip said, reaching out to shake his hand. Pike had a firm, gnarly grip.

'I'm here to take a look at the guttering,' he said. 'Leaked bad in the last storm. Told Francesca that I've got to fix the bridge over the gully. It's broken, you shouldn't walk on it. Don't walk on it.'

'I won't.'

'We had a flood. And the timbers are rotten. Needs to get fixed.'

'I'm sure you'll take care of it. How have you been, Pike?'

'OK.'

'That's good. And your mother?'

'Why haven't you been up?' he said accusingly. 'I wanted to talk to you.'

'What about?'

'I have a message for you. From Mitch.'

A gust of chill, stale air blew from the barn. Philip suddenly wanted to leave the barn very badly but Pike, a big man, was standing in his way.

'Mitch?' he said. 'But Mitch is gone, Pike.'

'I have a message,' Pike said stubbornly. 'He left one. For you.'

Forty-Seven

'Mom, I'm here. Philip is with me.' Pike opened the door and stood back to let Philip go in first. A large velour sofa sat against the wall. A matching armchair was piled with dolls in frothy dresses. The curtains, wallpaper and carpet were patterned with flowers. The scheme was so busy that it took Philip a moment to pick out Pike's mother, sitting in another easy chair with sewing in her lap. She was working on a doll's outfit, a gingham pinafore.

'Hello, Mrs Pike.'

'Philip, you came at last. We were hoping you would. Will you have a cup of coffee?' She set down her sewing and stood up.

Philip agreed to a cup, wondering what this was all about. He'd known Pike and his mother for years to say hello to, but this was the first time he'd been invited to their house. Mrs Pike picked up an armful of dolls to clear space for him to sit.

Philip had always hated dolls, and as he took in the details he realized they were everywhere. They were sitting on tables, perched against the sideboard, reclining on shelves. There were even two on top of the curtain rail.

A filing cabinet stood in one corner. It was covered with a hand-embroidered tablecloth. Pike lifted the cloth and began going through the drawers muttering to himself. Through the kitchen door Philip could see Mrs Pike pouring coffee into mugs and arranging cake slices on a plate.

'There we go,' she said, clearing a couple of dolls off the coffee table to make room for the tray. 'You found Mitch's message yet?' she called to Pike.

'It's here, Mom. I put it here for safe keeping, just like you said.'

Philip sipped his coffee and at Mrs Pike's insistence took a slice of cake.

'Do you like dolls?' Mrs Pike asked brightly. 'I made all their costumes myself.'

'Mom is great at sewing.' Pike's voice was muffled because he appeared to have his head completely in the filing cabinet.

'Never liked dolls when I was little,' Mrs Pike said. 'That's the funny thing. I had one, a cloth doll called Annie, but I didn't care for her much. It happened later, after Alfred came along.' She nodded towards Pike, who didn't appear to be having much success in his search.

The cookies were good. Philip took a second one.

'It was such a shock,' Mrs Pike said. 'We couldn't believe it when we heard, could we, Alfred?'

'Couldn't believe it,' Pike echoed, studying a sheet of paper closely before discarding it.

'We knew Mitch for years and years. We knew their parents. A lovely, lovely couple. A real shame that God took them so young.' Mrs Pike sipped her coffee delicately. 'I know that He has a plan but I have to be honest with you, there are days when I wonder what it is.'

Philip thought of his own father and said nothing.

Mrs Pike picked up a doll and stroked its hair absently. It had lipstick red cheeks and an expression that managed to blend complacency and surprise. It was beautifully dressed in a fitted tweed jacket and breeches. A tiny tie was knotted about its neck and a small riding crop dangled from its stiff outstretched hand. The jacket seemed familiar to Philip, although he couldn't think where he might have seen it.

'I made this from one of Mitch's coats,' Mrs Pike said. 'Francesca came by with a load of clothing for Alfred and most of it he's had good wear out of, haven't you, dear?'

'Good wear,' Pike agreed. A small forest of files was growing up on the carpet around him but he seemed no closer to finding whatever it was he was searching for.

'But this one didn't quite fit him. Too tight around the shoulders, so I cut it up and made a little outfit for Constanza.'

'It's beautiful,' Philip said truthfully as Mrs Pike unbuttoned the jacket to show that she had lined it with deep purple silk. The handiwork was exquisite.

'And that's where we found it,' she said. 'In the lining of Mitch's jacket. The pocket had a hole in it, you see, and it had slipped through the hole and worked its way around towards the back, so it was no wonder you never received it. I'm sure he meant for you to have it. It had your name on the front, you see.'

'What did Mitch want me to have, Mrs Pike?' Philip tried to control his impatience.

'The letter of course.' Her wrinkled face split into a wide smile.

'Found it!' Pike held up a piece of paper in one hand, knocking over one of the piles he had created in his enthusiasm to get the letter to Philip. 'It was here all along, just waiting for you. We kept it good and safe, Mr Ross.'

The envelope had Philip's name on it but no address. The handwriting was so familiar that Philip almost wept.

He carried the envelope out to the car, put it on the passenger seat and drove south. At Armenia he pulled into the parking lot of a mall. He wanted somewhere banal to do this. Mitch was talking to him from beyond the grave. He was shivery as he ripped open the envelope.

There was no date, just a couple of pages in Mitch's neat cursive.

> *Philip,*
>
> *We haven't had much time to get together lately, which is a shame. I've got lots on my mind and could use a willing ear. You always were a good listener, buddy. I miss that. I wish that we could be as close as we were in college. Things*

were simpler back then, your friends and your life were all wrapped up in one sweet package. The time we spent together was the best time of my life. Remember when I could just drop by your dorm room? And how we seemed to have so much fun on so little money? How the hell did things get so complicated? I guess you could say things have been going downhill for me lately.

I guess the best place to start is with Grace. It cuts me to say this, but there's something wrong with her.

I know it's hard to believe. You look at her and you think, she's perfect, right? So beautiful, so sweet. But it's all a lie. She is not who she says she is. In fact, I don't know who she is at all. It's as if she's constructed a persona, like a wall, and won't let anybody inside.

It took me a while to figure this out. A couple of months after we married I started to get a feeling that what she said and what she did didn't fit. It was little things. She said she loved living simply, didn't want any fuss, and yet somehow we ended up with a bigger apartment, new furniture, new clothes, the works. The money we spent, you wouldn't believe it. And then she started on at me about selling the house and getting somewhere in the Hamptons.

I can hear you saying, but that's every Upper East Side wife, going to hear the Dalai Lama one day and spending three thousand dollars at Gucci the next. Nothing unusual about that. I work a bit harder to keep her happy, that's all, so she can afford her spa treatments and those little trips to Madison Avenue. No big deal, every other working Joe is doing it.

But then one day I overhear her on the phone to this guy called Whitney. She's talking to him saying she'll get the money and don't worry, Mitch will never find out. And he says something that I can't hear obviously and she says, and this is the part that kills me, 'Don't worry, I know how to handle him. I'll get the money. My husband doesn't ask, he just pays up.'

It was terrible, I felt as if she'd punched me. Her tone was so cold and dismissive.

I should have confronted her about it. Right there. But I'm ashamed to say I couldn't. I couldn't bear to hear what she might say. So I don't know who this Whitney person is and what their relationship is. But I can't help thinking the worst: that they sized me up for the patsy I am just to rip me off.

I want to talk to Grace, to look into her eyes and have her tell me that she loves me and only me. But I'm really afraid that she won't be able to do that. It's the worst feeling you can imagine and I pray that you'll never have to experience it.

I see the gaps and silences in my marriage grow and every day I wonder. Some days, the dark days, I think that all I have are my suspicions and let me tell you they don't make good companions.

Philip's hands were shaking as he read on.

This is the thought that wakes me in the night.
This is the thought that tortures me: is Grace just
using me? Does she want me out of the way?

Forty-Eight

Philip sat down in the driver's seat, closed the door, turned on the engine, put the car in gear and drove out of the mall. He turned left on 44 and headed for the Taconic. He drove slowly. He probably shouldn't have been driving at all. He was numb.

Philip thought back to what Grace had told him about that night. She said Mitch had driven up to the Berkshires. They had stopped for dinner in Brewster and driven on up to the house. She had gone indoors and he had said something about taking care of things in the barn. He'd hooked up the hose to the gas pipe and sat in the driver's seat.

But if he'd done that, if he had driven up from the city, why were the driving mirrors all wrong for a man of his height?

Why would Grace lie about a little detail like that?

What if it wasn't a lie? What if it was an oversight, concealing a much greater crime?

The thought came unbidden, swooping out of the blue like a bird of prey. It struck him with such force that he felt sick and he pulled the car over to the shoulder of the road and got out, walking round in circles, breathing deeply.

He needed a second opinion, some perspective.

'Hi,' Poppy said. 'Come in.'

Her apartment was warmly familiar. The radio was on low and her perfume, sweet and spicy, mingled with the smell of clean laundry. She moved a pile of clothes on the sofa so that Philip could sit down.

'You've made some changes.'

'I finally bought a new couch. Moved some other stuff around.'

'Looks good.'

'Thanks.' Poppy drew a very deep breath and decided that she would go out and buy herself something special and expensive if she held it together for this. A new handbag or a pair of shoes. To try and keep calm she held the picture of a nice bag that she'd seen in Macy's in her head.

'I guess this is a surprise,' Philip said.

Poppy shrugged. *The surprise will be how coolly I can handle this*, she thought. *No more scenes, not ever again.*

'The thing is, I'm in kind of an awkward situation. And I really need help.'

Poppy looked at Philip, saying nothing. This was new. Philip was self-contained to the point of obsession. He never asked for anything. It was almost as if someone had literally taken the stuffing out of him. Even though he was as smartly dressed as ever, he seemed frayed and lacking substance.

'What sort of help?'

'I thought of you.' Philip drew a deep, ragged breath. 'I thought of you because you said some things about Grace that have . . . that might turn out to be true.'

Poppy sat up a tiny little bit straighter.

'I found this letter.' Philip fumbled in his pocket for a long time. Handed it to Poppy. 'Do you have something to drink?'

'There's wine in the fridge.' Poppy took the envelope.

'Anything stronger?'

'Whisky in the cupboard above the stove.'

She opened the letter and began reading while Philip poured himself a glass of Scotch.

'Well,' he said when he had finished. 'What do you think? What should I do?'

'What do you want to do?'

'I don't know,' Philip said, downing the Scotch in one and getting up for more.

'Mitch committed suicide, Philip. That means he wasn't of sound mind, to say the least. This Whitney guy could be anybody. Grace could simply have owed him money. You said yourself she borrowed from you. Maybe she saw a nice handbag that she simply had to have.' Poppy couldn't resist that.

'I know this Whitney guy. Paul Whitney. I met him one night. In a bar. Grace didn't seem very pleased to see him but then later, after she left me, she went back and spoke to him.'

'How do you know she did that?'

'I . . . er . . . I went back too. I wanted to talk to Whitney. Find out a few things.'

'Do you know who he is?'

'Someone she used to know, that's all she said.'

'It doesn't sound like a big deal,' Poppy said. 'It sounds like Mitch was a bit delusional, that's all.'

'There's more,' Philip said. 'She lies about the money she spends. She buys things, expensive things, and tells me she got them on sale or at the consignment store.'

'Philip.' Poppy almost laughed. 'Every single married woman in the world does that. My mother has a wardrobe full of clothes that my father has no idea of the cost of. Look, you want my advice, here it is. Why don't you just ask her? Give her the letter and tell her where you got it. And talk it over. She'll say something that will put it all in perspective and you'll be fine.'

'I can't do that.'

'Why not?'

'It's not that kind of relationship.'

'What kind of relationship is it?'

'It's . . . It's . . .' Philip struggled to find the words. 'It's . . . I don't know what it is. It's up and down.'

'Up and down?' The shoes and/or bag were definitely in sight, Poppy thought with some satisfaction. Hell, she was doing marriage counselling for her ex! Maybe she should go right ahead and buy both.

'It's like that feeling that Mitch is trying to get across in his letter. I know that feeling. That you don't know the real Grace. Will never know her. It doesn't stop you loving her but you feel as if . . . I don't know. You feel confused.'

'Can you give me an example?' said St Poppy. Her mental shopping spree had begun at Macy's, moved quickly through Bloomingdale's and was now at Barney's.

'I think Grace might have worked as a stripper at this club in Jersey. Somebody I know thought he recognized her. So I went out there and asked about it.'

'Why didn't you just ask her?'

'The person who recognized her said she had this ram's head tattoo on her hip. Grace has a scar on her hip and when I asked her about it she said she'd had a melanoma.'

'She might be telling the truth.'

'I really didn't get that,' Philip said miserably. 'When I went to the club and talked to the staff they said they didn't know her but I couldn't shake the impression that they were lying to protect her.'

'Why would they do that?'

'I don't know.' Philip finished the second glass and placed it down on the coffee table.

Poppy drew her knees up under her. The beginnings of a feeling were starting to spread across her chest. A novel feeling. Once you cut away the façade, there wasn't much about Philip to admire. *He really is a bit pathetic*, she thought.

'I think you should go home and talk to your wife,' she said firmly.

'There's something else, Poppy. I think Grace may have lied at the inquest. She said that Mitch had driven all the way from New York up to the house. But I saw the car today and the mirrors are all wrong for a man of Mitch's height.'

'So somebody moved them.'

'Francesca told me ages ago that the car hadn't been touched. She'd been meaning to get rid of it but hadn't.'

'I fail to see the significance.'

'What if Grace drove that night? What if they stopped for dinner and she slipped something into his drink so that by the time they got to the house Mitch had passed out. And then all she had to do was put him in the driver's seat and turn on the gas.'

'You're accusing your wife of murder,' Poppy said.

'I'm not accusing her. I just . . . wonder.'

'Do you think she's really capable of such a thing?'

'I don't know.' Philip slouched over his empty glass. 'I just don't know any more.'

Forty-Nine

'Did you have a good meeting, darling?' Grace greeted him at the door.

Philip started. Meeting? How could she possibly know that he had been talking to Poppy?

'The prospective client. What was his name? Rivkind?'

'Client? Oh . . .' He collected himself. 'Oh yes. Of course. I'm sorry, I'm a little tired from the drive.' He kissed her on the cheek, marvelling at his new ability to dissemble. The old Philip Ross would not have been quite so smooth. 'The traffic was hell,' he added for extra veracity.

'You look tired. Would you like me to run you a bath?'

'No thanks.'

'A glass of wine?'

'No thanks.'

'Put your feet up then, I'll give you a massage.'

'It's OK. I just need a little quiet.'

'I'm roasting a guinea fowl for dinner. From D'Artagnan.'

'Sounds great,' he lied. 'Now, I'm going to sit in the

study and think inspired thoughts about my new client. While the meeting is fresh in my mind.'

'I know you'll build him something wonderful. And perhaps you'll become friends and he'll invite us to all his wonderful Hollywood parties.'

Always figuring the angles. The thought was deep and cold; it didn't show on his face.

'I'm sure he will.' Philip took off his tie and went into the study, dropping his bag on the floor and kicking off his shoes. Grace had become like one of those computer-generated dot puzzles that one can discern a pattern in if one stares at it in just the right way. And once you see the pattern, you can never go back to not seeing it.

Funny how quickly love can die. It was as if somebody had turned off the light.

Philip sat behind his desk, massaging his temples.

What happened to you today, honey?

Oh, I fell out of love.

Or perhaps it had never been real to begin with.

Maybe we package up lots of different things and call them love just because we yearn for it so much, he thought miserably.

He put his notebook and Mitch's letter side by side on the desk. He read it through again slowly, more aware than ever of the bitter irony of his situation. He had taken his dead friend's wife, not knowing that Mitch's marriage, like his now, had been an illusion of happiness. A trick.

He awoke to Grace shaking his shoulder. 'Goodness,' she said. 'You must have been tired.'

He sat up, confused, trying to get his eyes to focus.

'What's that?' Grace asked, pointing at Mitch's letter.

'Just some notes I made,' he said, pushing the letter off the desk and into his back pocket.

'It doesn't look like your handwriting.'

'It's the client's. He jotted down a few things he wanted me to think about.' Grace looked puzzled for a moment, then her face cleared. 'Dinner's ready,' she said. 'Would you like to open some wine?'

They sat at the table. It was a beautiful table, a fine example of modern American craftsmanship, and it was beautifully set. What a wonderful life this looks like, Philip thought, as he poured an excellent California Zinfandel into two glasses. If somebody could magically rise up from the street and look in our ten-foot windows, what a perfect image of domestic harmony and discreet good taste they would witness.

And what a lie it would be.

Grace served the food. She was a good cook, he thought absently. That was one thing he knew about her for sure.

'I've had an idea.' Grace leaned forward to grasp his hand across the tablecloth and her eyes gleamed in the candlelight. Philip let her hold his hand, even squeezing a little back, but it was as if he was watching the scene through thick glass. 'If we sell all your father's property we can afford a really nice vacation home.'

'I'm not selling my father's house. I grew up in that house. Besides, Nyack's practically the country.'

'But what about a place for the summer? I'd love to be near the beach.'

'Like the Jersey shore?'

'Or the Hamptons.'

Philip hated the Hamptons. He hated the people who went there and the mini-Manhattan, McMansion hash they'd made of it.

'You don't even swim, Grace. You hate the water.'

'I could learn. It'd be so much fun.'

Suddenly there were brochures on the table. 'I've called a few places. We can schedule some appointments for next weekend if you like.'

Philip looked at one of the brochures and resisted the urge to shudder.

'We'll see,' he said. 'I've got a lot of work on. I may be busy this weekend.'

'But if we're agreed, then we shouldn't delay. Summer will be here before we know it. Oh, wouldn't it be fabulous to have our own place right on the beach! We could throw great parties.'

'We're not agreed and none of our friends go to the Hamptons,' Philip pointed out. Even social-climbing Herb had the good sense to avoid it.

'Not friends. Contacts. For building your business.'

Philip shrugged. Grace's vision was sounding more vile with each sentence. 'Most of the people who go out there don't want the sort of architecture that I do,' he reminded her patiently. 'And to buy a house on the beach costs millions of dollars.'

'We've got millions of dollars.'

'I'm not blowing my father's investments on one house. Let's talk about this some other time, OK?'

Grace closed her mouth in a sullen line. She shifted the brochures on to her lap. Like a hen with her eggs, he thought. Nurturing quietly until the idea came to fruition.

Was this going to become a joke marriage? Would he look back in years to come, perhaps at a party, and ruefully admit that he had once been married for two weeks?

Philip's head was becoming cloudy, even though the second glass of wine remained half drunk. He had another thought. If he divorced Grace, she would fight him for his father's money.

He felt so very, very tired. Like one of Mrs Pike's dolls ready to be folded up and put away.

'You look exhausted,' Grace said. 'Go to bed, darling. I'll take care of the dishes.'

He was too tired to argue. He barely made it into the bedroom. He stripped off his clothes and sank on to the bed, his eyes closing as he did so. He didn't clean his teeth. He didn't take off his socks. And he forgot all about Mitch's letter, which was neatly folded in his back pants pocket.

Fifty

'For someone who says she's staying out of this you're not doing a very good job.'

Poppy had made a photocopy of the letter Philip had shown her. Marvel ran his index finger down the page. He really had very nice hands, Poppy thought. His fingers were long and he took care of his nails.

'Philip now thinks Grace killed Mitch.'

'Just from this letter?'

'No. He went to the house and sat in the car and discovered that the mirrors were wrong. Grace testified at the inquest that Mitch drove all the way to the Berkshires the night he died but Philip thinks the mirrors were not set for a man of his height. Also, he's been checking into her background and thinks she used to work as a stripper. And he's found that she's lying about the amount she spends on clothes. He's a bit upset.'

'Philip doesn't know about Mitch's fraud?'

'Didn't mention it,' Poppy said. 'You think he might be on to something?'

'There's no evidence that she benefited, and that's the first place the company looked. Still looking, in fact, but they haven't turned up anything. What do you think?'

'I think Philip became infatuated with Grace, married her too quickly and is now regretting it and can't bring himself to admit it.' Poppy put her feet up on Marvel's desk. 'Like my new boots?'

'Very nice.'

'Four hundred bucks. From Barney's.'

Poppy was looking much better, Marvel decided. There was a lightness in her manner that he hadn't seen before. A good sign.

'For services rendered?'

'If you can't treat yourself after providing marriage counselling to your ex-boyfriend, when the hell can you?'

'That's always been my motto.' Marvel picked up the letter. 'This isn't evidence of anything except Grace Falco's unique ability to drive the men in her life nuts, except perhaps her other ability to overspend and get into trouble.'

'Precisely,' Poppy said, leaning forward to remove a smudge from the toe of her boot. 'That's what I said to Philip, although not in so many words.'

'So you don't believe Grace Falco killed her husband?'

'I didn't believe it the way Philip said it,' Poppy grinned, 'because it sounded like a big whinge.'

'I have a present for you too,' Marvel said, pulling a folder out. He put it on the desk in front of Poppy, who quickly removed her feet.

'What is it?'

'It's the autopsies of Jake Connor, Sarah O'Reilly's boyfriend, and Mitch Browning.'

Marvel's reward was a big, slow smile from Poppy. She was even more beautiful when she smiled.

'I have a feeling this is going to be better than the boots.'

'It's certainly better than the letter.'

Poppy began reading Mitch's report. *The victim was six feet tall with brown eyes, a muscular, well-nourished, well-developed adult Caucasian.* Sounded like Mitch. She didn't understand a lot of the terminology and the police and medical jargon was tedious.

'Skip to the interesting part,' Marvel said. 'Toxicology.'

He took up Jake Connor's report, folded back the page and laid it on the desk so that she could look at both.

'Well, well, well,' Poppy said. 'That *is* the interesting part.'

'Secobarbital roughly the same amount in both cases. Of course it could just be a coincidence.'

'Or it could be that if you find something that works, you stick with it.'

They stared at each other for a moment.

'What was the cause of death for Jake Connor?' Poppy asked, scanning the document.

'Drowning. But he had rather a nasty bump on the head.'

'Could have got it falling out of the boat drunk.'

'Could have.'

'Here's a scenario for you,' Marvel said after a pause. 'Mitch and Grace stopped for dinner. We know that. Grace drugged his Coke and insisted on driving the rest of the way. She didn't want him running off the road with both of them. By the time they reached the house he was out of it. All she had to do was move him to the driver's seat, turn on the gas and leave him there.'

That was exactly what Philip had said. But it sounded more credible coming from Marvel.

'How did she move him? He would have been dead weight.'

'It could be done. If you're jacked up enough on adrenaline.'

'Maybe she had help,' Poppy suggested. 'What about this Whitney guy mentioned in the letter?'

'Maybe.'

'But why? She didn't get anything out of it. There was no money, nothing.'

'Maybe there's another reason,' Marvel said. 'One that we don't know about yet.'

Fifty-One

Philip woke the next morning with a heavy, drugged feeling. He could hardly open his eyes.

He dragged himself out to the kitchen. The coffee machine was on and the coffee was warm. It was late. Grace had left a note saying that she was at the gym.

She had abandoned all pretence of looking for work, he noted. How easily she had fallen into the leisurely ways of the Upper East Side trophy wife.

And they didn't even live on the Upper East Side.

He poured himself a cup of coffee. He had to make a decision, any decision. What clothes to wear, what to do next.

To anchor himself, he decided to read Mitch's letter through again. Carrying his coffee, he went back to the bedroom and searched through his trouser pockets.

The letter was in the left pocket, not the right pocket where he had put it.

He took the train to Rockefeller Center. A homeless man came lurching down the aisle of the subway car. He was wearing three hats on his head secured with a grubby silk tie. The rest of his clothes were just as filthy but his sneakers were brand new. He stopped right in front of Philip and stared with wild, sad eyes.

'Will you help me?' he asked. 'Will you?'

Philip reached into his pocket for some change. All he had was a twenty. He took it out. Fuck it. He was rich.

'Here.'

The man took the note, studied both sides before jamming it into a crevice of one of the many garments he was wearing. 'God bless you, brother,' he said. 'May God bless you and cause his face to shine upon you. And may you dwell in the house of the Lord forever, all the days of your life . . .'

The train stopped and Philip, with relief, made his escape.

Rockefeller Plaza was crowded with people united in their gratitude for a warm, sunny day after a spell of rain. Francesca looked out of place in this carefree oasis, sitting stiffly on a bench. She was, as ever, thin and black-clad.

'Hey, Franny.' Philip kissed her on the cheek.

'Hello, Philip. What's so important?' She took off her dark glasses as she spoke and the lines around her face were more pronounced.

Philip handed her the letter. 'Pike found this in one of Mitch's jackets. He gave it to me yesterday.'

She looked at it sideways, replacing her glasses.

'What is it?'

'It's a letter Mitch wrote to me. I guess he never got around to sending it.'

Francesca handled the sheets of paper as though they were radioactive. Philip looked at the tourists and the office workers making their way through the open space. You could tell the two sets apart quite easily. The tourists and their cameras and video recorders looked up, the workers with their Palm Pilots and cellphones looked down.

'Well, well,' Francesca said when she had finished, her voice low and rough. 'And what am I supposed to do with this information? Use it to miraculously raise him from the dead?'

'I thought you might want to see it.'

'For what purpose?' Francesca turned towards him, her thin body tense and coiled. 'For what purpose, Philip? Do you suppose perhaps that I haven't suffered enough? Do you imagine I want to go over and over the circumstances surrounding my brother's death in perpetuity? Do you really think that's what I want?'

'Fran, there are some issues in here that, well, affect me.'

'And whose fault is that?'

'He's talking about murder, Fran.'

'He isn't,' she snapped. 'He's talking about marriage.'

'Can we discuss this without getting angry?'

'I don't want to discuss it. I don't want to discuss it at all. I'm sick of it. I don't want to talk to any more private detectives. And I don't want to have any heart-to-hearts with you or Poppy.' Francesca didn't look at him. She looked straight ahead, her right boot tapping smartly on the ground. A pigeon landed in front of her and she kicked out at it. The bird moved gracefully away from the arc of her foot. 'Why can't you all just leave it alone?'

'Private detectives?'

'Some guy called Marvel. FirstVenture is investigating Mitch's death. At least that's his story.'

Philip's shoulders slumped. 'Can it get any worse?'

'Don't come to me for pity. I don't do pity.'

'Do you think they were happy?'

'Do you?' Francesca turned towards him again. 'Do you think they were, Philip? Or do you hope they weren't?'

He flinched. 'What do you mean?'

'You snapped her up pretty quickly. I wasn't the only one to notice that. Perhaps you always wanted her too. And perhaps you're feeling a little guilty now. And if you are it's scarcely my problem.' Francesca jerked a cigarette out of her bag, lit it and dragged deeply. 'Nobody's innocent here. So let's not pretend, OK?'

'I . . .' Philip didn't know what to say. Francesca's hostility level was intense, even for her. 'You can't believe that. I didn't even like Grace when she and Mitch were together.'

'You swooped in pretty fast afterwards though. He hasn't been dead a year, Philip. What am I supposed to think?'

'That's ridiculous.'

'Exactly my point.' She sat back, cigarette in her mouth, arms folded. Any other person would have looked a wally, Philip thought. Francesca just looked like she was posing for a photo shoot. 'Things are not always what they seem.'

'Were they in trouble?'

'Must we, Philip? Must we really?'

'Please, Fran. I'm . . . I don't know what I am. I just need to know something. Anything.'

Francesca breathed out smoke. It might as well have been fire. 'Talk to the detective, he seems to be up on this, and, as I hope I've made clear to you, I really don't care. I've got his number here somewhere.' She picked around in her handbag and came up with a packet of cigarettes. 'Want one?' She held out the packet.

'No thanks.'

'Sure? They make life easier.'

'That's what you told me fifteen years ago,' he said. 'I tried it once, remember? Burned the rug.'

Francesca shrugged. 'Once isn't enough. You've got to persevere.'

'So this Marvel guy might know about Whitney?' he said. 'You don't know who he is.'

Francesca took Marvel's card out of her wallet, then lit a cigarette. She took two puffs, dropped it to the ground and stepped on it.

'Here's a crazy little notion,' she said. 'Why don't you just ask Grace what the story is?'

'It's a little more complicated than that, Fran. I wish you'd try to understand.'

'How dare you!' Francesca stood up and for a minute Philip thought she was going to strike him. 'How dare you! He was my only brother, the only family I had left. And I'll never see him again. And you know what? This is hell for me too. I suppose if I was feeling particularly indulgent I could run around cooking up conspiracy theories. But I choose not to because I hope that one day I'll be able to move on from this ghastly experience and live what approximates a normal life.'

'Fran, I'm sorry. I didn't mean it. You know I didn't. I'm just feeling lost and confused.'

Her look was as cold and pale as snow. She shrugged her thin shoulders.

'Yeah, well, welcome to the club.'

Fifty-Two

Grace Falco went to the Reebok Club, but not to work out. She retrieved a small black bag from her locker, then walked west to Central Park.

She loved Central Park, because it was green but it was also indisputably in the city. She didn't much care for the countryside. As somebody who had grown up in it she had always considered its charms over-rated. In her experience the people who extolled the virtues of the rural life generally did so because they had a bank balance which said they didn't have to be there all the time. Living in the sticks was no fun when you had no other choice.

But Central Park had the best of both worlds, and she loved the beautiful apartment buildings that could be seen wherever you went. Eventually, she hoped to persuade Philip to move uptown and buy somewhere on Fifth Avenue. He was very attached to his present apartment, but she wanted to convince him that it would be better for his practice if he lived somewhere more fashionable.

A rollerblader snapped past her, missing her by inches and bringing her back to the problem at hand. She had to make some important decisions and make them quickly, otherwise there would be no Fifth Avenue future with Philip. There'd be no future at all.

It wasn't as if this moment had come as a surprise. She had known since the night Jake Connor died that he would come back in some form or another; it was the law of the universe.

So why couldn't she think what to do? She was resourceful and intelligent and she'd survived much worse. Why was it now that her resourcefulness had failed her?

It was important not to panic, she told herself. She had to put aside the look that she had seen in Philip's eye last night. That look had told her almost as much as the letter had done when she had retrieved it from his pocket while he slept.

That letter had been a hard thing to read. She had known things were not exactly rosy between her and Mitch, but she hadn't known they were quite that bad. And he had had to go and spill his guts to Philip. Why the hell had he done that?

Damn Mitch had messed up her life. Again.

And damn Whitney too.

She had to figure out what to do, and quickly. Time was important; her marriage was withering.

'You can do this,' Grace said out loud to herself as she passed morning commuters clutching huge cups of coffee. 'You've survived before and you can do it again.'

The words did not have their customary bracing effect. She felt alone and, worse, she still didn't have a single idea.

Her phone rang.

'It's me.'

Grace Falco drew a deep breath. And she knew at that moment that her fantasy she could control this situation was just that. As of now she was stepping into the storm.

Marvel had woken half an hour before his alarm went off, with an unexplained sense of anticipation.

'Today's the day,' he thought, apropos of nothing, as he laced his running shoes, gathered his keys and went out for a run.

It was a clear day and the skyline of Manhattan was in sharp relief against an early sky. Marvel nodded at the other joggers and dog-walkers he routinely saw in Fort Greene Park. He wasn't a particularly enthusiastic runner and would by no means have described himself as an athlete. He seldom pushed himself too hard, content just to put in the time and enjoy the opportunity not to think about anything too taxing.

But today he ran hard several times around the park and finished by pounding up the stairs to the Martyrs' Monument, a single column that graced the highest point in Brooklyn.

Gasping for breath, he didn't take a moment to appreciate the view as he usually did, but turned and trotted down the hill towards his apartment.

He drove into the city that day because he had an appointment in Yonkers later in the day, but even the lazy-moving traffic – it took him forty minutes to get from his house to the Manhattan side of the Brooklyn Bridge – could not put him in a bad mood.

When he eventually got to the office his first message was from Philip Ross, asking him to call immediately.

Marvel picked up the phone.

'Hello, Grace.'

'Philip. What are you doing here? Why aren't you at the office?'

Grace had reached the breakfast bar before she had realized Philip was in the apartment.

'I want to talk. I think it's time, don't you?'

'That's a lovely idea, darling, but I really do have to run. I have a . . .'

'Job interview? C'mon, Grace, you don't seriously expect me to believe that old line any more?' Philip's voice was cold, knotted with fury. 'Really, you must think I'm pretty stupid.'

'Philip, this is very important. I do have to go right now.' Grace reached for the drawer where she knew the car keys were kept.

'An appointment with Whitney perhaps? Does that take precedence over a heart to heart with your good old sucker of a husband? What am I anyway except the poor sap who pays the bills?'

'It seems like you don't need me for this conversation,' Grace said coolly. 'Seems like you've got all the answers.'

Philip snorted, and Grace was reminded of her

very first impression of him – a stuck-up twat. She pushed the thought away. Philip was under pressure. They both were.

'I have to go,' she said wearily. 'I have to be somewhere. I'll explain everything when I get back. The whole story, I promise. Please just trust me for a few hours more.'

'Going with Whitney?' Philip raised a hand and for a moment Grace thought he was going to hit her. *Underneath they're all the same*, she thought bitterly. *They're weak.*

Philip lowered his hand.

Grace's closed around the keys. But Philip was now blocking her exit. There was no way she could make a dash for it.

'Please move, Philip.'

'I'm not leaving till I get some answers.'

'I told you, I can't. Not now.'

'What's more important to you than our marriage, Grace?'

'The trust of my husband when I ask for it,' she snapped.

'I'm not letting you go.' He moved closer.

Grace pulled the gun out of her black bag. It was only a .22 but it could inflict reasonable damage close up. 'In that case, I really must insist.'

Philip stared at the gun and then at Grace.

'You're insane,' he said.

'Get out of my way.'

'Give me the gun.'

'Get out of my way.'

Silently Philip stepped aside.

'I'm going to take your car,' she said. 'Out to the country for a little drive. I'll return it tonight. I'd consider it a great favour if you didn't call the police and report it stolen.'

'You're going to regret this, you bitch,' he said as she opened the door.

Grace didn't reply. She dashed down the stairs, pushing the dreadful scene from her mind. She would figure out a way to get him back. She'd tell him the truth, or at least a version of the truth, but right now she had to act.

'Have you got a car?'

'What?' Marvel was a little surprised to be met by Philip Ross at the door of his apartment, looking wild.

'A car! My wife has stolen my car.'

'What do you want me to do about it?'

'I told you. I want your car. To follow her. To see where she's going.'

Marvel shook his head. 'Sorry, pal. I don't have the insurance coverage for car chases. The premiums just got too expensive.'

'This is no laughing matter.' Philip Ross looked as though he wanted to take Marvel by the shoulders and shake him. 'We have to go.'

'Go where?'

'Wherever she's going. She pulled a gun on me. My own wife.'

That was a little more interesting.

'Paul Whitney have anything to do with this?' he asked.

'We'll never find out if we stand here yakking.' Philip Ross pulled him towards the elevator.

This is wild, Marvel thought as they drove to Philip Ross's garage. *Poppy'll get a laugh out of this.*

'Hang on here, I'll be right back.' Philip jumped out of the car and spoke to the attendant. A few moments later he was back.

'She asked the parking-lot attendant about traffic on the West Side Highway,' Philip said, fastening his seat belt. 'I guess that's the best place to start.'

Normally Marvel liked to listen to talk radio when he drove, but Philip's story was much more compelling.

'She didn't say where she was going?'

'All she said was she'll be back tonight.'

'She's not going too far then. What's the car look like?'

'Red Alfa.'

Of course, Marvel thought. Of course he drives a sexy sports car.

'So tell me about this Whitney guy.'

'He's an old friend of my wife's.' Philip's voice was so quiet Marvel could hardly hear him.

'What kind of friend?'

'I don't know. Somebody from her past. She doesn't talk about him but I know he has contacted her.'

'Does it seem like a friendly relationship?'

Philip swallowed. 'She gave him money.'

'How much money?'

'Ten thousand dollars.'

Marvel sat up a little straighter. This was new.

'Where'd she get ten thousand dollars?'

'From her ex-husband's estate. Money from the house he owned in the Berkshires.'

'The house wasn't in her husband's name. How'd she do that?'

Philip ignored the question. 'Can you tell me the truth about how Mitch died?' The pain in his voice was unmistakable, but Marvel refused to feel pity for him.

What goes around comes around, he thought. *I fucking love that rule.*

'Where'd Grace get ten thousand dollars?'

'She persuaded Francesca, Mitch's sister, to give her some money.'

'And she gave it all over to this Whitney guy?'

'So it would seem.'

'Did she discuss it with you?'

'No.'

'Then how do you know she gave him money?'

'I saw . . .' Philip swallowed again. 'I looked through her things this morning and saw the withdrawal slip from her bank. She took it out in cash.'

Aha, Marvel thought. *Beneath that upright exterior, a snooper.*

'But you don't know for sure it went to Whitney.'

'I know he was after her for money,' Philip said flatly. 'Had been for some time. While she was still married to Mitch. That's all I know.'

'Paul Whitney was recently released from prison

after serving a sentence for aggravated robbery,' Marvel said. 'He held up a gas station upstate. Beat the clerk till he nearly died because he didn't think the takings from the cash register were worth the effort he'd put into the venture. He's what you'd call lacking in the social graces.'

'How'd you find that out?'

That little piece of news had to hurt, Marvel thought. New wife being blackmailed by a con.

'The Corrections Department of the State of New York keeps very good records. Not surprising when you consider prison is one of our growth industries.'

'Jesus Christ.'

'Sounds like Whitney is blackmailing your wife,' Marvel said helpfully, in case Philip Ross hadn't already reached that conclusion. 'Any idea why somebody would want to do that?'

'I was hoping you could tell me.'

'Maybe if we catch up with her we can ask her ourselves.'

Fifty-Three

Poppy didn't go to strip clubs as a rule, but during the course of her work in south-east Asia she had visited a few.

The Silver Stiletto was different from its Asian counterparts, the clubs that drew the sex-obsessed from all parts of the globe – the paedophiles, the perverts, the obnoxiously drunk – just looking to see if what they'd heard about Asian women was true.

Two women were dancing on stage, ostensibly with each other, but nobody appeared to be taken in by the act. Most of the customers' eyes were on a football match being shown on a shabby television that was chained to the wall. Poppy looked at the dancers. They were older than her and not in the best shape – another way that the Silver Stiletto differed from Asia, where the girls were often heart-breakingly young and as slender as the bamboo reeds they had grown up among.

'Beer?' The man who had introduced himself as the manager was also working behind the bar, but he was so fat it was only with some difficulty.

'No thanks.'

The manager poured himself one.

A cheer went up and Poppy looked at the television screen to see what the cause of the excitement was. Something had happened in the game but she had no idea what. She didn't understand the rules of American football – just another example of how, whatever her passport said, she was, in most functioning ways, a foreigner here.

The manager put his beer on the bar. Poppy showed him the photo of Grace that Marvel had given her.

'This woman used to work here,' she said. 'And it's very important that I find her.'

The manager looked at the photo. 'She's popular these days.'

'I know what you told Philip Ross and you needn't repeat that story with me. Whatever reason you or your staff had for doing it doesn't exist any more.'

The manager regarded Poppy with one eye closed.

'See, here's the thing. This place? Whatever it looks like to you, it's a different place to every single person who works here. And for a lot of the girls that means it's a place to hide. I understand that, and I respect my girls' reasons for keeping below the radar. Whatever the reason, I don't ask. And I don't tell. To nobody, OK?'

'It's vital that I speak to her,' Poppy repeated. Not for the first time in her life she was glad of her lack of height and her relatively small frame. Nobody could call her physically intimidating. 'I'm not a cop or anything.'

'No kidding,' the manager said.

The game on the television cut away to commercials and the men's eyes drifted back to the stage. Poppy noticed that most of them were dressed in business suits and were wearing wedding rings.

'If you don't tell me what I want to know I'm going to go over to your customers and tell them I'm a private detective who's been hired by their wives – or their companies – to check up on why they're not at work on this nice sunny afternoon.'

'They won't believe you.'

'I can be pretty convincing.'

'Perhaps it's your lucky day then.' The manager lifted one fat finger and one of the dancers on stage came and sat next to Poppy.

She was wearing body make-up which had a sharp, metallic smell. Her breasts were unnaturally huge. Poppy wondered if it hurt to have something that immobile attached to living tissue.

'This is Daisy,' the manager said. 'She's been here for a while.'

'I went away,' Daisy said. 'I was gone for two years. But I had to come back.'

Poppy nodded sympathetically. She'd known jobs like that.

'This person.' She showed the photo to Daisy.

'Katalina Lake,' Daisy said promptly.

Katalina Lake was where Jake Connor had drowned.

'She wore a blonde wig,' Daisy went on. 'We thought she should've called herself Veronica Lake. Not that any of the Einsteins who come here would know what that meant.' Daisy shot a glance at the manager, who shrugged.

'What does this look like?' he asked. 'Fucking Princeton?'

'What did you know about her?'

'No much. She didn't talk. Very private. Not that that's unusual. Nobody's exactly bragging about their résumé here.'

'She have any special customers? Any regulars?'

Daisy shook her head. 'Nah, but we weren't often on the same shift so I couldn't say for sure.'

'What about boyfriends, friends? Anybody pick her up after work?'

Daisy snorted. 'So they could carry our books home?'

'She ever say anything to you that stuck in your mind?'

'She was out of it a lot of times.' Daisy indicated the stage, the pole. 'She had a fairly serious habit. Not that that's so unusual. Like I said, she didn't stand out.'

'She had a tattoo,' Poppy prompted. 'A ram's head. On her hip.'

Daisy shrugged. 'Maybe, I don't know. Hang on a minute, yeah, I remember. It wasn't a ram's head. It was a woman. With snakes in her hair. Like in that old story.'

'Greek myth,' the manager added. 'Athena or something.'

'Medusa,' Poppy said automatically. 'All who looked at her were turned to stone.'

*

Paul Whitney left the parole office and bought a coffee before getting into the Chevrolet he had borrowed from a buddy and miraculously managed to get a parking space for almost right outside the building his interview was in. He'd even fed the meter, a first for him.

The interview had been amusingly predictable. No, Whitney still had not been able to find work. Yes, he was looking (a small lie). Whitney had not let his disdain for the whole post-incarceration process show. In many ways being an ex-con suited him. Everybody expected you to have trouble finding work and so you could, if you were so inclined, milk that particular bovine for almost as long as it suited you. And now that he had his own little cash cow squirting out the green stuff on a regular basis, that time period could extend for a good comfortable stretch.

Who said prison didn't prepare you for real life?

Whitney unlocked the car, threw a paper bag containing a bagel onto the front seat and folded his big frame into the car. He groped underneath him and his fingers touched the Glock pistol that his pal had provided as part of the asking price.

'We try harder.' Whitney laughed aloud at his own little joke as he put the car into gear and lurched into the northbound traffic, causing the guy behind him to step on the brakes and yell a string of insults that impugned him and all of his female relatives.

His cellphone rang at exactly the time he expected it would. Whitney knew that it was against the law to drive while talking on the phone without a hands-free device, but he answered the call anyway, even though there was a cop one lane away.

'It's ready,' Grace Falco's voice said. 'All you have to do is come and get it.'

'There she is! Up ahead on the right.'

Marvel edged a little closer to the red car.

'Not too close,' Philip said. 'She'll see us.'

'She'll see us anyway, eventually,' Marvel said. 'Those movies where the hero follows the bad guy all on his lonesome? That's fiction. You need a fleet of cars to follow somebody so they don't know it's happening.'

'There's no need to be patronizing,' Philip snapped.

'Just saying,' Marvel said calmly, wondering if he could stand much more of this man's company. Sure, his wife had just pulled a gun on him but that was no excuse for being a prick.

Grace Falco kept to the speed limit, stopping only to pay the toll on the Henry Hudson Bridge. The traffic thickened as they followed her on the Henry Hudson Parkway through the Bronx and slowed even further on the Cross County Parkway.

'Big intersection coming up. Go north,' Philip said. 'She'll probably take 87, that's the best.'

Marvel said nothing. He knew there were any number of alternatives and no special reason to take 87, which could very well be choked at this time of day. But he saw Grace move the car into the turning lane and he did too.

'Where do you think she's going?' he asked, just to fill up some empty air space.

'To meet Whitney. Bring him some more money, no doubt.'

'Does she have any more money? I thought she just paid him ten grand.'

'How the hell should I know?' Philip said bitterly. 'I'm finding out new things about her every . . . watch out!'

It was a risky move. As the mighty flow of traffic turned to go north, Grace Falco had shot straight ahead, riding the little sports car up on to the shoulder of the road until the eastbound traffic loosened to let her in.

'Damn!' Philip slapped the dashboard. 'Damn.'

'I guess she saw us,' Marvel said. 'Nifty driving though.'

Philip, slumped in the passenger seat, did not reply.

Fifty-Four

Poppy had a dislike of tunnels that went under water, so although she could have returned to the city more quickly through the Holland or the Lincoln Tunnel she chose instead to detour a mile or so north to cross the George Washington Bridge.

Her phone rang just as she was paying the toll. 'It's Daisy, at the Silver Stiletto.' Poppy held the phone away from her ear. Daisy was shouting to be heard over the music. 'Good thing you gave me your number. After you left I remembered something. This guy came one night to pick her up. He came back to our dressing-room. She introduced me.'

'What was his name?'

'I can't remember,' Daisy said. 'It was a long time ago.'

Poppy held the phone away again while she gave a snort of frustration.

'But he was real skinny and tall. And he had a scar on his lip. That was what I remember.' Daisy produced the finding triumphantly.

'What kind of scar?'

'Like one of those surgeries? You know for when your mouth doesn't work properly?'

'A cleft palate?'
'Yeah, that's it.'

Bill Brady had not been at work so Poppy decided to
try him at home. His house had not been too difficult
to find. She'd stopped at a gas station, bought a map
and asked the sulky kid behind the counter if she
could borrow a phone book. Ten minutes later she
was parked outside a modest split-level ranch house
on a quiet street.

It was a balmy afternoon but there were no signs
of life in the six or seven houses on the street. No kids
played on the street, no lawns were mowed, no gar-
dening was being done.

Bill Brady's curtains were drawn and the windows
were dark. Poppy went up to the house and rang the
doorbell. She could hear the chimes respond somewhere in the house but nobody came to answer.

She went around the back of the house. It was
larger than it looked from the front and the back yard
stretched into some kind of nature reserve.

Just for a laugh she tried the back door. It was
locked. There was nobody at home, she had wasted
her time.

She got back in the car and turned the key. Just at
that minute a guy in a pickup with the lettering 'Brady
Motors' drove past. The garage door rose and Poppy
could see another car inside, a dark green Subaru.
Brady drove into the garage, got out of the truck and
into the station-wagon, and drove out of the garage.
From Marvel's description it had to be him.

He drove out into the street and turned left.

Poppy didn't have to return the rental till the next day, so she decided to see where he went.

They were heading north, she knew that much. She saw a sign for Brewster, a town she recognized from the train trip she had taken to join Francesca the weekend they had gone up to the house to sort out Mitch's things. She wished Francesca was with her; that way it would seem more like an adventure and less like complete insanity.

Should call Marvel, she thought. No, Marvel wouldn't approve. *Best just to ride this thing and see how far it takes me.* She found a rock station and turned up the volume.

More miles passed. North of Brewster they turned west, heading to a town called Pawling. Hadn't Marvel told her that was the town where Sarah O'Reilly had lived?

Perhaps it was time to call Marvel.

'Something's weird,' she said, and told him about Daisy and the Silver Stiletto. 'And now I'm following Bill Brady and guess where he's going. Pawling.'

'Looks like Grace might be headed that way too,' Marvel said, glancing at Philip. 'And by extension, me and Philip.'

There was a brief silence on the other end of the phone.

'Look, I'll call you back. I need to concentrate on this for a moment.'

Marvel shut his phone and put it on the dashboard.

'We got lucky,' he said. 'I think I know where Grace is headed.'

Poppy followed Bill Brady about two miles out of town and watched as he turned off down a dirt track that appeared to lead into the middle of a forest. She drove about a hundred metres past, parked the car about five hundred metres down the road and began following him on foot.

She found the track easily enough. It had rained recently and several cars had been down it, judging from the tyre tracks. Poppy checked her cellphone battery. It was very low. She put through a call to Marvel. He answered immediately.

'Tell me where you are. We're coming to get you.'

'North of Pawling, about . . .' was all Poppy managed to say, as a hand grabbed her throat in a vicious grip.

Fifty-Five

Poppy had taken self-defence classes in Hong Kong. She stamped down on her attacker's instep and brought her elbow up to his eye. And then she ran.

He was fiendishly fast. He grabbed her again, this time by the arm, and flung her to the ground. Her head struck a tree root.

'What are you doing here?' His face was close to hers. 'What do you want?'

She kicked him in the kneecap and scrambled to her feet but he knocked her down again. She heard a high-pitched whine and then darkness.

'What's happening?'

'I don't know,' Marvel said.

'What did she say? Did she mention Grace?'

Marvel said nothing. The last thing he had heard was Poppy weeping in pain, a sound that chilled him to his marrow.

He prayed that she was OK. Prayed that she would pick up her phone and tell them where to find her.

Because he couldn't help her if he didn't know where she was.

And if he did, Pawling was still a long way away.

When Poppy came to she was tied to a chair in a small room. A cabin with one window and one closed door. It was filthy and smelled rancid. The side of her head was throbbing and she was so thirsty she felt sick from it. Outside the cabin she could hear voices, but they were too far away for her to discern what was being said.

A wave of nausea washed over her again and she felt unconsciousness beckoning. The ropes chafed against her wrists. She rubbed against them harder. Pain would keep her awake at least. She felt the top layer of her skin start to give way, a dull, hot ache.

The rope firmly tied her hands and feet to the chair. Even though the rope was old they were good knots, she couldn't loosen them. She stood up, balancing the chair on her back. If she waddled this way she could get to the window, see what was going on at least.

She took one tentative step, then another. Testing her balance each time. She had to be very careful not to fall. Bound to the chair, without the use of her arms there was no way she'd be able to get up.

The voices outside were raised now. It sounded like an argument. Poppy took a step further. And then another. Only one more to go until she would be able to see out the window.

The gunshot sounded fake. It was a low popping sound, like a firecracker or a car backfiring. Still, it surprised Poppy and she lost her balance.

She could feel herself topple, unable even to put out a hand to break her fall.

She crashed to the filthy floor of the cabin, feeling her cheekbone shatter.

And then she knew for sure it was a gunshot because she could hear a person crying in great pain.

Poppy cried herself as she lay on the floor. She had never felt more helpless and ashamed and foolish. Her face was throbbing and the fetid smell in the cabin choked her nostrils, making her more nauseous.

I'm going to die, she thought. *And it's my own stupid fault.* And she cried more, till tears and mucus covered her face.

It was then she realized, as she instinctively moved her hand to wipe her face, that she could move one of her arms. The next realization was even sweeter. The chair was so old that her fall had snapped the back support that bound her right hand. Loosening her arm, Poppy cried harder. She was going to get out of here.

She opened the door a fraction at first, peering through the gap. She couldn't see anybody. Good. A clear coast was exactly what she wanted. She had lost her own phone in the struggle with Bill Brady and her plan was to run as fast as she could to the nearest telephone and call the cops.

She opened the door a fraction more, just enough to squeeze through, and stepped out on to the damp earth. She was going to walk straight ahead, into the forest and not stop till she came to civilization.

But before that she could not resist looking back. And what she saw made her gasp in horror.

'You,' Grace Falco said. She was holding a gun.

Marvel caught a break in the traffic. North of White Plains it thinned out. He put his foot to the floor and drove like the devil. He ran two red lights once he got off the highway in Brewster.

Philip had completely given up pretending to be cool and was gripping the dashboard with both hands. Periodically he looked around for cops, but unusually for this stretch of road – and he knew it as well as anybody – there was none to be seen.

They screeched into Pawling. Marvel parked the car, grabbed his bag out of the back seat and dialled a number he'd written in his diary.

'This is Doreen.'

'Doreen, it's Frederick Marvel from New York. I need your help. It's urgent. Is Ralph there?'

'Sure, hon. He's outside chopping wood. Let me get him.'

'Ralph here,' he said after ten thousand years had passed.

'Ralph, I'm in town. Can you tell me how to get to the lake?'

'Which lake, buddy? There's a few around here.'

'A guy, years ago, he drowned there. Jake Connor. It was before your time but I wondered if you knew where it was?'

'Katalina Lake,' Ralph said promptly. 'Where did you say you were again?'

'Main street. Outside McDonald's.'

'Well, that's real easy,' Ralph said. 'You got a pen?'

When she saw Grace Falco's gun pointed right at her, Poppy felt every last vestige of hope fly away. It was as if hope had never existed and never would again.

'What are you doing here?' Grace asked.

Weren't you supposed to talk to people with guns? Say soothing and confident things like, 'Put that gun down and let's see if we can work this out?' Poppy was sure she must have heard or read that some-where. And perhaps it made sense to other people, in other situations, but it didn't to her. Not right now. Because it occurred to her, in a flash of inspiration that seemed particularly pertinent to her situation, that guns weren't just things to kill with. They were symbols of power, like money. And the person who doesn't have the power can't tell the person with the power what to do.

'I said what are you doing here?'

'Bill Brady,' Poppy stuttered. 'I wanted to talk to him.'

'You chose a bad day. But I guess you figured that out already.'

Poppy nodded dumbly.

'What are you doing?' she asked after her wits began to return.

'Good question,' Grace Falco said. 'I think I might be here to save a worthless scumbag's life. And I think I'm going to need your help.'

As they came out from behind the cabin a man she didn't recognize was standing in a small clearing which led down to the beach. A rowboat was dragged up on shore. The sun was setting, spraying the whole tableau with a filmy golden light. It would have been quite beautiful except that the man was bleeding profusely from a wound in his thigh. Even from a distance Poppy could see that his jeans leg was soaked in blood. Bill Brady stood in front of him, his arms stiff at his sides like an action figure. A woman stood beside him.

Grace dragged Poppy roughly out into the clearing. 'Hey, guess who I found trying to escape.'

'Grace, what are you doing here? I told you we could handle this. And who the hell is she?'

'This is Poppy Adams,' Grace said. 'She's got some kind of death wish or something. She followed Bill up here. I guess he thought he got the situation squared away tying her up and everything, but shit happens. So she's here now. Poppy, that's Paul Whitney, whose blood we sincerely hope is clotting. This gentleman is

Bill Brady and the lady beside him is his lovely wife. She was christened Grace but everybody these days calls her Sarah.'

The car with the Maryland plates, that had to be her rental. Marvel started breathing again. She wasn't too far away.

Marvel took a Maglite from the glove compartment. It didn't fire bullets but it was better than nothing. He put the flashlight in his jacket pocket. 'Come on,' he said to Philip. 'Pray that we're not too late.'

Fifty-Six

Poppy stood completely still, staring at Sarah. She looked similar to Grace, certainly. But what really struck her was the way she sounded. It was like hearing the same voice from two different people.

'Poppy represents a problem, of course,' Grace Falco said. From the tightness of the grip on her arm Poppy knew that Grace was much more nervous than she was letting on. And then she saw the reason why. Bill Brady was also carrying a gun.

'The chick made a phone call. The cops will be here.'

'We have to finish,' Sarah said. Bill Brady nodded.

'Finish it and you're finished,' Grace said crisply. 'It's not like last time. Witnesses.' She gave Poppy a shake.

'Kill the fucking witness as well as Whitney,' Bill Brady growled.

Grace Falco's voice shook. 'For Christ's sake, Bill, this is bone-headed even for you. You kill somebody and you go to jail. That's what happens.'

'You didn't.' Bill Brady took a step towards Grace. 'Cut the crap moral lectures. This is all your fault. You put your fucking wedding photo in the *New York* fucking *Times*, if you hadn't done that Whitney never would've figured out there were two of you. He didn't even know Grace Falco existed till then. He never would've found Sarah and me and figured he could squeeze us the way he squeezed you.'

'Irrelevant,' Grace Falco snapped. 'Really, what are your options? There's only one thing to do. We talk; we sort out a deal. Everybody goes home happy.'

'All right for you, married to a fucking millionaire. We got a business to run. Kids to feed. We live in the real world.'

'And how am I going to explain a gunshot wound to my parole officer?' Whitney whined. Nobody was listening. Sarah was looking at Grace.

'Grace is right, Bill. We have to think of the girls.'

Bill Brady did not appear to be listening. His jaw was clamped shut and he was clenching and unclenching his fist. Poppy feared that he was ready to launch himself at Whitney.

'I don't like people who threaten my family. You threaten my family and I come after you.'

'Yes, all right, Bill. But the clock is ticking and we really do have to apply a little more realpolitik here,' Grace said. 'So let's just hand the gun over to me and everybody gets to go home and sleep in their own bed. C'mon, Bill, I'll shoot you myself if it means plugging some sense into you.'

There was silence while everybody stared at Bill. Poppy had no doubt that Whitney was right and Bill and Sarah had lured him here to kill him. But why was Grace trying to stop it? Surely it would be better for her if Whitney were out of the way?

The sun and the temperature were dropping. Poppy started to shiver violently. Her injured head throbbed harder.

A movement in the forest caught her attention. Two figures moving slowly, quietly. She looked around the circle. Nobody else seemed to have noticed.

Poppy strained to see them better. Marvel? Could it really be Marvel? How the hell had he managed to find her? Who cared? God, she had never been happier to see anybody. Marvel would know what do to. Everything was going to be OK.

Then she noticed Philip standing slightly behind him. And she realized with the clarity of somebody who is facing mortal danger that whatever she had once felt for him had gone.

OK, now this is officially weird. She leaned against Grace, who pushed her gently away so she could give her full attention to Bill Brady.

They were losing light fast. Marvel was wearing dark clothes and it was hard to keep her eye on him. Even harder to keep her grip on reality. Were they really all standing out here in the forest, some of them bleeding, with guns and accusations of murder and blackmail? Or was this just something she had dreamed up, a terrible end for Grace Falco, the woman she thought she hated but who just at this moment was impressing the hell out of her?

Philip and Marvel were right here. Perhaps she could slip away and nobody would notice. She could just walk over to them, right now. Head injuries were kind of cool in some respects. The rest of your problems just seemed to fade away. Like a two-martini buzz, everything became woozy yet clear at the same time.

Here he was. Philip, walking out of the forest towards her. Tall, debonair, in control. And saying something. What was it?

Time stuttered and then stalled. Poppy saw things in separate tableaux, like a jerky home movie. Philip walking towards Grace, hand outstretched, saying something. Bill Brady turning, taking his attention off Paul Whitney. Whitney with a black gun. Where did that come from? Sarah shouting. Brady turning. Brady lunging for Whitney. A blur of movement, a scream, two screams, Brady and Whitney together, arms up, like they were pointing at a single star. Then a gun shot. Then another. And a single cry stretched out across the still dark water of the lake.

Fifty-Seven

'Jake Connor was a prick. He drank and when he drank he got violent and angry. He hated his life and he took it out on those around him, especially if they were weaker.

'And then one day he got his big break. He bought some marijuana off some guys from Texas and he arranged to sell it on. It was going to be his big start. The new Jake Connor. The Jake Connor with the fancy cars and that thing he desired more than anything: respect.

'So the deal goes smoothly and he decides to celebrate. He calls my cousin and says come over. And she goes. I told her not to. She didn't listen.

'So I'm sitting home in the trailer, me and my uncle, and I say I'm going over there. I'm going to see if she's OK. He says she can take care of herself, but I have a bad feeling. I've seen what he does to her.

'So I walk over to his place, it's just through the woods there, actually.' She pointed northwards. 'It's a creepy walk. I don't like nature at night.

'And I get there and surprise, surprise, Jake is drunk. And he's yelling at her. I come in the back door – it's open – and I wait in the kitchen for the right moment to walk in. I don't want to embarrass her. So I wait by the sink. The tap's dripping. I stand there listening to it. And then I hear a scream and a thump and she's crying. And I rush in. He's standing there with his hands on his hips, swaying because he's so drunk. And there's a bunch of pills as well, sitting beside his whisky bottle. And I go over to see if she's OK. She's just lying there with her eyes closed. And then she opens her eyes, says she's OK and she's going to leave now. And I say fine, let's go. I'll help you. And she says, no, I just have to get my stuff and you wait outside. So I go back out to the kitchen.

'And in a few minutes she comes out with a bag. And I ask her what's in it. She says the stuff that she kept at Jake's and the money from the drug deal. And I say what about Jake? I go back inside and Jake is lying on the floor. There's a baseball bat. She follows me in and says she's killed him and she's taking the money. I check his pulse and he's not dead. So then we have to make some decisions. Quickly.'

Poppy pulled the blanket more tightly around her. It had come from Philip's car and felt expensive. She picked at the label. Tasmanian merino.

'I tell her that no court will convict her. She has every right to defend herself and she's got the bruises to show that Jake was an asshole. But she's seen the money and money changes everything. Plus, she's juiced by the violence. Suddenly she's full of plans. She wants to get away and start a new life, with Jake's money.

'We take him down to the lake. This lake. And we put him in the boat, along with his fishing gear and a bottle for veracity. She said he liked to go out on the water and get tanked. She rows out to the middle of the lake and tips the boat over. Jake sinks. She swims back to shore, changes and we go back to the trailer. My uncle knows something's up but he doesn't say anything. Until Whitney calls, middle of the night. Says he saw her. He wants money or he's going to the cops.

'My uncle sends him away but makes us tell him everything. And he comes up with the plan. It's a perfect plan, I had a lot of respect for my uncle for thinking of it. Of course, we had to pay him, too.' She grimaced. 'But that's what happens when you have money, lots of people want to part you from it.'

'What was the plan?' Poppy asked.

'It was based on the simple notion that Whitney didn't know I existed,' she said. 'I came to town and was too depressed to go out so I didn't meet any people. The other part of the plan was that my mother had left me some money but only if I went to college. I'd lost both my parents in a matter of years, I wasn't ready for college. All the plans that they had made for me just didn't seem to make sense when they were no longer around. So I took the drug money.'

'Honey, you don't have to say any more.' Bill Brady put his hand on his wife's arm.

'I want to say it. It's been unsaid for too long. Sarah O'Reilly became Grace Falco a few days after that and went off to college. Kind of ironic really. She said she'd always wanted to be me. My mother used to send out these photo cards every year. My cousin told me she envied my life so much that she once put her own photo on the card so she could become Grace Falco.

'I went to New York and became nice, anonymous Sarah Clarke and was quickly parted from all my cash. Too many bad habits. Too many bad memories. Ended up in a strip club in New Jersey trying to make money to pay off a couple of loan sharks when I ran into Bill again. He saved my life.'

'What happened to John O'Reilly?'

'He did the same as he always did – moved around to avoid the people he owed money to. He died a few years back. Emphysema. He never told. He was proud; in many ways it was his finest hour.'

'We took care of him at the end,' Bill Brady said. 'He didn't want for anything.'

'And Whitney went to prison and we thought we had a good old-fashioned happy ending,' Sarah Brady said, looking about the clearing and the buzz of official activity. 'We were wrong, I guess.'

Fifty-Eight

Paul Whitney died instantly. Grace Falco, shot in the head at medium range, miraculously lasted till she got to hospital but died on the operating table. Poppy was admitted to the same hospital and dismissed after a few hours. Her cheekbone wasn't broken, the doctor told her, and she displayed no signs of brain damage.

Philip was sitting in the lobby when Poppy came out. Poppy sat next to him and put her hand on his. He put his arm around her and held her while she wept.

Marvel, who'd been outside talking to the cops, stopped when he saw them. Swallowed. Didn't come any closer.

'What'd you tell the cops?' Marvel asked later, after Philip had left.

'Just what I saw. A struggle, an accidental shooting. I guess it's all going to come out now.'

'No way to stop it.'

'What about Sarah Brady's story about what happened the night Jake Connor died?'

'It'll hold up.'

'What do you mean it'll hold up? It wasn't the truth?'

'Sounded good, didn't it? Bill Brady told me that Grace – the original Grace – was a champion swimmer and high diver. I checked with Philip and he said the Grace he knew – or Sarah as I suppose we should call her – was petrified of water. Wouldn't even get in a swimming pool. And Jake Connor died from drowning. So who do you think is more likely to have rowed him out into the lake and given him a little help over the side?'

'You gonna tell the cops?'

'I'm sure they'll find it out if someone decides they need to know,' Marvel said. 'That would be up to Bill and Philip. Besides, Sarah and Bill will have enough to deal with from last night alone. No sense in making things more complicated, not with them having two little girls to take care of. What do you think?'

'I think you're right,' Poppy said. 'And I think Grace would approve. She wanted to do the right thing, even though she could have stayed well away. A dead Whitney would have made life easier for her. No more blackmail.'

How's Philip?' Marvel asked.

'Went home,' Poppy said. 'He's pretty cut up. Blaming himself. He was furious because Grace had pulled a gun on him in their apartment, which was why he tried to grab it off her later on in the forest. All righteous anger. Didn't think it through.'

'Patently.'

They sat in silence, their shoulders touching.

'You OK?' Marvel said.

'I will be,' Poppy said, touching her cheek, although she knew Marvel wasn't referring to her injury. 'I will be.'

Fifty-Nine

Marvel dressed carefully the day of Grace's funeral. He had bought a new suit because his old one had fitted better thirty pounds ago. He'd gone to Bergdorf's and bought a new tie and the snowiest and most expensive white shirt that he had ever owned.

Not too bad, he thought when he saw himself in the mirror. He hoped Poppy would like it. He hadn't seen her since he'd driven her home from hospital and he still hadn't asked her out to dinner.

Perhaps today would be the day, he reflected as he smoothed his tie – one advantage of military training was that tie-tying came easily.

It was a cold blustery day. Poppy wore a black trouser suit which made her hair glow brightly in the thin afternoon sun. The bruise on her cheek had faded and she looked, he thought, more beautiful than ever.

Philip looked distinguished and gaunt standing next to Sarah and Bill Brady and their two girls. He smiled grimly at Marvel, who inclined his head in return.

The service was brief and soon they were walking back to their cars

Marvel walked over to Poppy. He was looking startlingly good, Poppy realized. And she suddenly hoped it wasn't on account of a woman. At least a woman who wasn't her. The thought made her blush.

'Can I give you a lift back to town?' he said, suddenly shy.

'That would be terrific.'

They made idle and stilted small talk until they stopped at the Triboro Bridge toll and Marvel pulled into the cash lane, which was long.

'You should get the electronic pass,' Poppy said as she dived into her handbag for change. 'Much easier. Francesca just shoots through in the Audi. Barely even slows down. They send you a bill at the end of the month.'

'And in return our wise and magnificent leaders know where you are at all times.' Marvel accepted the money from Poppy to pay the toll but his thoughts were suddenly far away.

Francesca. There were two things that he had flagged but had not followed through with about Francesca. The first was that he hadn't checked what time she had actually left Manhattan the night Mitch died. And the second was, why had she paid off Grace so readily? Not from the goodness of her heart, and there was no legal need to. The house in the Berkshires was in her name.

'What's up?' Poppy said. 'You look weird.'

'Is it OK if I just drop you off? Just remembered some things I have to take care of.'

Poppy's face fell. 'Oh,' she said. 'I thought we could

go out afterwards. Perhaps have dinner or something . . .' her voice trailed off.

'Gee, I'd love to,' Marvel said. 'But this can't wait.'

Once back in his office Marvel got out the first notebook he had started on the case and turned to the
page where he had written down the details of Francesca's interview. She had gone to a party at the
Cloisters, she said. Which meant she would have
taken the Henry Hudson Bridge out of town, just as
he had done with Philip. He had written down her
licence plate number and the fact that she had an E-Z
pass, an electronic pass that automatically paid bridge
and tunnel tolls and, more importantly, kept them in
a database that nosy people could get their hands on
if they had the right contacts.

Marvel had the right contacts. Whistling a little
tune, he called a friend in NYPD who owed him a
favour.

Half an hour later his phone rang.

'Nada,' his friend said. 'Not the Henry Hudson
Bridge that night and not any night near it. She did
however take the Triboro. At nine o'clock in the
evening.'

'Doesn't make much sense if you're in the
Cloisters.'

'But it does make sense if she was lying about the
Cloisters,' his contact said helpfully.

Marvel checked back through his notes again. He
had spoken to one of Francesca's colleagues, who had
said she was definitely at the party. But as he well

332

knew, parties were confusing, noisy and frequently intoxicating affairs. Easy enough to slip away, and who would notice?

Why had she lied?

Marvel made another call, to the police department in Pawling, and asked the sergeant on duty if anybody else had requested the details of Jake Connor's autopsy in recent months.

The information took less than ten minutes to recover.

He made more phone calls, called in more favours. And by eleven that night he was fairly sure he knew what had happened to Mitch Browning.

Sixty

'Mr Marvel,' Francesca said crisply, lighting a cigarette. 'I keep running into you.'

'Thought I'd walk you to work,' Marvel said. It was a mild day for the time of year, half an hour after a light rain. Manhattan glistened with possibility.

'I usually get a taxi.' Francesca gave him the Sub-Zero of icy stares.

'Exercise is good for the soul. Take some time. Stop and smell the dysfunctional drains.'

Francesca started walking at a surprisingly brisk clip given the height of her heels. Marvel ambled along slightly behind her.

'Wanted to run some ideas past you. I think Grace knew about what really happened the night Mitch died. Otherwise why would she have been able to get money out of you so successfully?'

'That's as wild a statement as any I've heard lately.'

'Well, she's gone now so I can't say for sure. But maybe she saw or heard something that didn't make sense at the time but did later. Perhaps the sound of a car that was not supposed to be there. Your car, perhaps, parked nearby but out of sight. Or the voice of a person whom she didn't recognize?'

'Hilarious,' Francesca said. 'I must thank you for providing such a humorous start to my day. And may I congratulate you on your good taste in implying that I lied about my brother's suicide.'

'But what if it isn't suicide? Why kill yourself if you've got all that money stashed away? Why not find someone else to die for you? A homeless person or a drug addict, somebody that nobody will miss?

'And then you get your sister to cover for you. Bring the guy up in her car, knock him out on sleeping pills. Load him into your car, turn on the gas. Make it look like a tragic end. Which it is, of course, just not of you. Where is he, Francesca?'

'This is preposterous.'

'Grace left a confession,' Marvel lied. 'With her lawyer in the event that she died. 'Very revealing.'

'She did not.'

'How did Mitch get away?' Marvel switched tactics. 'Did you smuggle him out the next day? Put him on a plane at Hartford airport? Somewhere small?'

'How could we fake his death? The autopsy, that would show that it wasn't Mitch in a minute.'

'The medical examiner in Great Barrington has a gambling habit,' Marvel said, inspecting his finger-nails. 'Very sad. The local cops just told me his wife left him and apparently the house is being sold to pay back his creditors. I imagine it would have been fairly easy to, shall we say, convince him to write up a report so that the dead guy looked like Mitch. You told me that Grace didn't see Mitch after he died, you identified the body. The cop was new in town, didn't know Mitch at all.'

Marvel took a missing persons report out of his pocket and held it in front of Francesca. A man in his late twenties with hollow eyes and a thin face. 'This guy fits the bill. He look familiar? He disappeared around the time your brother did. He did, by the way, have somebody who cared about him – a sister in Idaho filed this.'

'You're really stretching it, Marvel. What about FirstVenture? Mitch would never have done anything that stupid because he would have known they'd be all over him.'

'You had the body cremated before anybody could check. And just to muddy the waters a bit further, Mitch cast a little suspicion on Grace. It was neat, there was already something dodgy about her past, he got that from Whitney. All he had to do was do some checking and find out about Jake Connor's death and then leave little pointers towards it, which is why I guess both autopsies listed significant amounts of secobarbitol. And then there was the little to-do list and the convenient letters to Philip. I bet he even came up with the idea of adjusting the mirrors on the car so that if anybody was checking it would look as if Grace had lied about who drove up to the house. Why'd he do that? Just for the hell of it? What kind of man was your brother anyway?'

Francesca took the cigarette from her mouth and regarded the burning tip with interest. 'You tell me,' she said. 'You seem to know everything.'

'Not everything, alas,' Marvel said. 'I don't, for instance, know where your brother is. But I'm sure that you do. And if you see that guy standing over there . . .' Marvel pointed to the opposite side of the street. 'The one who looks like a Fed, because he is? He's very interested to know. And here's what I think: if you tell him where Mitch is, it'll be easier for you.'

'I'm not saying a word without my lawyer.'

'Good. Your lawyer will tell you the same thing I am: save yourself because nobody else is going to.'

Sixty-One

Death threads the fabric of my life now, Philip wrote in his journal.

> *I no longer foster the illusion that it will not
> eventually touch everything and everyone I
> know, including me. There are some days when
> I would welcome it for myself.*
>
> *My life has withered away and I am often
> surprised at the pace of the atrophy. A year ago I
> had an enviable life. It's almost all gone.*
>
> *I don't see much of my friends these days. I'm
> not much company, to be honest. Herb and
> Tiffany ask me over every now and then, I
> decline. Poppy calls every now and then but
> I sense that it's more out of pity than anything
> else.*
>
> *I sit in my apartment alone most nights. It is
> as beautiful and clean as ever. I could sell it for
> much more than I paid for it. I'm thinking about
> doing that, moving up to Nyack to the old man's
> place.*
>
> *I have my work. There's always that. The
> commissions come in fairly steadily, perhaps*

*even more so than before. I achieved some degree
of notoriety, you see, after the story about Grace's
death came out in the newspapers.*

*Yes, I still have my work. Perhaps later in
my life, if my career ever achieves prominence,
critics will look at what I built after this year and
say that it had lost a certain exuberance and
sense of possibility and they will probably be
right. I'm not as American as I used to be. I don't
feel optimistic about the future. I'm just getting
through each day by sheer will. But I'm never
alone. I have my ghosts. Dad and, of course,
Grace. Would she still be alive if I had trusted
her? Was I wrong to act the way I did, no matter
how guilty I thought she was? These are just a
couple of the questions that keep me up nights.*

Sixty-Two

One month later

Marvel was late. And unusually for him he was flustered. He'd just come from a meeting with his old buddy Leigh Sampson at FirstVenture.

'Good work,' Leigh said, handing him a cheque that bore no relation to any of the invoices Marvel had submitted. 'A bonus. Token of the board's appreciation.'

Marvel looked at the zeros lined up, all nice. 'More than a token,' he murmured, slipping it into his jacket pocket.

'Yeah, I told them not to bother, that you'd spend it all on booze and loose women, but they never listen to anything I say.' Leigh grinned. He looked younger since the news had broken that Mitchell Browning had been found in South America and battalions of lawyers had been dispatched to address the delicate issue of extradition.

'Everything fine?' Leigh asked.

'More than fine.'

'Jenny wanted to know if you could come for dinner tonight. Last minute, I know, but she knows you're always embarrassingly available.'

'I'd love to,' Marvel said, 'but the thing is, I have a date.'

He hadn't had time to change between the meeting and the restaurant, so he arrived at the restaurant in the suit and was glad he did. It was a smart place filled with smart-looking people. Poppy sat at the bar. She was wearing a red dress which showed off her perfect figure. An embroidered Kashmiri shawl draped her shoulders and black jet earrings dangled from her ears. Marvel caught a glimpse of himself in the distressed mirrors that covered the walls. He didn't look too bad either, he decided. Slim, straight-backed. Reasonably clean shaven.

He walked over to her and his stomach knotted. She stood up to greet him and kissed him, her hand lingering at the back of his neck in a way that thrilled him. He kissed her back and decided he could stand a whole lot more of that.

'There's a fifteen-minute wait for our table,' she said and her smile crushed his heart. 'You don't mind, do you?'

'I guess we'll think of some way to fill it,' he said.